THE MISTLETOE KISSER

BLUE MOON #8

LUCY SCORE

Bloom books

The Mistletoe Kisser

Copyright © 2020 Lucy Score

Cover by Kari March

ISBN: 978-1-945631-69-6 (ebook)
ISBN: 978-1-7282-8272-5 (paperback)

Published by Bloom Books, an imprint of Sourcebooks
P.O. Box 4410, Naperville, Illinois 60567-4410
(630) 961-3900
sourcebooks.com

lucyscore.com

111021

Dedicated to...
Elaine from my newsletter.
The care you provide to your husband is a beautiful, true example of real love.

1

December 23, fifteen years ago
Blue Moon Bend, NY

*S*ammy Ames surveyed the holiday festivities with no clue that the trajectory of her life was about to change. She would never look at hot chocolate, mistletoe, or sheep the same way.

It seemed as though the entire town had turned out for the traditional Winter Solstice and Multicultural Holiday Celebration. As usual. The same old food stands were clustered on either side of the winding path. The same neighbors manning them. The same wild collection of crafts and homemade goods. The same greetings delivered with puffs of breath.

December in upstate New York was cold. *Really freaking cold.*

But it had never occurred to the residents that perhaps the festivities should be held in warmer weather or—what normal towns did—move them into the homes of residents where each family could choose to mark Christmas, or Hanukkah, or Kwanzaa, or Solstice, or secular family quality time, or nothing at all on their own.

This was Blue Moon. No one did anything on their own. Even if they wanted to.

Instead, they bundled up in parkas and mittens. And stood in line for latkes and lentils and lasagna. There were holidays to celebrate. Cultures to respect. Diversity to appreciate.

At fourteen, Sammy secretly appreciated the fuss. Secretly *liked* that her hometown's mission was to include, not exclude.

She was, by her own account, an average-ish girl with average looks and an average personality. The people around her, both peers and family, always seemed more vibrant, more sure of the space they claimed.

But in this tiny corner of the world, even though she wasn't sure where she fit, Blue Moon still made room for her.

"Ugh. Why do we have to do this every year?" her best friend, Eden Moody, asked, stamping her feet to stay warm. Her black tights—though a trendy, can't-miss proclamation that the girl in them was a budding rebel—weren't as warm as Sammy's practical long underwear and jeans.

Sammy was debating whether to engage in a rebellion of her own. While dressed appropriately for the weather, of course. After all, rebelling against expectations didn't mean she had to freeze to death.

Where Eden's parents embraced their teen daughter's desire to express herself and experience the consequences of those expressions, Sammy's mother, Dr. Anastasia Ames, seemed determined to micromanage her down the path of acquiescence.

"I'm building this veterinary practice for us, Samantha."

"I'm counting on you to carry on the legacy I started, Samantha."

"No, you may not skip college to join the Peace Corps, Samantha."

It would have been nice to be consulted before having her entire life decided for her. Just because Sammy loved animals didn't mean she wanted to join her mother's livestock veterinary practice. Maybe she wanted to work for a horse breeding program or study turtles in the Galapagos.

But her mother seemed more interested in her reputation and what it would mean to that reputation if her daughter joined the roster at her practice.

"You don't like this at all?" Sammy asked her frozen friend.

Eden's eyes followed Beckett Pierce's butt as it—and he—wandered by with his equally cute younger brother Jax. Moon Beam Parker, Eden's cousin, walked in step with Beckett, making puppy dog eyes at him.

Eden was on an accelerated path toward adulthood. She'd had her first kiss at twelve, Amir Lubarnas at the roller rink during Nancy Finkelstein's birthday party. The still-first-kissless Sammy sometimes wished she'd had a Moon Beam in her life to influence her out of her comfort zone.

"I'm almost fifteen," Eden said airily. "I'm exploring my hormonal-induced disdain for life."

The Blue Moon School District's health and sex education curricula were embarrassingly comprehensive.

"Textbook puberty," Layla quipped. Despite being the long-legged, blonde bombshell of the group, Layla was less interested in boys and more interested in protecting her friends from them... and from themselves. Responsible to a fault, she seemed to have skipped the teenage years entirely and jumped straight into adulthood.

Sammy landed squarely between the two. Not too much of a rebel or too much of a Goody Two-shoes. Just a girl waiting to find herself. Waiting for the universe to tell her who she was destined to be. A girl who was getting a little tired of waiting.

"Don't look now, but there's a Ryan Phillippe look-alike behind us," Eden whispered.

This was news. No one in Blue Moon looked like the bored,

wealthy boy from *Cruel Intentions*, which meant fresh meat. Layla peeked first. When she turned back to them, the height of her eyebrows concurred with Eden's assessment.

Sammy casually peered over her shoulder and found herself being grinned at by a tall, lanky boy in a yellow parka straight out of the L.L.Bean catalog. His blond hair flopped artfully over his forehead. Long lashes edged amused brown eyes. He had braces, and a soft, mossy green scarf tied jauntily around his neck. Definitely a Ryan Phillippe type.

Realizing she'd been staring at him for much longer than acceptable, Sammy flashed him a weak smile and whipped around to face forward.

"Smooth, Sammy," Layla teased.

Eden let out the barely audible, high-pitched squeal of a teenaged girl delighted for her friend. "He's totally into you," she whispered knowledgeably.

"Yeah. I don't think so," Sammy hedged. She was used to being the least interesting out of their little group. Layla was the boobed goddess next door who didn't try too hard. Eden was the spunky rebel too busy dancing to the beat of her own drum to care if anyone thought she was cute.

"Hey," a voice said behind them. A cute, teenaged, *boy* voice.

They whirled around as one.

"Hey," Eden said with enviable chill.

"Hey," Layla said with distinct distrust.

"Hi," Sammy squeaked.

The boy grinned again and looked directly at her. "So, how's the food here?" he asked, gesturing at the fried tofu stand in front of them.

"Great," Eden said. "Layla and I have to go. We'll catch up with you later, Sammy." She hooked her arm through Layla's even as Sammy started to shake her head. She wasn't prepared to be abandoned.

"Are you new here?" Layla asked the boy, digging the heels of her sneakers into the ground. It wasn't personal interest. She was making sure a stranger interested in her friend wasn't a future criminal in the making.

"Yeah," the boy said. "I'm in town visiting my great-uncle. Kinda lame," he said with that flirty smile. This time, he gave a little head toss, dislodging the hair that had fallen over his eye.

Sammy wondered why he didn't just cut it shorter. His neck probably got sore by the end of the day from all the hair tossing.

"Who's your uncle?" Layla demanded while Eden tugged on her arm with more determination.

"It doesn't matter who his uncle is," Eden hissed.

Sammy pitied Layla's future children—if she decided to have any—when they tried to bring dates home to meet the parents.

"Uh, my uncle is Carson Shufflebottom," he said, eyeing her friends as if they were a sideshow at a discount circus. "He lives on a farm outside of town."

All information reported after "Carson" was unnecessary of course because this was Blue Moon and everyone knew everyone else.

"How old are you?" Layla asked.

"Fifteen."

"Okay then. We'll be around," she said ominously as Eden hooked her by the hood of her jacket and dragged her away.

Sammy waited a beat and then worked up the nerve to face the age-appropriate heartthrob. He was extremely cute up close.

"Your friends are... interesting," he observed. Then, as if to take the sting out of any undertone of judgment, he flashed her that smile again.

She felt her hormones spiral into a riot. On one hand, he was very good-looking. Like "Jason Priestley on *90210*" good-looking. Normally, she was more of a broody Luke Perry girl, but she was willing to make an exception.

"They are," she agreed. "I'm Sammy, by the way."

"Yeah, I caught that," he said, amused. "I'm Ryan."

A Ryan Phillipe look-alike named Ryan? Yes, please!

"I'm from Des Moines," he added, saying it as if it made him geographically superior.

"I'm from here," she said, daring him to object.

Instead, his gaze warmed. "Well, Sammy from here with the beautiful blue eyes. What do you say we forget about fried tofu?"

Beautiful blue eyes. Gulp. Okay, she could be into a Brandon Walsh type if he handed out compliments like that.

"What do you have in mind?" she asked. She might have been crushing hard, but that didn't mean Dr. Anastasia Ames had raised a fool. If the next words were "Want to check out the back of my older brother's van?" she was out of there regardless of his cuteness and compliments.

He glanced around. "Hot chocolate? My treat," he offered with another little hair toss. This time, she found it endearing.

Ryan from Des Moines held out a hand. She looked at it and debated. He either thought she was cute *or* he thought she was a lost eight-year-old who needed to be reunited with her parents.

"I'm fourteen." She blurted out the words to his ski glove.

"Really? I thought you were at least sixteen," he said.

It was official. Sammy was in love. She slipped her mitten into his glove and reveled in the fact that she, Samantha Ames of Science Club and long underwear, was holding hands with a cute stranger who thought she looked as if she had a driver's license.

Sammy did her best to fall in step with him as they headed in the direction of molten chocolate. His legs were longer, but he walked slower than she did. She was accustomed to propelling only herself forward. Having the bulk of another human in tow took some getting used to.

They finally—and a bit awkwardly—arrived at their destination, a tricked-out Airstream trailer. Lesbian lovers and chocolate aficionados Winona and Bettina spent their retirement years traveling New England and parts of Canada. In the winter, they sold gourmet hot chocolate. In the summer, they switched it up to organic lemonade and iced tea.

She ordered a Butterfinger hot chocolate with whipped cream from Bettina.

Ryan grimaced then ordered the same. "I'm trusting you, blue eyes," he told her.

Bettina gave her a girl-to-girl wink and Sammy relished the confirmation that she wasn't imagining the flirtation.

They took their steaming cups of delicious goodness and began a slow wander around the park. With their hands still entwined, she was forced to drink with her left hand. The sacrifice of her dominant hand made her feel grown-up in a way that the boobs that had started to sprout last summer hadn't.

"Merry Christmas, Sammy," Mrs. Nordemann called out from her place in line at the wassail and eggnog stand. She was wearing an ankle-length black cloak, elbow-length gloves, and a black knit beret.

"Happy Hanukkah, Mrs. Nordemann," Sammy said with a lift of her cup.

"Was that a Christmas witch?" Ryan asked incredulously.

"No. She's Jewish, not Wiccan. She's on the town council."

Sammy always found it hard to describe her Mooners to outsiders. No list of facts could ever fully encapsulate them. Besides, the relaying of the facts often said more about the person relaying them than the person being described.

She could have told Ryan that Mrs. Nordemann handed out the best candy at Halloween. But what if fifteen-year-olds in Des Moines didn't trick or treat anymore? She could have told him that when Sammy's grandmother died, Mrs. Nordemann showed up with a big bottle of wine for her mom and a box of ice pops for Sammy. But what if he thought it was weird to be sad about a grandmother?

"This place is definitely weird," he said. Before she could take offense, he added, "But if I knew Uncle Carson had access to girls like you, I wouldn't have waited so long to visit."

Hair flip.

Heart flip.

Sammy committed the compliment to memory so she could rehash it with Eden and Layla later.

"Hey there, Sammy." John Pierce, handsome and rugged in a flannel coat and muck boots, hailed her from his farm's petting zoo. Temporary fences contained two woolly sheep, half a dozen fluffy chickens, and a swayback Jersey cow wearing a Moo-rry Christmas bandana around her neck.

John was too old to be the unrequited crush of a teenage girl. But she still adored the man. He was quiet, calm, and just a little grumpy.

"Do you know everyone here?" Ryan asked when Joey Greer, all long legs and dark, straight hair, waved. She and Jax, the youngest Pierce, led pony rides around a makeshift ring.

She shrugged. "Mostly."

Carter Pierce, the oldest and, in her opinion, handsomest due to the broody factor, worked behind a folding table, exchanging cash for tickets. Beckett—the middle and object of Moon Beam Parker's current affection—distributed baggies of organic feed to the participants.

"I don't even know my next-door neighbors," Ryan told her. She couldn't tell if he was bragging about that pitiable fact or not.

"What's Des Moines like?" she asked.

While he described the city, she watched as one of the Bowler twins, troublemaking four-year-olds with distracted parents, upended his biodegradable container of fried tofu on the sidewalk in front of the petting zoo. He tugged on his mom's sleeve, announcing he'd finished his supper and was ready for dessert. Mrs. Bowler was mid-gossip session with Bruce and Amethyst Oakleigh and absent-mindedly patted the kid in the face.

Ryan had moved on to the merits of his school, which had a good wrestling team and high-speed internet access in the typing lab. She was doing her best to appear enthralled when a group of Mooners meandered by, animatedly discussing the new movie release *Crouching Tiger, Hidden Dragon*.

She recognized Bill "Fitz" Fitzsimmons, a skinny, bespectacled hippie. He was walking backward, performing some sort of martial arts choreography while clutching an ICEE, when the sole of his winter Birkenstock landed squarely on the mound of fried tofu.

It happened in slow motion. His foot slid out from under him. He tried to compensate, but his other shoe landed in the now flattened goop and skated through it. In cartoon fashion, he stepped, slid, and scrambled half a dozen times before gravity finally won. Flailing backward, Fitz toppled over into the petting zoo's temporary fence. Purple ICEE soared through the air and splattered all over the bigger sheep, who looked startled by the unexpected bath.

The fence *and* Fitz went down with a clank and an "oof," respectively.

"Wow," Ryan said, abandoning his description of his collection of sneakers.

"Uh-oh," Sammy said, already shoving her hot chocolate into Ryan's hand.

Pandemonium erupted. Both sheep bolted for the opening. The purple one didn't exactly vault the prone Fitz. It was more like plowing over him. Fitz squeaked, and the sheep raced down the park's path baa-ing. The chickens were next, scrambling and clucking frantically over their newfound freedom. The cow trotted forward, slowly gaining speed.

Carter vaulted the table and dove for the cow as she charged for the opening. Beckett made a grab for the closest chicken. John went after the regular-colored sheep that had stopped to nibble at Fitz's socks.

The ponies in the riding ring eyed the chaos balefully until Fitz, trying to pull himself to standing, accidentally unlatched the gate.

"Hold onto the lead!" Sammy yelled to Jax, who was gaping at the chaos from inside the fence and not paying attention to the dappled gray pony he led or to little Becky Halgren in the saddle. A chicken flapped Beckett right in the face. The little rider gave a high-pitched laugh, startling the pony.

It bolted, with its sticky-fingered novice rider clinging to the saddle, still laughing.

Farmer and fatherly instincts must have alerted John to the potential disaster. He gave up helping Carter drive the cow back into the enclosure and pivoted just in time to pluck Becky from the back of the pony.

"I'll get the purple sheep," Sammy called.

"You will? Don't you want to hear about my Air Jordans?" Ryan asked, but she was already running down the sidewalk. She spotted Eden and Layla sprawled on a park bench, watching the action with popcorn. "Need to borrow this," Sammy said, snatching the bag of popcorn away from Layla.

"Hey!"

"Sheep on the lam," she yelled over her shoulder. *Ha. She was totally funny.*

"Where do you need us?" Eden called after her, springing to her feet.

"Cut between the incense stand and the latkes truck. Try to

head it off. I'll come up on the flank, and we'll herd it back to the Pierces."

They split up, and Sammy slipped around the side of Velma Flinthorn's free-range chicken egg stand. The sheep appeared to be enjoying its freedom and was romping in an enthusiastic zig-zag through the grass and snow. Eden and Layla jumped into its path, startling the sheep. It made a 180-degree turn and loped away from them, heading in Sammy's direction.

Thinking fast, Sammy stepped out and sprinkled popcorn on the ground in front of her. "Come on, sheep. Come have a snack." She shook the bag. "Who wants popcorn?"

Thankfully, the purple sheep was feeling peckish. He trotted over and gobbled up the first few kernels.

"Good boy or girl," she said, unsure of the gender.

"Definitely a boy from this end," Eden said, eyeing the sheep's back end.

"Just follow me and the popcorn," Sammy instructed, sprinkling more kernels onto the ground.

"What do we do now?" Layla asked.

"Walk behind it with your arms out in case he turns around and tries to run," she told them, shaking the bag and walked backward. "And tell me if I'm going to run into something.

"Watch out for the chicken," Eden called.

"The what?"

Sammy blinked when the next piece of popcorn was gobbled up by a red hen that elbowed her way into the snack train.

"Is that a Pierce Acres chicken or someone else's free-range fowl?" Layla wondered.

It took patience and every kernel of popcorn in the bag, but they made it back to the petting zoo with the sheep and the chicken. A grinning Beckett opened the gate, and Sammy dumped the remainder of the popcorn on the ground.

Once everyone was officially corralled, the usually stoic John gave Sammy a hard, one-armed hug. His wife, Phoebe, who had missed the action while sampling mulled wines with her friend Elvira Eustace, gave her a noisy kiss on the forehead.

"What would Blue Moon do without you, Sammy?" Phoebe asked.

Sammy felt her cheeks flush at the praise.

"Nice going, kiddo," Carter said, ruffling her hair and making her feel even more breathless.

"It was a team effort," she said modestly to her shoes. The chaos had been quelled, the animals corralled. And the pigtailed Becky Halgren was getting a second, free ride to make up for the first near disaster.

"Thank you, girls, for your heroics. Last time this sheep got out, he wandered halfway to Cleary. Who knew David Bowie was such a huge fan of popcorn?" Phoebe mused.

"Uh. He is?" Sammy asked.

"She named the sheep David Bowie," John explained, giving the animal a slap on the rump. "You've got a hell of a way with animals, Sammy."

The praise made her feel warm inside.

"You also seem to have a fan," Phoebe observed, nodding across the park path. There stood cute Ryan still holding two cups of hot chocolate, his hair still in his eye.

"Kid needs a haircut," John grumbled. Phoebe elbowed him in the gut.

Eden gave Sammy a push in Ryan's direction. "Go make out with his face."

Sammy gave the Pierces and her friends a parting glance before crossing to Ryan.

"I saved this for you," he said, holding up her hot chocolate.

"Thanks," she said, attempting to wipe the snow and mud off her mittens. She was making more of a mess, so she gave up and stuffed them into her pockets. She accepted the cup and, following Eden's shooing motions, towed Ryan away from the crowd.

"Are you cold?" he asked.

She shook her head. The sheep chase had actually left her a little sweaty. "I'm fine," she said.

"Here." He unwound his scarf and looped it around her neck.

It was so soft and smelled like cologne. She didn't know what kind of material it was, but it felt expensive. She hoped her sweat wouldn't ruin it. "Uh. Thanks."

"You were pretty cool handling those animals," he told her as they strolled toward the end of the park, leaving the crowd, the smells of lasagna and patchouli incense behind them.

"Thanks. My mom's a veterinarian," she explained.

"Cool. My parents own a property management company. They want me to follow in their footsteps and join the family business. But I don't know."

Sammy felt a spark of commonality. "I know the feeling," she said. "Are all parents like that? I mean, is there a rule that says if your kids go to the same college you did or into your profession that means you made the right choices?"

"Whoa, blue eyes. That's deep," he teased.

A trickle of sweat worked its way down the back of her neck, and she hoped it wasn't burning a hole through the scarf. "Uh. So, do you want to go into property management?" she asked, steering the conversation away from any potentially off-putting philosophical questions.

Ryan seemed to be more comfortable when the conversation centered around him. And she felt more comfortable when other people were comfortable.

He shrugged. "It's okay. But if I *do* decide to do what they want, I can still do it on my terms, right?"

She stopped abruptly on the path. "Right," she said, the truth of it hitting her like a bolt of lightning.

As he rambled on about not wanting to work five days a week and shopping allowances, Sammy's brain turned the idea over.

There was nothing that said she had to go to Ohio State like her mother. Or that she *had* to use a veterinary career to build a legacy and a reputation. She could do it the way *she* wanted to. Heck, she didn't even need to join her mother's practice. She could practice veterinary medicine anywhere she wanted, and it wouldn't be because her parents said so.

Maybe, just maybe, she could find a happy medium between rebelling and conforming.

"Oh. Hey. Look at that."

Sammy followed the direction he pointed. Straight up.

"Mistletoe," she said, her pulse fluttering. *Oh boy. Oh boy. Oh boy. She forgot all about her potential future and focused on the present moment.*

She'd caught the eye of the cute guy, saved a sheep, and potentially solved her own "rebel or conform" debate. And then accidentally wandered into Mistletoe Corner.

It was a secluded little section of the park where a tall spruce wore hundreds of colored Christmas lights. In front of the tree, the Decorating Committee always strung a canopy of lights interspersed with mistletoe plants.

Maybe the Solstice magic wasn't over yet.

She wet her lips nervously, wondering if she should make the first move. *Did she know what the first move was? Should she stand on tiptoe? Tilt her head?*

Mid-worry about what to do with her hands, Ryan leaned down. That shock of blond hair tumbled across his forehead again. It was the last thing she saw before his lips touched hers.

Her first kiss was utter perfection. Under the mistletoe on a background of Christmas lights. She half-expected it to start snowing in further confirmation of a Solstice miracle.

But instead of fat, falling flakes, she got a shriek of dismay from a tall woman dressed in a puffy, lime green jacket and yellow ski hat.

"Ryan Shufflebottom! You get your fanny over here right now!" The woman stormed into the clearing like a principal about to start doling out detentions.

Sammy jumped back guiltily.

"Uh-oh," Ryan said.

"Yeah, uh-oh," the woman agreed. "You're *so* grounded. We're leaving. Now!"

Sammy wished the ground would swallow her up. *Was he in trouble because he kissed her? Would he think it was worth the punishment? Or was he already regretting it?*

"See you around, blue eyes. Maybe we'll meet again," her teenage Lothario said, giving her a little wink and one more hair toss.

She watched as Ryan Shufflebottom from Des Moines was dragged away by his mother, who was reciting the words "military school" like a mantra.

"What the hell just happened?" she wondered out loud.

2

_____

Friday, December 20, present day

"*What* in the hell is happening?" Ryan growled as yet another VW Bus cheerily tooted its horn while the driver tossed him a jaunty peace sign. "Stop waving. I don't know you."

In his opinion, it was too frigid for friendliness. There was actual snow on the ground. Not the kind of flaky crap that fell from the sky in Christmas movies. But frozen crusts of it, just lying there glistening like icy death traps in the fading afternoon sunlight.

He didn't bother wondering why he gave the driver a half-hearted wave—despite the fact that his life had imploded, he wasn't a complete asshole—but he did give passing thought to why this hippie hellhole had so many Volkswagen vans.

It seemed unnatural, as did everything else regarding his current situation. Including the fact that his knees were embedded in his armpits because the last rental car on the lot had been designed as a child's toy and not for a six-foot-two-inch-tall man.

"Turn right on Dharma Street," the car's snooty French GPS voice announced.

Ryan grudgingly took the turn. He was pissed off, unsettled, and several other adjectives along those same lines. The trip had been a whim. He didn't have whims. He had plans. Goals. Lists. Whims led to situations like *this*.

After a long-ass cross-country flight, he was careening through upstate New York—which was *significantly* colder than downtown Seattle in December—in a tuna can of a car heading into the unknown.

Mistake.

He should have spent the day in his comfortable, organized office, meeting with clients, saving them money, building their empires. But as of last week, that was no longer an option. Instead, he was shoehorned into a ridiculous electric car, off to save his great-uncle from whatever trouble he'd gotten himself into—Ryan's mother had been a little vague on that part.

Meanwhile, back in Seattle, his carefully planned and meticulously executed life was in shambles.

He felt like one of those razed casinos in Las Vegas. One push of a button, and years of hard work gone in an asbestos explosion.

So instead of having his usual dinner at his usual restaurant after his usual ten-hour Friday at work, he was cruising through Blue Fucking Moon's downtown. Which clearly had its halls decked by elves on hallucinogens.

To his left was the requisite small-town park. Except the normal open space and meandering paths had been replaced with an army of festive inflatables, including but not limited to a red and green peace sign, a ten-foot-tall menorah, and what looked to be a Kwanzaa unity cup.

Signs stabbed into the frozen ground shouted messages like "Oy to the World!" "Have a Cool Yule!" and "Merry Christmas!"

He was scoping out the huge spruce tree draped from top to trunk in thousands of multicolored lights when his phone rang. It took him half a block and three tries before he managed to stab the Answer button on the car's minuscule touchscreen.

"Yeah?" he snapped.

"Ryan! My favorite nephew," his great-uncle Carson's voice wheezed tinnily through the car's speakers.

They came from a big family. Ryan doubted he was even in the top five of favorite nephews.

"Hey, Carson. I'm almost there," he said, checking the GPS route. The too-friendly, too-festive town was thinning out and beginning to recede in his rearview mirror. He fervently vowed never to return.

"About that," Carson said. "I won't be there to greet you. You can let yourself in. Door's unlocked."

"I can wait outside for you," Ryan insisted, trying to keep the impatience out of his tone. He wasn't the kind of person who just barged into someone else's house.

Carson's cackle echoed inside the pumpkin orange Micro Machine. "You'll be waiting a long time, boyo! My sister had an emergency. I'm on my way to help."

Ryan's frown deepened.

"Turn left immediately," the French GPS robot announced briskly.

He slammed on the brakes and barely made the turn onto what was apparently some sort of unplowed, rutted path to nowhere.

"You don't have a sister," he reminded Carson. It was a big family, but the mandatory attendance of the Annual Shuffle-bottom Reunion ensured that all of the generations were reasonably familiar with each other.

Now he was going to have to report to his mother that her third favorite uncle was showing signs of mental decline. Fucking great.

"Did I say sister? I meant second cousin on my mother's side. She's like a sister to me," Carson said. "Anyway, that's why I'm on a plane to Boca."

Ryan came to an abrupt halt in the middle of the lane. "You're what?" he asked.

"On a plane."

"I thought you were the one with the emergency," Ryan reminded him.

He'd flown across the country and rented the world's stupidest clown car on zero sleep for nothing. He could have been home in sweatpants, halfway through that expensive bottle of whiskey he'd been saving for the special occasion that had never arrived.

"I *do* have an emergency," Carson insisted. "But that doesn't mean I can't help others. It's the Blue Moon way. My sister's emergency—" His uncle's voice cut off, and Ryan thought he heard someone else murmuring on the other end. "I mean my *cousin* just broke her... fetlock joint. She's having surgery."

Fetlock joint? Ryan was an accountant, not a surgeon. Even so, he was ninety-seven percent certain that the human body was devoid of fetlock joints.

"Okay," he said, blowing out a breath and counting backward from ten. It wasn't Carson's fault he'd gone batshit delusional. "Why did I fly across the country if you're not even here?"

"Because while I'm helping my cousin, you'll be helping me," Carson shouted from the speakers. "I need you to save my farm by Christmas Eve."

Christmas Eve was four days away.

"That's *not* an emergency, Carson," Ryan said, pinching the bridge of his nose and wondering if this was what an aneurysm felt like. "That's a damn Christmas movie."

He'd made the mistake of dating Marsha, a TV Christmas movie enthusiast. It had taken a valiant effort to overlook her obscene love of the campy, predictable entertainment. But her pluses should have evened out that annoying quirk. She was a smart, practical, well-dressed actuary with an impressive retirement account.

On paper, they made sense. However, in real life they just didn't add up. The entire relationship had been a misstep, putting him a full year behind on his plan to add a partner to his life before he made partner at the firm.

They'd broken up three days before last Christmas Eve when he found her planning the perfect outfit for the surprise Christmas morning proposal she was expecting. Apparently Marsha's practicality only extended to her career and wardrobe, not her love life.

A ridiculous, romantic proposal after only six months of dating was *not* in his life plan.

Ryan's Life Plan
   1. Make partner at the firm.
   2. Buy a bigger condo with solid resale potential.
   3. Find a suitable girlfriend to date for 18-24 months before proposing. Maybe an attorney or a financial advisor. No Christmas movie enthusiasts allowed.

"Christmas movie? You always were a joker," Carson wheezed.

Ryan had never once in his life been accused of being a joker.

"I'm counting on you, kiddo," his uncle continued. "I'm in a bit of a financial bind."

With gritted teeth, Ryan eased the car farther down the lane. Low banks of snow piled up on either side made it difficult to see what was beyond the driveway. He despised not knowing where he was going.

"What kind of trouble? Is some evil real estate developer going to take over your farm and build a bunch of environmentally unfriendly condos?" Sarcasm was Ryan's second language. He'd seen *that* movie four times. Or maybe it had been four movies with the same plot line. Either way, they'd all starred one of the actresses from *Full House*.

"Huh. Yeah. That!" his uncle said cheerfully. "Everything you need is in the house. It's unlocked. I'm counting on you."

"Counting on me to what?"

"Save the farm. Save the day. You're my only hope. Uh-oh. You're. Breaking. Up. Going through... tunnel."

This time Ryan very definitely heard someone else hiss in the background. "Not a tunnel, you nincompoop! You're on a plane."

"Oh, right. The plane is going through a sky tunnel. Bye!"

The call disconnected at the same moment his headlights cut through the gloom to illuminate a white clapboard farmhouse and a barn that had seen better days. Dusk had fallen like a heavy, wet blanket thanks to an unsettling lack of streetlights.

There was a lone rocking chair on the front porch. Limp garland hung unevenly from the railing. He hoped the unnatural blinking orange flames in the windows were electric candles and not several small fires since he didn't have the energy to play firefighter.

Romantically inclined visitors would likely be charmed by the country simplicity of the snowy scene. To the pragmatic and weary Ryan, it looked like the kind of place where innocent city dwellers went to get murdered.

He *really* didn't want to go inside. If he stepped foot on that front porch, he was actually going to have to spend the night there instead of driving back to the airport and demanding a one-way ticket home.

But he'd given his word. He needed to stop doing that.

He got out of the car, cursing the snow that swamped his expensive loafers and the wintery chill that squeezed him like a fist. Muttering his way through every four-letter word in his vocabulary, he wrestled his bags out of the back of the car and sullenly climbed the porch steps.

The welcome mat said Thanks for Dropping By. He wiped his feet harder than necessary across the cheerful sentiment. He didn't *want* to be thanked for "dropping by." He hadn't wanted to "drop by" in the first place. Trying the scarred brass knob, he found the front door unlocked as promised.

He dumped his suitcase and briefcase unceremoniously on the threadbare rug inside the door and searched for a light switch. He found it under a wad of sticky notes. The notes appeared to be in no particular order.

Buy new overalls.

Remember to turn off candles and fireplace.

Leave Ryan instructions on feeding chickens.

Breakfast with the BC.

The living room was a cramped rectangle. Built-in shelves crammed with tractor and chicken figurines surrounded a bulky TV set on top of a stand with a built-in electric fireplace. Next to an ancient recliner was a stack of yellowing *Monthly Moon* newspapers. The couch looked like something a drunk ninety-year-old picked out for her Florida condo. In 1984. It had orange and pink flowers and sagged in the middle under the weight of what looked like two dozen shoeboxes.

An upright piano partially blocked the front window that looked out onto the porch and whatever god-awful pastoral scenery was visible in the daylight.

To his right, oak-stained stairs with a worn green carpet runner went up to the second floor. Straight ahead, he could see the kitchen and dining room.

"Home sweet home," he grumbled to the empty house. As if on cue, the electric fireplace flickered to life. Apparently empty houses didn't get sarcasm.

Giving in to the exhaustion, he flopped down on the recliner and made a new plan.

Ryan's New Plan
1. Find a liquor store.
2. Drink half a bottle of whiskey.
3. Call Mom and break the news that her third favorite uncle had officially lost his damn mind.
4. Book flight home.

He felt good about everything except Number 3. But he was nothing if not efficient when it came to accomplishing unpleasant tasks.

The pink and purple tie-dye letterhead on the metal TV tray at his elbow caught his eye, and he picked it up. The paper smelled like the inside of one of those stores that sold dragon head letter openers and bongs.

Dear Mr. Shufflebottom,
It is with the deepest of regrets that the Blue Moon Bank must remind you that the balloon payment on your loan is due by 11:59 p.m. on Christmas Eve.

If you are unable to make the attached payment, we will be forced to collect the collateral—your farm—and remove you from the premises.

Wishing you and yours the happiest of solstice celebrations! Don't forget to cast your vote for us as Local Bank of the Year with the Chamber of Commerce!

Best wishes,

Rainbow Berkowicz, Blue Moon Bank President

Ryan flipped to the attached notice. The amount due made him pinch the bridge of his nose again.

"Fuck me."

New #4: Save Great-Uncle Carson's farm from foreclosure.

He needed to see a copy of the loan, the statements. Maybe the bank was pulling something over an elderly, not-right-in-the-head farmer? It wouldn't be the first time a financial institution screwed over the little guy. The accountant part of his brain started sifting through possible tactics.

He could use a win. Even if it was against some small-town, patchouli-scented bank that had probably never even heard of mobile deposit.

The stack of shoeboxes on the hideous couch caught his eye again. He shoved out of the chair to examine them. Each one was labeled: Receipts, Important Papers, Family Stuff, More Receipts and Paperwork, Stuff I Might Need Sometime.

There was a sticky note on top of the first box.

Ryan, Everything you need is here.

Curious, he lifted the lid. The box was crammed full of

crumpled receipts, a collection of rubber bands, and coupons for soap that expired in 1988.

"Nope. Whiskey first," he decided.

Grabbing his coat and keys, he headed back outside in the frigid December air, got into his roller skate of a car, and started to bump his way slowly down the snowy lane.

A large, white blob lumbered out of the dark several feet in front of him. The car's sensor beeped frantically. Ryan slammed on the brakes just as the navigation's French voice flatly announced an "object in road."

The dull thump seemed to come a second too late, but it still made his stomach turn.

3

---

*D*r. Sammy Ames's festive Santa scrubs smelled like cat pee. The love bite from an ornery parrot throbbed a little under the candy cane-striped bandage. And her Peace of Pizza lunch special had gone cold hours ago in a breakroom decked out in holiday decorations.

Her vet tech would have doubled over with laughter if he could see her now. But Demarcus was celebrating Hanukkah with his in-laws so there were no witnesses to her temporary foray into clinical veterinarian medicine.

It hadn't been a *bad* day, she decided, taking another bite of stale pizza.

She'd enjoyed the challenge of filling in at the veterinary clinic. But she was very much looking forward to returning to her own large animal practice in the morning. Her days were typically filled with house calls to inoculate livestock, perform ultrasounds on pregnant mares, birth calves. She was outdoors more than in, her patients much larger than the ones she'd seen today, and her clients were down-to-earth farmers.

Rolling out her shoulders, she checked the time on the kitty cat clock mounted to the wall. Its eyes ticked to the left as its tail tipped right. Closing time was twenty-seven minutes away. Which meant she was only an hour or so from a hot shower, clean pajamas, and some serious crafting time. If she didn't get her ass to a craft store and block out some serious hours over the next three days, her "great fundraiser idea" was going to be a gigantic failure.

"Hey, Dr. Sammy. Thanks again for filling in for Dr. Turner," Nimbus Miller, a swarthy former high school football star turned vet tech, greeted her as he bopped into the room and headed for the vending machine. The puffball on the end of his Santa hat swayed as he considered his options.

"It was no problem," she said. "I hope he's feeling better."

"Bet he'll rethink the family hot dog eating contest next time," Nimbus predicted, pressing the buttons for an apple walnut granola bar.

Dr. Turner had called in the favor at midnight the night before. *Diagnosis: Listeria-induced diarrhea.* He'd been on the schedule at the clinic for a twelve-hour shift. Still mostly asleep, Sammy had mentally kissed her own day off goodbye and agreed to take his shift.

It put her even further behind on Project Holiday Wreath, but this way, all the appointments were kept and animals were treated without delay. After all, that was the most important thing.

"Oh, hey. Think you'll have any wreaths with little icicles on them?" he asked.

"I'll save one for you," she promised, making a mental note to buy plastic icicles.

Her phone buzzed on the table. Nimbus threw her a salute as he chomped down half of the granola bar in one bite on his way out the door.

She wiped her hands on her scrub pants and answered. "Hey, Mom."

"Samantha." Dr. Anastasia Ames managed to convey quite a bit with one word. Aggravation, expectation, a vague annoyance that always accompanied her conversations with her daughter.

"What's wrong?" Sammy asked, biting back a sigh.

"First of all, I heard that you're working at the Turner Clinic today."

Her mother had retired from the practice to pursue more academic challenges. Those challenges required her parents to move closer to New York City, but the Blue Moon grapevine was long and tangled, delivering gossip to a wide network of past and present Mooners.

"You heard right. Dr. Turner had a medical emergency—a human one," Sammy explained. "He's taking my calls on Christmas Eve."

"I fail to see how you're going to build up the reputation of your own practice if you're too busy swapping shifts with some run-of-the-mill spay and neuter office."

"Mmm," Sammy hummed and took another big bite of cold pizza, knowing a defense wasn't actually expected.

"I'm sure I don't need to remind you how hard I worked to establish the practice you now run."

"Of course not," Sammy agreed, picking up the garden center's seed catalog.

"Not to mention how I think further dividing your attention by starting this non-profit is a huge mistake that you'll live to regret," Anastasia continued.

While her mom plowed through the list of baffling disappointments, Sammy paged through the catalog. Some daughters got guilt trips about not getting married or producing grandchildren fast enough. Sammy got lectures on carrying the family mantel. Dr. Anastasia Ames may have moved on from actually practicing livestock medicine—she taught it and spoke at conferences about it—but she still expected Sammy to somehow make her proud... without outshining the original Dr. Ames.

It took three pages of alfalfa and grass seeds before her mother's lecture began to wind down.

"Oh. While I have you," she said as an afterthought, "your father and I aren't coming for Christmas Eve. I'm giving a lecture the night before in Boston, and we've been invited to brunch with the Secretary of Agriculture. I don't want to have to rush off. So your father will put your gifts in the mail, and we'll touch base after the holidays on rescheduling."

Only Anastasia would put "by the way, I'm not spending Christmas with my only child" in the back seat in favor of leading with a lecture on duty and family responsibility.

"Okay. Well, I'll miss you guys," Sammy said because it was expected.

"Yes, well. Have a Merry Christmas," Anastasia said, also because it was expected. "Talk soon."

And just like that, her mother was gone. Dr. Ames was an important, busy woman who didn't have time for things like goodbyes.

Sammy hadn't even put the phone down when it buzzed in her hand. It was a text message from her father.

Dad: Already missing you, Sammy Girl! I had big plans for getting your mother drunk on eggnog so she'd go to bed early and we could watch Die Hard together without her complaining about "unrealistic stunts".

There was a collection of characters after the text, and Sammy guessed he'd been trying to send a frowny face.

Sammy: I'll miss you, too! Maybe we can watch it together after New Year's?

Dad: Sounds like a plan. Good luck with your fundraiser! Send pictures of your sold-out stand! Merry Christmas, kiddo. Love you.

Sammy: Merry Christmas, Pops. Love you.

It wouldn't be the same, and they both knew it. But overt sentimentality wasn't tolerated within the Ames family. Sammy and her father had learned to sneak it past Anastasia wherever possible.

She opened a separate text conversation and started typing.

Sammy: Okay. Who had my parents canceling Christmas on the 20th?

Layla: Yes! Me! Suck it, bitches!

Eva: Oh no! I'm so sorry! Does this mean you'll be alone for Christmas? That's so sad!

Sammy couldn't help but smile at Eva's response. She was the newest addition to the group of otherwise life-long friends. Not only was the woman a romance novelist who couldn't tolerate unhappy endings, she was also pregnant and hormonal. When she wasn't throwing up, she was crying.

Sammy: You're crying right now, aren't you, Eva?

Eva: Who would leave their only daughter all alone on Christmas? It breaks my heart!

Eden: What did I miss? Davis just made me orgasm twice in the kitchen, and I blacked out for a minute.

Eden was Sammy's best friend since third grade. They'd bonded over the unfortunate death of the class hamster while he'd been in their care. Mr. Biscuits had died of natural causes, but Sammy's mother still held a grudge for the dent it put in her reputation as a veterinarian.

Sammy: Eva, stay hydrated. Eden, I hope you sanitized the work surfaces after your orgasmic bliss.

Layla: Hey, remember the good old days when we used to all be single and no one was getting laid?

Eva: Layla, maybe it's the pregnancy hormones or writer's instinct, but I get the feeling your sexy next-door neighbor wouldn't mind making you not single.

Layla: N-O. Huckleberry Cullen is NOT my type. Besides, Sammy was the one at the top of the Beautification Committee's victim list.

Sammy shuddered. The Beautification Committee was a thin disguise for a diabolical matchmaking organization.

Sammy: I have zero mental energy to start a relationship right now. If the BC tries to pair me up with some bachelor Mooner right now it might just push me into the nunhood.

Eva: We're pretty busy with our nude calendar sales at the moment though. But our record speaks for itself. True love waits for no mental energy!

Eva and her sister Gia were the newest Beautification Committee recruits.

Layla: Don't waste your time. Unless the BC is planning to deliver the Mistletoe Kisser to Sammy's front door, you'll all be wasting your time.

Sammy: Do NOT give them any ideas. They burned a house down in the last match.

Eva: Allegedly! ALLEGEDLY burned a house down. And that was an accident. Also, it totally worked out in the end. You're welcome, Eden!

The Beautification Committee had—through accidental arson—managed to end a fifty-year feud *and* match Lunar Inn manager Eden with the next-door winery general manager Davis. The two were happily having sex everywhere and planning on building a house that would sit astride their respective property lines.

Eden: Hang on. Does this mean Christmas Eve Pajama Happy Hour is back on?

Layla: YES! I'll bring a slightly nicer veggie tray purchased with my new gambling winnings. I've also been saving this bottle of moonshine I got from some crazy West Virginia town. Bootleg Straps? Springs?

Eden: You can count on Davis and me for the wine and the dogs as if you need more animals running around your place.

Eva: Donovan is working Christmas Eve and I can't drink, but I'll bring snacks and freezer bags for me to throw up in.

Sammy: Best Christmas Eve ever.

She meant it. She didn't mind quiet holidays. She had good friends, great pets, and plenty of Christmas movies to keep her entertained in between naps and eating all of the cookie trays her clients insisted on giving her. It was a damn good life.

Sure, it would be nice to have someone around to swap stories of the day with in front of the fireplace with a tall glass of wine. Someone to have regular, awesome sex with. But where in the hell was she going to find a guy who didn't mind sharing a half-renovated house with three weird cats and a significant other that ended every day smelling like a barnyard?

For now, she'd stick with the plan. Finish the damn wreaths. Get her damn farm fixed up. And officially start the damn rescue.

"Get back here, Horatio!"

Sammy jolted as a humongous, hairy, half-washed dog bolted into the breakroom.

Jonica, the long-legged vet tech, slid into the room in soaking wet scrubs. The reindeer antler headband on her Afro was crooked.

Horatio, ninety pounds of mischievous mutt, evaded his captor by ducking under the table.

"Express his anal glands and he's fine, but try to give him a bath and he loses his damn mind!" Jonica complained as she crawled under the table.

A chair tumbled to the floor as the wrestling match ensued. Sammy was just getting ready to join the fray when a pissed off tomcat hissed in the doorway.

"How did Mufasa get out?" she yelped.

Horatio stopped squirming and made a mad dash for the evil cat.

Sammy did the only thing she could, executing a flying leap and tackling the dog one foot from the bad-tempered tiger cat.

The dog went pancake-flat under her and then wriggled

around to give her face and hair a lick with his giant pink tongue. She swore he was laughing at her as the hissing cat wandered off.

"You big doofus," she said, getting a firm grip on the dog's collar.

"My hero," Jonica said, shimmying out from under the table. Her antlers were around her neck.

"Just another day in veterinary medicine," Sammy quipped.

"Dr. Ames?" Another tech poked her head in the door. "We've got something for you to see in exam room two."

So much for closing on time. Sammy mentally pushed back her dreams of a shower by half an hour.

"What have we got?" she asked, dumping the remains of her lunch in the trash on the way to the door.

"It's kind of better if you don't know in advance."

There was a crowd in front of the open door to room two. Delighted snickers carried over the yowl of overnight kitty guests and the incessant yapping of Mrs. Chu's four-pound barking machine.

"What have we got?" Sammy asked, making a beeline for the hand-washing sink in the hallway and praying it wasn't a serious emergency.

"Don't tell her," tittered the receptionist who bore a jolly resemblance to Mrs. Claus in tie-dye.

Whatever was in the room, she'd probably already experienced at some point since veterinary school.

4

She was officially wrong. Inside exam room two, Sammy found one very handsome—married—man, a full-grown goat glaring at him, and three baby goats in holiday pajamas.

"Oh," she drawled out.

The office staff exploded in laughter, and she promptly closed the door in their faces.

Two of the babies ran around the exam table and took turns leaping onto and off the stainless-steel surface of the exam table. The third, in pink Hanukkah pajamas, was cuddled in the man's lap.

"Sammy! Thank God!" Jackson Pierce said, rising. The mama goat butted him in the ass with her head.

"What the hell, Jax?" Sammy laughed, grabbing a box of gloves out of Baby Goat #1's mouth.

"It's Thor," he said, gingerly placing the goat on the table. "I think she might have broken her leg. She's limping." He sounded like he was near tears. At least until the bigger goat gave him another headbutt. "Knock it off, Clem."

Clementine, mama goat and Jax's sworn nemesis, changed tactics and nibbled at the pocket of his jeans.

Sammy swallowed the laughter that bubbled up and started her physical exam of the pajamaed baby goat. "Clem, if you behave yourself and get your kids out of the sink, you can have treats," she told the other goat. She'd been Clementine's vet since taking over the practice from her mother. Now that she thought about it, her mother reminded Sammy a lot of the yellow-eyed cantankerous goat.

With the promise of treats hanging in the balance, Clementine coaxed her able-bodied babies out of the sink and into a corner.

"I hate you," Jax told the goat.

Clementine grinned evilly at him.

Man and goat had maintained a contentious relationship since she'd appeared on the family farm years ago. Clementine was friendly to everyone except Jax. However, they'd formed a tentative truce when the goat—that the entire family assumed was just getting fat—broke into Jax and Joey's house and had three babies on his side of the bed. The babies ignored their mother's hatred of the man and followed him everywhere.

"Is it broken?" Jax worried. "Is it caprine arthritic encephalitis? *Are her feet rotting?*"

"Get a hold of yourself and stop Googling shit, Jax," Sammy said, gently lifting the goat onto her feet to stand on the table. "Can you walk for me, Lady Thor?"

The little goat's tail flicked happily as she limp-skipped toward Jax at the end of the table.

"See? It's broken, isn't it?"

The poor guy looked like he was going to be sick. Thor nuzzled him and playfully bit at the string on his hoodie.

"It's going to be fine, goat dad." Sammy gently felt down the goat's front leg to confirm the diagnosis. "It's just a kid sprain.

She should be all healed in three or four days. It happens a lot with baby goats. Their bones are still soft."

Clementine grabbed Jax's sleeve and pulled hard enough to rip the fabric.

"Relax, you abominable douche. Your kid is going to be fine. You're sure, right?" He gave Sammy a side eye.

The man was unfairly good-looking *and* a hugely successful screenwriter. His gorgeous wife, Joey, was a partner in the stables and breeding program at Pierce Acres. Sammy bet they had crazy sex under the Christmas tree when their kids went to bed.

"Right. Listen, I'll put some tape on Thor's leg here to help keep it stabilized." Sammy told him. It wasn't totally necessary, but it would make Goat Dad Jax feel better. "How are the kids? The human ones," she added, turning to dig out the vet tape from the drawer.

Jax puffed up with pride as he stroked a hand down Thor's back. "Reva got into Centenary's equestrian program."

"Following in Joey's riding boots," she mused, carefully wrapping the fluffy little leg in hot pink tape.

"We're both secretly hoping she'll come back and help run the stables when she graduates, but Jojo doesn't want to 'pressure her' into anything." He made a single air quote with the hand that wasn't holding the baby goat still. "Caleb's kicking ass in school. Except for math."

"Joey said he's been following Carter around like a puppy on the farm," Sammy said, finishing off the wrap job and giving the goat a pat on the head.

"Another generation of farmer," he said proudly.

Pierce Acres was a family farm that raised crops, rescued livestock, and now bred some of the finest horses in the state. The land had also sprouted three very handsome men. Each married now, continuing the circle their parents had started by growing families of their own.

"All set here," she said, placing Thor on the floor, then raiding the pet treat jar. "A couple of days, and she should be fine. If she's still limping after Christmas, give me a call, and I'll come check her out."

He threw his arms around her. "You're the best, Sammy."

"I know," she said, giving him a squeeze. The Pierce brothers were excellent huggers.

"You smell like cat piss and wet dog," he whispered.

She sighed. "I know."

With treats and treatment dispensed, Sammy walked him out to the—thankfully—empty waiting room.

"You didn't bring this circus in your car, did you?" she asked. Jax drove a sexy vintage Chevy Nova that he treated almost as nicely as his wife and their adopted kids.

He gave her that mischievous grin that had been melting hearts for a few decades now. "I stole Jojo's SUV. If I can get it back in the next twenty minutes, she'll never know."

Sammy found Jax's delusion adorable. In her experience, a woman *always* knew when someone stole her vehicle and used it to transport farm animals.

Clementine jogged over to the scale and jumped up on it. She put her front hooves on the wall and stretched to reach the anything-but-tasteful nude Beautification Committee calendar. The goat took a bite out of December while the two babies not cradled in Jax's arm jumped onto the first vinyl chair and romped onto the next, the whole way around the room.

The receptionist was laughing so hard that tears slid down her cheeks as she swiped Jax's credit card.

"Need help herding them out?" Sammy offered, checking her watch. It was five past closing, and that shower was calling her name.

38

She'd help shove these goats in a car, lock the front door, and be elbow-deep in craft wire and pine boughs in no time.

Jax was just scrawling his signature on the credit card slip when the front door burst open.

"What the—" Sammy's brain couldn't quite keep up with she was seeing.

A sheep wearing what looked like a makeshift halter of a leather belt and mismatched tie-down straps careened into the waiting room, dragging a body behind it.

The humans in the room froze.

The goats gleefully raced to investigate the intruder. As the baby goat in the Happy Kwanzaa onesie nimbly hopped up onto the sheep's back, the body behind the sheep raised its head and then began a slow scramble to its feet.

His feet.

His *big* feet.

Big feet clad in fancy loafers caked with mud. Stylish, low-slung jeans were wet at the knees and smeared with more mud. The man's sweater had—until recently—been a blinding white. Now it was damp and dirty. Sammy could see the point of one manly nipple through the wet fabric.

Then there was his freaking face. *Holy guacamole, that face.*

Eyes: Cloudy winter gray and troubled. Jaw: Chiseled with a dusting of new stubble. Mouth: Sternly frowning. Hair: Medium brown. Neatly and expensively cut. Currently accessorized with a few leaves and at least half a cup of dirt.

There was something deliciously grumpy and broody about him.

The sheep bleated and trotted up to her, raining baby goats onto the linoleum floor. It stopped at her feet and looked up expectantly.

"Is there a sheep and a hot, dirty guy in front of me, or am I hallucinating?" Sammy whispered.

39

"Girl, we're both hallucinating," Jonica sighed, appearing next to her, her brown eyes glued to the man glaring at the sheep. "Dirty hot is *so* my type."

"You are aware that I can hear you, aren't you?" Dirty Hot Stranger said snidely with a gravelly voice.

"Whoops. Sorry," she said, recovering.

"Are you the vet?" he demanded, eyeing her skeptically.

"I am. How can I help you?"

"Here." He shoved the end of the leash at her and turned for the door.

5

How could she help him? Ha.

The veterinarian in ridiculous, stained Christmas scrubs with her blonde hair exploding out of a crooked ponytail didn't look like she could help herself, much less him.

Besides, he was beyond help. And that was before he may or may not have accidentally hit the sheep with his teeny-tiny stupid car.

"Hold it," she said as he headed for the door.

Despite her disheveled appearance, the vet's voice was steely enough that it stopped him in his tracks.

"You can't just abandon your sheep," she warned him.

"It's not *my* sheep," Ryan argued. "This woolly mammoth belongs to some irresponsible hippie. He ran out in front of my car. I don't know if I hit him or if he's hurt. Or if he's a he," he supplied, refusing to resume control of the makeshift leash he'd made with his own belt and supplies he found in his stupid car's tiny hatch. "He answers to Stan."

After "Hey, sheep" and "Stupid, jackass livestock" hadn't elicited a response from the animal, Ryan had to get creative.

It had been easier than he'd thought to stuff the sheep into the passenger seat. Stan had hopped right in. Catching him had been another story. Ryan's shoes were ruined. His jeans were wet from the snow he'd fallen in five or six times. And his hands were so numb he had serious concerns about losing digits.

Now he appeared to be in a stare down with the bigger, non-pajamaed goat. Ears flicking, it stalked toward him. Ryan took two steps back. *Great. He was going to die by goat.* It was a fitting end to a disastrous week.

"Back off, demon," he said.

"She's mostly friendly," the man cradling a baby version of the yellow-eyed monster assured him. "She only hates me."

As if to prove his point, the goat changed directions and head-butted the guy in the thigh.

"You mother-effer," the guy hissed through his teeth.

Ryan wondered if he was cleaning up his language for the sake of the baby goats. This town was insane.

"Knock it off, Clementine," the vet said sternly. The goat actually looked contrite.

Kneeling face-to-face with the sheep, the doctor stroked competent hands over Stan's thick wool. The sheep's tail fluttered like he—or she—was enjoying the attention. Ryan hoped it was a sign of sheep happiness and not an impending sheep shit.

"He ran out in front of me. I slammed on the brakes. I couldn't tell if I hit him or a pothole. It took me half an hour to catch him and load him up," he explained, still not quite believing this is what his life had come to.

"Where did you find him?" Goat Guy asked.

"On a farm," he said, shoving his hand through his hair and finding more mud there.

"Whose farm?" the vet asked without looking up from her examination of the sheep's legs.

"My great-uncle's. Carson Shufflebottom. I think everyone here knows him as—"

"Old Man Carson," Goat Guy filled in.

"Yeah."

At the mention of his uncle's name, the vet gave him a weird look.

"Carson doesn't have any sheep," the vet said, blowing a hunk of honey blonde hair out of her eyes. "Just chickens."

Freaking small towns. Where everyone knew who had what livestock.

She stood, still avoiding his gaze and coaxed the sheep to walk with her around the waiting room. The beast pranced like a show pony next to her. He caught a glimpse of a bright, shiny smile as the vet beamed down at Stan.

She had one hell of a smile. The kind that if it was aimed in his direction had the potential to knock him back a step. People who smiled a lot made him suspicious. No one should be that happy all the time.

"You're not Ryan, are you?" she asked, snapping him out of his suspicion.

He debated lying. God only knew what unstable Uncle Carson had told his hometown about him. Then decided it didn't matter what a reasonably attractive veterinarian in a town he'd never visit again thought of him.

"I am," he admitted.

"Listen, Sammy. I gotta get the kids and Jojo's car back," Goat Guy announced, hooking his thumb toward the door.

"Better hurry, Jax, or Joey will make sure you never finish that screenplay," the vet—Sammy apparently—said. "Call me if Thor's limp doesn't get better."

Jax—what kind of a name was that anyway—leaned in and gave the vet a kiss on the cheek. Ryan moved the too-charming man onto his Things to Dislike About Blue Moon list right between "the weather" and "free range farm animals".

"You're my hero, Doc," Jax said with a wink and grin that in Ryan's opinion weren't at all charming. "Good luck with your sheep," Jax said to Ryan.

"He's not my sheep," Ryan said. But his argument was lost in the chaos of the other man rounding up his four-legged army of weird and heading out the door.

A pretty, reindeer-antlered tech held the door for him and stood there grinning after him.

"Are you going to help him, Jonica?" Sammy asked the tech.

"I'm gonna watch and laugh for a minute before I offer any assistance," she called over her shoulder before ducking out the door.

Sammy laughed and shoved a wayward curl out of her face. It flopped defiantly back into place.

"Good news," she said, crossing the gray linoleum tile and holding out the leash. "Your sheep is fine. No cuts or swelling. No limping. I don't think you hit him."

Ryan blew out a breath. At least he hadn't run over a sheep. That was the one and only tick mark in the Reasons Life Doesn't Suck column.

"Good. But he's still not my sheep," he repeated.

Now the damn thing was staring at him. So was the vet. She jiggled the end of the belt leash at him.

"Can't you keep him? Find his family?" Ryan asked, staring dumbly at the leash. If he reached for it, if he touched it, the sheep was his responsibility. He was familiar with the rules of No Takesies Backsies.

Besides, he had a small-town bank to destroy and a plane ticket to book.

"We don't have the facilities to house livestock here and we can't just let him roam free," she insisted.

44

"Look. I just got into town an hour ago for a family emergency—"

"Is Carson okay? I talked to him this morning, and he didn't mention an emergency," she asked, looking worried.

Her eyes reminded him of a field of lavender. Fresh and bright. Maybe he was coming down with something? He didn't have romantic notions about attractive strangers and lavender fields. He slapped a hand to his forehead, but everything felt hot compared to his frozen palm.

"He's fine," Ryan said, shoving his frozen hands back into his pockets. She couldn't *make* him take the sheep. "He had to fly to Boca to help his second cousin after her surgery."

"He's eighty-five-ish years old," she said with the faintest smile on unpainted lips.

"Apparently the cousin is ninety-nine."

"That's some longevity you've got in your family." She took a step toward him, still holding the makeshift leash.

He took a step back like she was asking him to hold her pet snake. The backs of his legs caught the edge of the waiting room bench, and he half-fell, half-sat.

She reached out and took his hand, and for a split second, Ryan felt something besides the cold, besides the frustration and despair that had lodged in his very soul for a week. It was a warm shock to the system. For a second, he craved more with an intensity that made him rather nervous.

But that shot of heat dissipated when she firmly placed the end of the belt in his hand and closed his fingers around it.

"No," he insisted, tossing the leash back at her.

"Yes," she said firmly.

"I have no sheep experience, and I'm in the middle of several personal crises. So *you* can take this sheep and do *your* damn job."

"Are you staying on Carson's farm?" Sammy asked, ignoring his very logical argument.

"Yes, but—"

"Put him in the barn tonight and then let him into the south pasture in the morning. The fence is in good shape, and there's tall fescue in there for grazing."

"You're a veterinarian. You can't turn your back on a sheep in need. I almost ran him over. I have no idea what fescue is. Stan is in mortal danger in my care."

She laughed. "I have faith in you, Ryan."

"Great. A stranger in wet Santa scrubs who smells like animal urine has faith in me. That means the world," he ranted. He was tired. Hungry. Grumpier than usual. And had concerns that he was careening into a full-blown nervous breakdown.

She released a sigh nearly as weary as his soul felt. "You don't remember me, do you?" she asked.

"Why in the hell would I remember you?" he demanded. He'd never been to this bizarre, little, special-brownie twilight zone before and he highly doubted she'd come to him for accounting advice. He would have remembered that face, those lavender eyes.

"Winter Solstice Celebration? Fifteen years ago? One Love Park?" she pressed.

"I know very few of the words that just came out of your mouth."

Fifteen years ago, his parents had announced their divorce. He'd spent that Christmas morning in his father's bare-walled condo eating cold cereal and opening a plastic bag of unwrapped presents. That afternoon he'd been shuttled to his mother's new townhouse to repeat the process. It had sucked. Every Christmas since had pretty much sucked too.

Great. An hour in this damn polar hamlet, and he was already suffering from Seasonal Affective Disorder.

"You seriously don't remember?"

Now she looked annoyed. *Good.* Ryan liked annoyed better than amused. "Look. I don't know you. I don't know this sheep. And I have shit to do," he announced.

With that, he spun on his heel and pushed through the door.

"It's not like I don't know where you're staying," she called after him.

"I'll be gone by lunch tomorrow," he predicted.

Without a backward glance at Goat Guy chasing the big goat around the parking lot, Ryan headed in the French-accented direction of the nearest liquor store.

The Monthly Moon: *Apocalypse Recovery a Long Road: How to Grow Out Your Perm by Anthony Berkowicz*

6

———

*L*unar Liquors was located across the street from a grocery store called Farm and Field Fresh. Ryan zipped his car into a spot at the back of the lot. On reflex, he pulled out his phone and tried to check his work emails. When the app prompted him for his new username and password, he remembered there was no work, therefore, no work emails.

He did, however, have a text from Bart Lumberto, one co-worker he wouldn't be missing. Bart was a pot-bellied ass-kisser who stole clients and dumped all the work on the firm's book-keepers. His aunt was a partner which meant Bart had never been taken to task for his assholery.

Bart: *Trying it on for size. Thanks for the bigger office, dipshit.*

Ryan gripped his phone so hard the case cracked. The jackass had sent a picture of *his* feet propped on *Ryan's* desk.

"Fuck."

Any tiny scrap of hope he'd been holding on to that the partners would reconsider their decision and give him another chance extinguished. There was only one thing left to do. Ryan pried himself out of the car and shivered his way to the door of the liquor store.

He stepped inside and was blasted with both heat—a welcome sensation for his mostly frozen face—and "The Twelve Days of Christmas" wailing from the speakers in the ceiling.

Ryan had been in his share of liquor stores since turning twenty-one a decade or so ago. They all seemed to have the same displays of the same bottles, the same moderately depressed clientele, the same bitter employees.

However, as with everything else in this trippy town, this particular liquor store was different. Instead of avoiding eye contact like respectable patrons, the shoppers here gathered and gossiped in aisles. Employees wore hideous holiday sweaters and Santa hats with mini liquor bottles attached where the requisite white puffball usually was.

Just when he thought it couldn't get more annoying, everyone in the store paused what they were doing to half-sing, half-shout "Fiiiive golden riiings!"

He gritted his teeth. One bottle of decent whiskey, and he could go back to Carson's and drink until he could pretend this entire week had never happened.

Usually, he had a much more proactive approach to problem-solving.

Ryan's Regular Problem-Solving Plan
  1. Analyze the problem.
  2. Identify the obstacles.
  3. Outline potential solutions.
  4. Choose the most efficient option.
  5. Craft and execute an action plan.

But being stuck in this holiday nightmare with a blurry family emergency while someone else tried on his chair and his clients for size called for a more intensive method.

Ryan's Emergency Disaster Plan
  1. Drink until he couldn't see straight.
  2. Pass out.
  3. Be so hungover he would forget about any and all problems for the 48 hours it took him to get over the hangover.
  4. Feel like an idiot.
  5. Humbly move on to Regular Problem-Solving Plan.

He'd only had to enact his Emergency Disaster Plan twice before. Once when he'd failed one of the sections of the Certified Management Accountant certificate. And then again when he'd been passed over for his first promotion at work. In both cases, he'd redoubled his efforts (after the hangover, of course) and accomplished what he'd set out to do.

He ignored the aisle of cheerfully labeled wines with names like Bohemian Riesling and Dirty Hippie Chardonnay, heading instead for the Whiskey/Bourbon sign. It was a popular aisle.

A woman with waist-length, silvery dreadlocks and a Peace of Pizza T-shirt winked at him as she passed with a bottle of Lagavulin. She had good taste, not that he was ever inclined to make small talk with a stranger.

Instead, he gave her a nod and then tried to maneuver around a couple so mismatched it was almost comical. The man was in Dockers and a starched button-down under a dreidel tie. The woman had jet-black hair in pigtails secured by skull clips wearing Santa hats. Instead of a sensible wool coat like the guy, she was wearing a floor-length, dark purple cape embroidered with silver thread. Her boots looked like they were less for snow and more for mosh pits.

The nerd and the goth princess.

They were being questioned by a skinny man of indeterminate age wearing a homemade Support Your Local Exotic Dancer T-shirt and breaching what Ryan considered to be the common decency standard of personal space. "So, if I build a shed over my bunker and store some of my used paperbacks and G-strings in there, can I write it off as a work expense?" he asked.

"Well, maybe," the nerd hedged. His glasses were fogging up. "I'd need more information. Like if you were also using the structure for personal use. And what the ratio between personal and professional usage would be."

Ah, the nerd was a fellow accountant. Ryan thought he'd recognized the resignation of a professional being pounced on in public for free advice.

"Why don't you make an appointment with Mason, Fitz?" goth girl suggested sweetly.

"Ha! Good one, Ellery! Then I'd have to pay him for his time," Fitz the exotic dancer fan, or—God forbid—the actual exotic dancer, chuckled.

"You know, tax preparation is a deduction," the accountant hinted.

Ryan skirted the free advice dispensary but accidentally made and held uncomfortable eye contact with the goth queen. Her dark purple lips curved up. Another smiler. *What was it with this town?*

Finally, he made it to the whiskey shelves. It was a decent selection for a town that was barely a blip on the map.

He was debating between a scotch and a bourbon when a very small redhead clutching a very large bottle of tequila bumped into him. In fuzzy pajama pants, pink boots, and a Pierce Acres sweatshirt she'd clearly stolen from an adult, the kid looked like the kind of student elementary school teachers hoped didn't land in their class.

"Oopsies! Sorry," she said, beaming up at him.

"Aren't you a little young to be buying tequila?" he asked.

She threw back her head and laughed until her tangled curls shook. "You're funny!"

"Aurora!" A guy with a nice suit, nicer wool coat, and a familiar-ish face rounded the corner.

"Hi, Bucket!"

"Short Cake, how many times have I told you not to wander off in here? Sorry," the man said to Ryan. "Last time I brought her in here, I found her behind the register asking to see Old Man Carson's ID."

Ryan let out a rusty, short laugh. Small towns meant small worlds, he guessed. "Carson is my great-uncle," he said, then wondered why he'd willingly volunteered the information.

"You must be nephew Ryan. I'm Beckett Pierce, attorney and mayor of this circus. This is my daughter, Aurora."

"Technically, Bucket is my stepdad," Aurora explained. "But we don't like to use that label in our family. He's my real dad just like my other real dad because s-e-x doesn't always equal family."

Beckett—or Bucket—looked a little misty-eyed over the whole "real dad" thing. Ryan didn't feel like he was up for an emotional family moment.

Thankfully, Santa's overanxious twin bustled around the corner into the aisle and interrupted. "Mayor Pierce!"

"Shit," Beckett said under his breath. Aurora looked delighted.

"Bruce, how many times do I have to tell you to call me Beckett?" the mayor said. "Aurora, put the tequila down."

"You know how I feel about disrespecting your office," Bruce, the Santa look-alike, insisted.

Beckett bit back a sigh. "Have you met Carson's nephew Ryan?"

Bruce glanced at Ryan. "Of *course* I know Ryan. He's from Seattle, even though the rest of his family is in Pennsylvania. You really should visit home more often, you know."

"Uhhh." Ryan didn't know what to say to that.

"We'll catch up later," Bruce said to him with confidence. "Mayor Pierce, I have a dire situation that I must discuss with you immediately."

Beckett closed his eyes for a moment. "Bruce. You are the town supervisor. I have complete faith that whatever crisis arises, you can handle it on your own tonight. Because I am spending the entire night alone with my wife while my saint of a mother takes the girls for a sleepover and Evan is with the debate club in Corning."

"I'm afraid some situations are a bit more urgent than a quiet evening at home," Bruce insisted as he fidgeted with the zipper on his coat.

Beckett gripped the man's shoulder. "Bruce. Nothing. I repeat. *Nothing* is more important than getting home to my empty house where my beautiful wife is waiting for me to show up with a bottle of wine."

Santa Bruce opened his mouth, but Beckett cut him off. "Nothing," he repeated. "Now, if you'll both excuse me, I need to get Aurora home to hand her off to my... Mom?"

At the end of the aisle, a woman wearing a floppy felt hat and glasses looked up. Her eyes went wide and she tried to duck behind a display of holiday-themed wine gift bags.

"Hi, Gram!" chirped Aurora, the underage tequila shoplifter.

"You're not invisible, Mom," Beckett said dryly.

The mayor's mother popped back up, abandoning the charade. Just then, everyone paused and shouted "Fiiiive golden riiings!"

"Oh, hi, Aurora, Beckett, Bruce..." Her gaze tracked to Ryan. "Man I don't know."

53

"This is Carson Shufflebottom's great-nephew Ryan," Beckett said.

"From Seattle. The one with the condo with the concrete countertops," Bruce added.

Ryan added Santa Bruce to his list of things he didn't like about Blue Moon right under "spontaneous singalongs in liquor stores".

"Hi, Ryan. I'm Phoebe. This one's mother and that one's grandmother," she said, pointing to Beckett and then Aurora with a large bottle of merlot.

"Uh. Hi," Ryan said, growing increasingly uncomfortable. He wished the aisle was wide enough to escape this conversation.

"What are you doing here, Mom?" Beckett asked. "I'm supposed to have the kids to your place in fifteen minutes."

Phoebe joined them in the aisle, crowding Ryan even further. "I'm preparing to babysit," she explained, shooting a pointed look at Aurora. "How are you liking Blue Moon so far, Ryan?"

Don't be an asshole, Ryan cautioned himself. It wasn't a babysitting grandmother's fault his life was a disaster. "It's uh... very festive," he said. "Full of livestock."

"It certainly is," she agreed. "What brings you to town?"

Bruce was making a suspicious slashing motion across his throat.

Phoebe's eyebrows rose over her glasses. "Oh," she said as if someone had answered her question. "Well, good luck with... everything."

Beckett rolled his eyes toward the ceiling while Bruce laughed nervously.

Ryan had the distinct impression that he was missing something. Not that he cared to figure out what that something was. No small-town shenanigans could measure up to the hell he'd endured this week.

"Gram, I picked this out for you," Aurora announced, proudly holding up her tequila. "You can have some while I give Grampa a makeover!"

The kid was going to be a menace in her teenage years, Ryan predicted. Mother and son shared a silent and pointed exchange. *You owe me*, Phoebe's face said to Beckett.

"Let Gram see that bottle," Phoebe said with a sigh. Aurora handed it over and her grandmother studied the label then shrugged. "Good enough for me and Grampa Glamorous."

"Yay!" Aurora squealed. "Mr. Oakleigh, can I pick something for you?" She was already reaching for a bottle of something called Sour Apple Pucker. It looked like NyQuil.

"That's quite all right," Bruce said, patting her on her snarl of red curls. "But you can tell your daddy how much I need his attention regarding an issue with the state auditor."

"Nah. I'd rather pick a drink for you," the kid said.

"What's the problem, Bruce?" Phoebe asked.

"Well, it seems that there is a problem with our paperwork—"

Beckett cut him off. "Bruce is town supervisor. He's going to supervise. *I* am going home to my beautiful, impatient wife, and *you*," he said, pointing at Phoebe, "are taking my children so Gia and I can speak in complete sentences for one whole night."

"But—"

Beckett cut off Santa Bruce with one raised hand. Bruce, looking like a recently kicked puppy, slunk off down the aisle.

Ryan tried to do the same, but his way was blocked by a store employee with a cart of stock for the shelves.

"I expect you to be feeling very grateful toward Franklin and me, favorite son," Phoebe said cagily.

"Extremely," Beckett agreed.

"*How* extremely?" she pressed.

"Day spa for you and Franklin at that place you like."

"The Hershey Spa? Hmm. Three treatments each," she said, cocking her head.

"Two treatments, plus lunch," her son bargained.

"Deal," Phoebe said smugly.

Ryan decided it was beyond time to extricate himself from the conversation. He attempted to squeeze past Aurora, but she very deliberately stepped in his way and grinned. *Diabolical child.* He turned to try the other way, but a couple in matching corduroy bell-bottoms was hogging half the aisle and making excited exclamations over some kind of organic wheatgrass vodka.

In desperation, he snatched a bottle off the employee's cart. "Well, I need to go take care of... this bottle," Ryan announced, holding up the bottle.

Phoebe clinked her tequila to his whiskey. "It was nice meeting you, Ryan. If you need anything while you're in town, let me know."

"Uh. Thanks," he grumbled. He'd be on a plane by tomorrow and doubted there was anything he'd need help with in less than twenty-four hours.

Phoebe turned her attention back to her son and grand-daughter. "I'll see you two in—" she glanced down at her watch. "Not very many minutes." With a wave, she headed toward the cash register.

"Don't drink all of the tequila before we get there," Beckett said, playing tug-of-war with Aurora over a cheap bottle of peach-flavored vodka.

The frustration and abject fear on Beckett's face made things click into place. Ryan snapped his fingers. "Goat Guy."

Beckett won the battle and pulled the bottle free. "What Guy?"

"Goat Guy," Ryan repeated. "That's who you look like. I met him at the vet clinic. Do you have a brother?"

"Two. Which one was it?" Beckett asked.

Ryan couldn't remember anything besides not liking the way the guy flirted with the vet. "He's the one with all the goats."

He assumed that would narrow it down enough. He assumed wrong.

"Big beard or short beard?" the mayor asked, stroking a hand over his own neatly groomed beard.

Ryan had never been asked to classify facial hair before. "More stubble than beard."

The mayor nodded. "That would be Jax. He's the youngest. The goat hates his guts."

Jax, the cheek kisser. Ryan still thought it was a stupid name.

Aurora giggled. "Clementine wants to eat Uncle Jax. It's sooo funny! Also, he looks nice in blue eyeshadow."

Ryan didn't want to know how she'd obtained that information. He didn't care for how the little girl was studying him like she was trying to figure out if he'd look better in spring or winter colors.

"Well, it was nice to meet you," he lied, thankful that the aisle had finally cleared, leaving him with an actual escape route.

"You as well," Beckett called after him.

"Bye, Ryan!" Aurora waved.

He ducked into the checkout line closest to the door. There was a display of hideous, hand-knit hats, mittens, and scarves. He averted his eyes from the rainbow of lopsided winter gear and stared at his shoes to thwart any more conversations with strangers. The bell jingled, and two more customers entered, bringing with them a cloud of frigid winter air.

Damn it. It was still fucking cold.

"Fiiive golden riiings!" shouted the customers around him.

With the regret of a man who enjoyed a tasteful wardrobe, he grabbed the scarf set from the display and threw it down on the counter next to the bottle. They would get him through the ride out to Carson's. And it didn't matter if anyone saw him in it. Because he was leaving and never returning to Blue Moon.

7

*S*howered, changed, and accompanied by one Stan the sheep, Sammy pulled up to Old Man Carson's farmhouse. The lights on the first floor were on, casting a cozy glow out into the winter night. There was an electric car the size of a ladybug parked out front.

The house looked the same as it always had. Sammy had been coming to the farm with her mother since she was old enough to hand the doctor the right instrument at the right time. Carson Shufflebottom was practically a historical figure in Blue Moon. He was in his eighties but looked closer to a hundred. His wife—an excellent gardener and horseshoes tournament champion—had passed away before Sammy was born. So Carson belonged to the community.

Neighbors brought him meals. Fellow old-timers kept him company at doctors' appointments and Saturday diner breakfasts. As Carson's age crept up, his ability to take care of the land and equipment declined, so farmer friends and visiting family stepped in to help with the upkeep.

It had been a favor to her to have Carson keep the scraggly flock of chickens she'd liberated from a neglect situation. He'd enjoyed having animals around again and spent hours in a lawn chair in the pasture, whittling and philosophizing with the newly free-range birds.

The bigger, higher-maintenance rescues were spread out amongst a network of soft-hearted farmers to foster rescued livestock until her own barn and pastures were ready.

If necessary, she'd give that list of farmers a call tomorrow to see if any of them would mind taking Stan the sheep for a few days while she worked on finding his owners. But for tonight, she was teaching Ryan "Why Should I Remember You and Here, Have a Sheep" Shufflebottom a lesson.

Sliding out from behind the wheel into the cold night, Sammy drew in a breath of sharp, crisp air that invigorated her lungs. "Let's go, Stan," she said, opening the back door.

The sheep happily followed her out of the SUV and trotted into the snow while she wrestled the bale out of the hatch and huffed and puffed her way into the barn.

The flock of chickens squawked at her from their temporary coop inside. "You guys can go outside tomorrow," she promised them. Finding the first stall clean enough, she made quick work of spreading the straw for a comfy, temporary sheep bed. She added a scoop of pellets to the feed bin then found and filled a heated water bucket.

"Okay, bud. Head on in. Your grumpy roommate will let you out to graze in the morning, and we'll go from there," she promised.

Obediently Stan shuffled into the stall and shoved his face into the food bin.

Sammy secured the stall door and headed back out into the December cold. She debated just leaving, but her first kiss had grown into an adult ass. Ryan Shufflebottom needed to understand he couldn't come to town, not remember her, and start abandoning livestock all over town.

There were rules, after all.

She'd just pop in, yell at him a little, and be on her way. If she kept the lecture short, she could finish a half-dozen wreaths before bedtime. *Okay. That was a little optimistic. Maybe three wreaths.*

Sammy took the porch steps two at a time and gave the front door an authoritative rap.

A muffled snarl sounded on the other side of the door.

In Blue Moon, that was good enough to be considered an invitation. She pushed open the front door and stopped short when she spotted him.

He was kicked back in Carson's favorite recliner, wearing one of Enid Macklemore's rainbow knit hats and one mitten. A mostly empty bottle of whiskey sat on the ancient metal TV tray next to him. It was wrapped in the matching scarf.

"You've got to be kidding me," she groaned.

"Hey, vet lady," Ryan crooned. Apparently Drunk Ryan was significantly more friendly than Sober Ryan. "How's Stan? He's a sheep, you know." He picked up the bottle and drank straight from it.

"I am aware," she said, crossing her arms and weighing her options. He was an asshole. But a drunk one. Her veterinarian's oath required her to use her skills in the "prevention and relief of animal suffering." Considering this guy's manners, he was on par with a misbehaving baboon.

On a heavy sigh, she stomped back into the kitchen. The room was an homage to the 1960s, complete with bile yellow appliances and brown, peeling linoleum tiles. She found a glass, filled it with water, and returned to the living room.

He was hefting the whiskey again, aiming for his mouth but on course to make contact with his eyeball when she snatched the bottle out of his hands.

"Uh-uh, buddy. No more. Drink this instead."

He took the glass from her and drank half of it down before making a face. "This clear whiskey is garbage," he said, sniffing the glass.

"Drink the rest of it," she ordered.

"You smell much better than you did," he mused. "It makes you more attractive."

If she slapped him now, he wouldn't feel a thing and likely wouldn't remember it. She'd save it for when he was sober.

"I'm so glad you approve," she said dryly.

"My approval shouldn't matter. You're fairly beautiful. You should know that without someone telling you." Drunk Ryan's level of snark rivaled Sober Ryan's.

"You've gotten really bad at giving compliments since we first met," she observed.

"Ha. Joke's on you. I was *never* good at it. 'Sides, why should I tell you you're sexy when you obviously already know you are? Waste of time." He hiccupped.

"What the hell happened to you, Ryan?" she asked. The guy she remembered had been mischievous, lively, flirtatious. The man he'd grown into was a grumpy pain in the ass. *Maybe it was the military school his mother had threatened him with all those years ago?*

She found a pack of lime green sticky notes on the skinny table at the foot of the stairs. The mirror above it was covered in Carson's nearly indecipherable notes to himself.

Find lightbulbs.

Buy overalls.

Breakfast with BC.

Her eyes narrowed when she read the last one. In Blue

62

Moon, BC stood for the Beautification Committee, and the Beautification Committee stood for trouble. Before she could puzzle out why Carson would be having breakfast with them, Ryan distracted her.

"Hey! Hey, Sexy Sam?"

She didn't turn around fast enough, and he pegged her in the back with a cross-stitched throw pillow that said *Farm Life*.

"What?" she asked in exasperation.

"Why do you keep pretending like we know each other?" he asked. His bloodshot eyes narrowed, presumably to keep her in focus.

"Because we *do* know each other." But only one of them had been memorable apparently. It was downright disheartening to know that she'd meant nothing to the guy who had given her her first kiss and set her on the right path.

She cringed when she thought of all those Solstice celebrations when she'd strolled past Mistletoe Corner, wrapping herself in warm, fuzzy memories.

Let Stan out into pasture, she scrawled on the note.

Looking around for a good place to put it, she settled on Ryan's forehead. She gave the adhesive an extra smack just to make sure it stuck.

"Hey," he mumbled.

"I seriously can't believe you don't remember me, you ass," Sammy grumbled, wrestling the first loafer off his big, stupid foot.

"Why in the hell would I remember you?" he slurred.

"Oh, only because you were my first kiss, jerk. Under the mistletoe, surrounded by Christmas lights."

He snorted with drunken derision. "That sounds like one of those stupid holiday movies."

"Just for that, I'm leaving your other shoe on."

"I was *not* your kirst fiss," he enunciated with arrogance.

"Yes. You were."

"Not. I've never been to this tie-dye holiday hellhole before today."

"I was fourteen," she lectured. "You were Ryan Shufflebottom from Des Moines visiting your great-uncle Carson Shufflebottom. We met in the park during the Winter Solstice and Multicultural Holiday Celebration. We were both in line for fried tofu."

He sat up abruptly, stopping mere inches from her face.

"Shufflebottom? Des Moines?" he squinted at her. "Tofu?"

"Ha. I told you," she said triumphantly. And then—because she was a good person, damn it—she yanked off his other shoe and threw it in the direction of the first. "You were so sweet. So much fun. What happened to you?"

"First of all, I would *never* eat fried tofu. That's dic-susting. Nextly, I was never sweet. And bullet point number B, that wasn't me."

Sammy threw her hands in the air. He could argue mistaken identity all he wanted. It didn't matter. He'd already ruined the moment for her. "Fine. Whatever. It doesn't matter what you were. It only matters what you are now."

"What am I now?" he asked.

"A miserable, grumpy, superior, snide adult who seems like he's never had fun in his entire life. I bet your bedroom walls are beige," she predicted.

He frowned, furrowing his brow. "Hey. Those are my feelings you're hurting."

"Yeah? Well, I'm not sorry." She took the empty glass and returned to the kitchen to refill it.

"Oh, come on," he called after her. "You're whining about some lame holiday peck from a guy who's too busy getting pedicures and visiting sketchy massage parlors to pay his own rent.

I'm the one whose life just unraveled. You don't hear me bitching about it!"

She practically ran back to the living room. "You've done nothing but bitch about everything," she scoffed, handing him the glass again instead of upending it on his head like she wanted to. "What's the matter, Crabby Patty? Sad about being stuck in this 'hippie hellhole' for the holidays?"

"I could give a steaming crap about the holidays," he said testily. "I'm much too distracted by the fact that my biggest client lied to my face for years, embezzled a fuckton of money from his own company, and got me fired because I damaged my firm's reputation."

Sammy eyed him in surprise. Maybe the Grinch had a reason to be grinchy. He flopped back in the chair, spilling water over the rim of the glass onto the crotch of his pants.

"They fired me," he said quietly. "Didn't even give me a chance to defend myself or remind them what I've done for them for the last twelve yucking fears."

"That sucks," she said, feeling the tiniest spark of empathy.

He eyed her suspiciously. "Yes. It does. I love my job. 'S my whole life."

She knew the feeling. "What do you do for a living?"

"Corporate accountant," he said. "And now Bart Lumberto, the buck-toothed weasel, is putting *his* ass in *my* chair behind *my* desk and gloating about it."

"For what it's worth, I'm sorry," she said. "I hope it works out."

"Works out? Ha. That's unpossible. Did I mention that I dislike this clear whiskey very much?" He raised the glass to her and then chugged it in two long swallows. While he was distracted, Sammy tucked the whiskey bottle behind the bizarre pile of shoeboxes on the couch.

"Oh! And"—he stabbed at the air wildly with one finger—"*now* I'm supposed to swoop in here and save the day."

"Whose day?" she asked.

"Great-Uncle Carson. 'S a family thing. I shouldn't talk about it." His attempt at a whisper came out in the realm of a shout.

Grumpy Ryan was kind of cute when totally shit-faced. The observation annoyed her. "Is Carson in trouble?"

"Pfft. Only if ending up homeless in an air tunnel at one million years old is trouble."

Oh, good. They'd gotten to the gibberish portion of the evening.

"It's on me, disgraced corporate accountant guy, to *swoop* in and save the day." To emphasize his point, Ryan slashed his arm through the air and knocked a tissue box and its crocheted cover to the floor.

"Where is your uncle?" she asked, trying to make sure there wasn't a real emergency that needed to be dealt with.

"He's in Boca with a fetlock."

"I don't think you know what that word means," she said.

"His plane went through an air tunnel," he told her.

"Oh, boy. Okay. Maybe let's get some sleep. Regain some sanity. I'll swing by in the morning and help you with the sheep and chickens. You can tell me more about the fetlock and the air tunnel then."

He opened one eye and looked at her with suspicion. "Why?"

"Why what?"

"Why would you come help me with anything? Don't you have other things to do besides help people do stuff?"

"It's what we do here, Ryan."

He screwed his face up. "That's weird. You're weird. You probably have a dumb gazebo that gets snowed on every Christmas Eve."

She'd officially had enough. "I hope your hangover is terrible," she told him. "Now go to sleep."

"'Kay." He obliged by closing his eyes and letting his head loll to the side.

She sighed, then pulled a green-and-orange knit afghan off the back of the couch. Just as she started to drape it over him, he came back to life.

"Pants!" Ryan yelled.

Sammy jumped back as he flung his limbs out wildly. Somehow, with an excessive amount of flailing, he managed to unzip his jeans. She caught a glimpse of absolutely no underwear and decided now was a very good time to leave.

"Uh. Yeah. I'll see you tomorrow," she said, backing away. "Merry Christmas."

"I don't want your pity Christmas spirit!" he roared. He shoved his pants down to his knees.

She was only human. At least, that's what she told herself when she peeked for one whole second. *Okay. Fine. Five seconds.*

From where she stood, Grumpy Ryan had nothing to be grumpy about below the waist. In fact, he should be the happiest guy on the planet.

"Night, Sexy Sam," he murmured.

Opportunistic ogling complete, she hurled the blanket at him and bolted for the door.

She was still thinking about him—and his bottomlessness—fifteen minutes later when she let herself into her own house. The fluffy, striped head of McClane—the surly six-year-old cat —popped out of a naked wreath on her dining table when she flipped on the lights.

"Hey, guys," she sighed, wishing she could just sink into that couch, light a fire, and watch TV until she fell asleep like a normal adult.

But her kitchen sink held four days' worth of dishes. Her

table was buried under what looked like a craft store explosion. Ribbon, wire, fake pine cones, sparkly berries on wire stems. Her collection of every size of jingle bell was scattered across table and rug. McClane's doing, most likely. He liked shiny things he wasn't supposed to play with.

One wreath, she decided with a yawn. She'd just double down tomorrow and block off some serious crafting time.

"Who wants to help me wash dishes and make a wreath?"

BLUE MOON COMMUNITY *Facebook Gossip Group*

Sammy Ames: If anyone is missing a friendly male sheep, please contact my practice immediately.

Edit: Please call only if YOU or SOMEONE YOU KNOW is DEFINITELY missing a sheep right NOW. Not two years ago or one time in college. A currently missing sheep.

Edit: A SHEEP. Not a cow or a cat or your car keys.

8

Very early Saturday morning, December 21

$\mathcal{R}$yan couldn't tell if the knocking was coming from inside his skull or from the outside world. Blearily, he pried one eye open. It was dark. But he wasn't certain if it was *still* dark or dark again.

The knock sounded again.

"I can *see* you staring at the door," a very smug, very female voice called. "Open up."

The pretty vet, he realized, then decided he was too hungover to find anyone attractive.

"Go. Away," he rasped, pulling the blanket up over his face. It didn't help though—there were so many knit holes in it. Even the blankets in this town were ridiculous.

The door opened, and he heard footsteps.

"Morning, sunshine," she called chipperly in a volume several decibels too high.

Morning. Okay. At least he hadn't lost an entire day to an over-

thirty hangover. Yet.

"You know, in the rest of the world, 'go away' means the opposite of 'come in,'" he groaned.

"Town Ordinance 17-06 of 1985 gives any Blue Mooner the right to enter the premises of another Blue Mooner if they are concerned that a crime or a crisis is in progress," she announced.

"Great. So you just legalized breaking and entering."

"Technically it's just entering since the door wasn't locked."

"That's not my fault," he insisted. Though who he could blame it on wasn't immediately clear either.

"No one locks their doors here," she said, sounding amused.

"Why the hell not? What stops someone from walking into your house and stealing your shit?"

"Oh, I don't know. Maybe being a good person?"

"This place is so weird." Ryan pulled the blanket tighter around his head and willed the world to stop spinning.

"Whoa there, tiger. I didn't come here to get an eyeful of Grumpy Junior."

"Grumpy Junior?" he rasped. The cold air from the open front door finally reached his unprotected southern hemisphere. Peering through one of the face-sized holes in the blanket, he realized he was completely naked from the waist down. *Fuck.*

He snatched the blanket off his head and hurled it over his lap. "What the hell happened last night? Or is it still last night?"

It was pitch black outside the farmhouse windows.

"It's six a.m."

Which made it his three a.m. Great. *He'd just managed to combine jet lag with a hangover.*

"Where are my pants?" he rasped. "Did you... did I... did we..."

She looked annoyingly pretty standing there in slim cargo

pants, scarred boots. A flannel shirt tucked in under a down vest and a soft green scarf. Her hair was a riot of thick curls in a color that made him think of honey. She was holding two to-go cups of what smelled like coffee.

She rolled those blue, blue eyes. Lavender fields, he remembered.

"I did *not* take advantage of you. You did *not* sexually harass me. And we did *not,* nor will we *ever,* have sex," she said.

He felt a rush of relief, then a vague dissatisfaction, which was almost immediately eclipsed by a wave of nausea.

"Why are you here?" he groaned, trying to work his way out of the recliner. He managed finally to climb unsteadily to his feet and wrapped the blanket around his waist like a holey sarong.

She plucked his pants off the singing bass fish mounted to the wall and handed them over. "You abandoned a sheep. Drank yourself stupid. Confessed to getting screwed over, losing your job and your way in life, briefly mentioned a fetlock emergency, then screamed and took your pants off. Surprised me with the whole commando thing, by the way. You seem like the kind of guy who not only wears underwear but irons them."

He rubbed at his eyes, headache throbbing. That all sounded vaguely, blurrily familiar. Also, he was pretty sure she'd insulted him a few times along the way in her recap, but he was too tired, too sick to care.

The holey blanket slipped off his hips and pooled at his feet.

Sammy gave a strangled sound and turned around to face the front door.

"That was an accident," he insisted in a dry-mouthed rasp. Bending over to pick up the blanket made his head feel like it was going to pop like an overinflated lawn ornament.

"I'm starting to have my doubts," she said wryly.

"Why were you here in the first place to witness my newest

level of shame?" His fingers brushed something on his forehead. A sticky note. He peeled it off and read it.

"I brought your sheep back," she told him.

She handed him one of the cups of coffee she held. Large and steaming.

"He's not my sheep." He took a long gulp of hot, glorious caffeine. It scalded his throat, but the pain was better than the rolling vertigo.

"You are currently in possession of said sheep until his owner can be identified."

He wanted to slink off into a dank basement and die in a corner somewhere. He also wanted to throw up. In a distant third, was the scenario where he curled up with his head in the pretty vet's lap and slept for three days straight.

He groaned. "What am I supposed to do with a goddamn sheep?"

"I'll show you. Since you're also in charge of Carson's chickens."

He made a grab for the jeans. The move had his head spinning, and he had to lean against the wall until the urge to puke his guts up passed.

"Just when you think things can't get worse," Ryan muttered.

"Are you always so cantankerous? Or is it just small-town life that does it to you?" she of little sympathy asked, patting his cheek on her way into the hideous kitchen.

"The world has enough happy-go-lucky dumbasses in it. I'm a realist," he yelled after her, shaking his jeans out and sending fragments of dried mud everywhere. He hated mud. Dirt. Puddles. Slush. Snow. Basically all nature and weather.

"Go shower, realist," she called over the bang of pots and pans. "I'll make you something greasy for breakfast, show you how to feed and pasture your animals, and then we can both go back to our regular lives, never to speak again."

He was too hungover to argue. Though he did wonder what was going to become of his "regular life." It was Saturday. On Saturdays, he went to the gym for leg day with Lars, the mean Icelandic trainer he was too afraid of to fire. Then he headed into the office for a few hours of uninterrupted work. In the afternoons, he'd catch up on his professional development reading, and—*Wow. He was so fucking boring. When had that happened?*

Deciding it didn't matter, Ryan stumbled into the bathroom on the second floor, vomited, and then gratefully slid under the hot water in the powder blue-tiled shower. He fell asleep standing up for a few minutes, but the smell of food woke him.

Five minutes later, dressed in clothes made more for business casual Saturdays in the office than sheep tackling, he returned to the first floor and found his way into the kitchen.

The room was still ugly, but the atmosphere had vastly improved thanks to the smell of actual food and the very attractive woman standing at the stove.

"You look better," she observed, tapping the wooden spoon on the pan of eggs.

"With my pants on?" he asked, helping himself to her coffee she'd left unattended on the tiny yellow Formica table.

She gave him a long look.

"What?" he asked, gingerly taking a seat. He was rather pleased when his head didn't separate from his neck and roll across the table.

"I'm trying to decide if you're human and just made a joke."

"Always assume I am inhuman," he told her. He considered it a kindness when she didn't comment.

With practiced efficiency, she dumped a handful of shredded cheese over the eggs and turned off the burner. "Check this out," Sammy said, wiping her hands on a dish towel before popping open the freezer door on the piss yellow refrigerator.

There were over a dozen neatly labeled casserole dishes stacked inside. "That's a lot of leftovers," he observed.

"That's a lot of love," she corrected. "These are all from your uncle's neighbors. Blue Moon makes sure he doesn't live off junk food and cold pizza. You can thank Carter Pierce for the cheesy, free-range eggs you're about to scarf down. Or maybe just not insult him to his face if you run into him."

"Pierce? I bet he has a beard and some goats," Ryan said as memories of last night coalesced in his brain. Mayor Beckett Pierce. His mother, Phoebe. And of course, Jax, the flirty big Hollywood deal.

"You met him?" she asked, sounding surprised.

"His brother. Brothers. And mother. Also, I'm not an asshole," he insisted as her previous comment finally sank in.

She set a plate of eggs and toast in front of him, delivered with a skeptical stare.

"Fine. I'm not *always* an asshole," he conceded. There were people who liked him. His clients. His bosses—at least they had until he'd brought shame to the firm. His family. Probably.

She gave a noncommittal grunt and surprised him by taking the chair opposite him.

He poked the food in front of him with a fork.

"Eat and talk, Shufflebottom. I have things to do today."

The final few pieces of last night's blurry puzzle fell into place. He rubbed a hand over his throbbing head. "You think I'm Ryan Shufflebottom."

"For the love of God, man. We're not doing this dance again," she groaned.

"I'm Ryan *Sosa*. Ryan Shufflebottom is my dumbass cousin. And if you think *I'm* an asshole, you should meet him."

The eggs flew off her fork and landed with a splat on her plate. If those blue eyes got any wider, he might fall into them.

"You're freaking kidding me," she said.

He shook his head then stopped when the motion made him dizzy. "His mom and my dad are brother and sister."

"And you're both named Ryan?"

He grimaced. "It's a big, competitive family. We've got two Ryans, three Katelyns—different spellings—and four Georges. You should see the family reunions. We've got nametags with family trees."

She leaned back in her chair and crossed her arms. "So you really weren't my first kiss?" He thought it was rather rude that she looked thrilled over that fact.

"I've never been to Blue Moon before last night. And if I kissed you, you'd know it," he added.

She leaned back in her chair, her knee accidentally nudging his under the minuscule excuse for a table. "Thank freaking God," she breathed.

Definitely offended now, he reached for her coffee again. "Excuse me. I'm an *excellent* kisser." He pushed back against her leg.

"Yeah. Sure," she scoffed, clearly not believing him. But she didn't move her knee.

"I am highly skilled at delivering all levels of pleasure." he said around a bite of toast.

"Your mouth is in a perma-scowl, which isn't remotely kissable. There's nothing sweet and romantic about you. You're too growly and grumpy."

"Growly and grumpy is part of my charm," he insisted. "Besides, romance is overrated."

"Is that your personal mantra or just your central belief system?" she asked smugly.

He pointed his fork at her. "You're one of those Christmas movie fans, aren't you? Everything's so sweet and romantic and boring and predictable."

That was exactly what Dr. Sammy Ames was looking for. A

small-town good guy who threw flour during completely unrealistic cookie baking fights. Growly and grumpy would never be the star of one of those stories. Besides, Ryan was too practical to throw flour. It took forever to clean up.

"You're a corporate accountant. I bet you worship boring and predictable," she shot back.

She had a point, and that annoyed him.

"You know what your problem is?" he asked around a bite of toast.

"Right, because *I'm* the one with the problem." She looked more amused than annoyed.

"You're one of those hopeless romantics," he told her with disdain.

She laughed in his face. "That's the *worst* thing you can say about me?"

"It's the worst thing I can say about anyone." *Okay, that wasn't true, but he knew arguments were built and won on vehemence, not facts.* "What's wrong with being pragmatic, practical? Why is a sense of responsibility not sexy? Why should we as adults make one of the five most important choices in life based on stupid butterflies that—let's be real—are just gas in the digestive system."

She put down her fork and took back her coffee. "I can't tell if you're joking or serious, but either way, I'm intrigued. What are the four other most important choices?"

"College, career, real estate, health, and personal and professional relationships." He ticked them off on his fingers.

She cupped her chin in her hand. "I find it very telling that you lump personal and professional relationships together."

He shrugged. "Not much difference."

"You're an interesting underwear-less man," she mused. "What criteria do you use to choose a significant other?"

"Compatibility, communication, shared beliefs around fiscal

responsibility, and sexual compatibility."

"Hang on. So physical attraction is pragmatic, but romance is what?"

"Inconsequential." The vomiting, shower, food, and argument made him feel more human than he had the right to after killing the better part of a bottle. "You might be looking for some small-town fruit farmer to bring you flowers and gives you a PG kiss for your Christmas cards. But that's not what works."

She pulled out her phone. "Hang on. I need to cancel your meet-cute with the fruit farmer this afternoon."

"Do I want to know what a meet-cute is?" he asked, devouring the last of his toast.

"Definitely not. So if it's not PG Christmas cards, what do *you* want, Ryan?" She dropped her second triangle of toast on his plate.

He pounced on it. "That's easy. I want a woman who contributes to her retirement savings while working a job that she enjoys and makes sense to me. That way I don't have to suffer through any office holiday parties or corporate picnics where her co-workers complain about shit like Instagram filters." He took a bite of toast and chewed thoughtfully. "I want someone who won't complain if I stay late at the office four nights a week. A woman whose life doesn't revolve around demanding more quality time from me."

"So a roommate then?" she said with a smirk.

He gave her a cool look. "Someone who goes to dinner with my boss and her wife and can carry on an intelligent conversation all while reminding me she's not wearing underwear under her dress."

That had her attention.

Those lavender eyes widened, and her mouth curved into a smile. "Just when I was starting to think you were a robot."

"Someone who asks for help reaching for something in the

kitchen and then ends up taking my pants off against the fridge. Someone who makes me do things I don't want to do so I don't miss out on life outside the office." Okay so maybe those last few weren't on his official list. But he liked getting a rise out of her.

Ryan's New Plan
> *1. Track down Rainbow Berkowicz.*
> *2. Solve Uncle Carson's financial problems.*
> *3. Fly home and save his career.*
> *4. Then find a woman who smiled at him like Sammy, enjoyed kitchen oral sex, and had a conservative investment portfolio.*

"Well, well. The accountant has an unsuspected kinky side," she said.

She didn't look appalled, he noted. If anything, she looked intrigued... and a little flushed. Her knee was still pressing against his.

"So, Sam," he said, leaning into her space from across the table. "You can keep your friendly first kiss with my idiot cousin. I'll find my naughty 401(k) contributor."

"I was fourteen," she said dryly. "I wasn't looking for reverse cowgirl or marriage. It was sweet, and so was he. You'd be surprised how the right kiss at the right time can change your path."

"You'd be surprised at how a good plan can keep you going in the right direction," he said, crunching into the toast.

"I bet Other Ryan is a much warmer, fuzzier adult than you are," she said, pointing her fork at him.

Ryan narrowed his eyes. "My cousin is a shiftless douche. And I know without a doubt that I'm a better kisser."

"Just keep telling yourself that, tiger," she said, turning her attention back to her food and moving her leg away from his. A careful withdrawal.

He felt the need to convince her, to arrange the facts for her and lead her to the correct conclusion. "Dipshit Ryan went to college for six years and never graduated," he began. "He changed his major every other semester and failed all of his classes because he was too busy 'falling in love' every five seconds."

"Some people like love," she pointed out, looking amused.

He rolled his eyes, then decided he'd wait a week or two before attempting it again when the room began to spin. "Now, he has a title at his parent's property management company and shows up to work once or twice a week. At least when he's not trying to 'find himself' in a yoga teacher training or a pastry chef workshop. He hasn't paid taxes since 2007. And he prefers dating wealthy married women because they give him shiny presents and don't expect him to be home every night."

"That's quite the assessment. You *do* come from a competitive family," Sammy mused, over the rim of her coffee cup.

"You have no idea," he told her.

In elementary school, Dipshit Ryan had challenged him to a hot dog eating contest and then stacked his own plate with cocktail wieners. In high school, the idiot had bet him ten bucks that he couldn't finish his trigonometry problems first. Ryan had whipped out the work and answers in record time only to have his shithead cousin slap his name on it and turn it in for class.

Then when Ryan had brought his college girlfriend home for Thanksgiving, Jackass Ryan had gotten her loaded on cheap tequila and tried to make out with her. She'd—rightfully—pushed him down the stairs.

Weiner Face Ryan had been in a neck brace for Christmas and blamed *him* for the whole thing.

"What would your cousin have to say about you?" Sammy asked.

"That I am loyal, dependable, responsible. All derogatory

insults to him," Ryan told her. "That I take everything too seriously and I haven't had any fun in twenty years. That I'd rather cross things off my to-do list than live life."

"So the real question is, which one of you is Evil Ryan?" she asked with the arch of an eyebrow, clearly enjoying herself.

"*He* is." Ryan was moderately offended that she hadn't picked up on that. "He's irresponsible, flighty, and an asshole. A *worse* kind of asshole," he insisted when she flashed him a pointed look. "He's not capable of caring about other people."

"And you are?"

"I'm here, aren't I? Instead of fighting for my job and defending my reputation, I'm in Full Fucking Moon attempting to solve some crisis for my great-uncle."

"Blue Fucking Moon," she corrected. "What's the crisis?"

He shook his head. "It's family business, and I don't know the details yet."

Dammit. He needed to get a meeting with that Rainbow Berkowicz at the bank. Once he knew what he was dealing with, he could figure out a solution and reward himself with a one-way ticket home.

"Well, we'd better get started then," Sammy announced. She picked up both their plates and put them in the sink.

"Get started?"

"You're living on a farm. You have chores to do."

Blue Moon Community Facebook Gossip Group

Lavender Fullmer: I'm not one to speculate, but I believe I saw our very single veterinarian pulling into Old Man Carson's farm last night. Rumor has it, Carson's nephew is staying there alone for a few days.

9
___

The sun was barely a pink sliver cresting the tree line when Ryan marched into the snow wearing a pair of two-sizes-too-small muck boots. He'd already ruined one pair of shoes in this winter wasteland.

"I can't believe I'm doing this," he grumbled to himself. At home, he was an early bird by nature. He liked to be in the office by seven thirty most mornings to enjoy the stillness before phone calls and meetings and "quick questions" overtook the rest of the day. The important delineation being that usually he was sober West Coast Ryan. Not Hungover Jet-lagged Ryan.

Sucking in a breath of lung-stabbing, icy air, he tromped toward the barn. The boxy, white structure looked like it could use a few coats of paint and maybe a new roof. A rusty tractor and a jumbled collection of metal farming implements resided in the open bay to the far right. The frozen ground was uneven and rutted with patches of gravel and weeds popping out of the melting snow.

Farming seemed like a dirty, disorganized job. Exactly the opposite of what he was comfortable with.

Sammy whistled for him from the door. "Nice hat," she called with a grin.

Not everyone could look like *her* in the morning. He refused to be charmed by the picture she made. Lavender blue eyes framed by those honey blonde waves under a green knit hat. She wore a scarf—more green—around her neck. Her vest was a pop of red against the gray-white of the barn wood. Just looking at her made him feel warm, which then annoyed him.

Pulling his stupid rainbow hat lower over his brow, he plodded toward her, toes scrunched at the ends of the boots. "Reluctant farmer reporting for first and last duty ever," he grumbled.

With that saucy grin, she tweaked the puffball of his hat. "It's a good look on you."

He batted her hand away, well aware of just how ridiculous he looked. Not that it mattered since she'd already seen him muddy, drunk, *and* naked. If this were a relationship, it would have taken him at least six to eight months before she saw all of those sides of him.

She dragged the old door open and he followed her inside, boots scuffing on the relatively clean concrete floor. There were stalls to his right and a bigger enclosure on the left. More rusty implements of questionable purposes hung on the far wall above a workbench of sorts. Bare lightbulbs hung from alternating rafters, casting light into the murky darkness.

Stan, his sheep buddy, clamored at the door of a stall, looking thrilled to see him.

"Hey, pal," Ryan said, reaching in to scratch the sheep's head.

Stan baa-ed a sheepish greeting.

"He really seems to like you," Sammy noted.

Ryan grunted, not wanting to acknowledge that it was kind of nice being greeted enthusiastically just for walking in the door. Maybe that's why people got dogs.

A flurry of activity in the enclosure caught his attention when Sammy pried the lid off a plastic bin. A dozen of the scraggliest chickens Ryan had ever seen clucked and pecked behind the wood of the fence.

"What's wrong with them?" he asked, eyeing them in horror.

"Nothing now," she said, shoving a metal scoop into a bin. "At least, nothing a little TLC won't fix. They were rescued from a neglect situation a few towns over. Carson's keeping them here for me until their permanent home is ready."

He eyed a particularly bedraggled chicken perched in the corner. It looked groggy, as if life had just delivered a surprise one-two punch. Ryan could relate.

"Pellets in the morning," Sammy lectured as she dumped the full scoop into a metal trough on the floor of the enclosure. The chickens reacted like kids after a broken piñata. "Just in case the snow is still too deep for hunting and pecking."

She pointed at the smaller bin outside Stan's stall. "Give our sheep friend a scoop of those in his feed bin. He should have plenty to graze on in the pasture with the snow melt, but we don't know how long he's gone without regular meals and this'll top off his tank for the day."

Because it was easier than arguing, Ryan obediently did as he was told. In the stall, Stan muscled him out of the way and shoved his face into the bucket after the pellets. "Now what?" he asked, watching as a dozen googly-eyed chickens squawked and pecked at the trough through the wooden slats in their enclosure.

"Now we put the free in free-range," she said, securing the lid on the chicken feed. "We'll let the chickens and your woolly pal out to pasture. They can graze and forage for the day."

"Is that safe?" he asked.

"It's a small pasture with double fencing. They'll be fine," she explained. She pointed to the side door. "Open that, will you?"

He tromped over to the door in his too-tight boots, and after a few false starts, managed to shoulder it open. A small, square pasture rolled out before him, running between the back of the farmhouse and the tree line. The sun cast a pinkish-purple glow on the icy crust of snow. Tall blades of grass broke through the surface in tufts.

"Heads-up," Sammy called. He jumped back as two NBA teams' worth of poultry raced past him.

"Poor idiots," he said, watching them scatter into the open. "They think they're free but it's just a bigger cage."

"Think of it this way," Sammy said, "that bigger cage keeps them from being fox or coyote food."

"Nature is fucked up," Ryan mused.

"Nature doesn't do anything for personal reasons. It's not purposely cruel. But people can be. Someone out there purposely starved these guys, kept them locked in a dark pen twenty-four hours a day," Sammy pointed out.

"People are fucked up," he said.

"A small minority," she said, watching the chickens flutter and race around in the open.

He caught a glimpse of something glittery on her face but before he could take a closer look, Stan bleated plaintively from his stall.

"Want to do the honors?" she offered, nodding toward the sheep.

"Sure," he said, then paused. "Wait. Won't Stan eat the chickens?"

Sammy's laugh was as bright as the early morning sunshine. If he weren't still hungover he might have appreciated it. "That's adorable," she said. "And no. Sheep are herbivores."

"Will the chickens organize and attack him?" The sheep had

been through enough trauma, in his opinion. A sneak chicken attack would just be adding insult to injury.

"They'll be fine," she promised.

He opened the gate to Stan's stall and watched the sheep trot for the door. Once his hoofed feet hit the snow, the woolly little guy jogged in an enthusiastic circle.

"I've never seen anything frolic before," he observed.

"Look how happy you made him," she said, stepping into the pasture.

He followed her, and they stood shoulder to shoulder watching the sheep and fowl enjoy the obscenely early morning. She was grinning and he guessed it probably felt pretty good to liberate animals from horrible situations and watch them thrive. To be the one on the front lines, instead of the one in the conference room or behind the computer screen. But there was room for all kinds of heroes in life. Some of them were just more... heroic.

"I still think he would have been happier and safer in your care," he said, resisting her upbeat mood. He had his own work to do here and taking care of farm animals hadn't been part of the deal.

"I told you. The clinic doesn't have the space to keep farm animals. Besides, I don't even work there," she said.

"Does this town let *anyone* walk in off the streets and treat Chihuahuas?"

"Very funny," she said dryly. "I was filling in for the food-poisoned doctor. I'm a livestock vet."

"There's more than one kind of veterinarian?" he asked, only half kidding. Growing up, his mother had stuck firmly to her no pets rule. In fairness, the woman already had five kids. Adding an unruly dog would have only added more unnecessary chaos.

"Just like I imagine there's more than one kind of accountant," she said, nudging him with her elbow. "I work mostly with farms."

"What a remarkable coincidence. Stan just so happens to be a farm animal. He can stay at your place," he suggested.

She was already shaking her head, sending her curls bouncing. "I moved in over the summer, and it took me this long to get the house livable. The barn and the pastures are next on the list. It's kind of a whole thing."

"He could stay *in* your house," he decided. "Problem solved. I'll help you load him up."

She put her gloved hands on his shoulders and looked up at him. "Ryan, Stan is staying here until I can find his owners or a foster farm. You can handle the fifteen whole minutes a day it will take to feed and pasture him while you're here."

"I'm *not* staying," he reminded her.

He felt her eye roll was a bit excessive. "You've mentioned that," Sammy said dryly.

Across the pasture, Stan pranced up to two of the chickens and then backed off when they ran at him. But something else caught his eye. Sammy was glittering again.

"What?" she asked, when she noticed him watching her.

"You're sparkling," he observed with a frown. He leaned in. The gold glints dusted one cheek and down her neck.

Her eyes widened and he realized they were practically in an embrace. "I'm what?" Her hands slid off his shoulders, but he caught them and held her still when she tried to back away.

"Are you wearing glitter?" he asked, turning her face toward the sun. Since he was there, he took his time perusing the rest of her face. Those almost purple eyes were wide and nervous. Her cheeks were flushed pink. Her lips were full and unpainted. A point in her favor since he'd never understood the need some women felt to cover everything up.

"Dammit," she groaned, bringing her gloved hand to her cheek. "I thought I scrubbed it all off."

"You're actually wearing glitter?" He couldn't imagine any of his female co-workers—ex-coworkers—showing up to the office sprinkled in bits of gold sparkle.

"Do not even *think* about making a stripper joke," she warned him.

"The thought never crossed my mind," he lied, picturing her in green pasties and a tasteful thong.

Mistake! With the hangover still present and accounted for, he felt light-headed the second his blood cruised south. Abruptly, he released her and took a self-preserving step back to think about sheep. Dirty, woolly, smelly sheep.

"I was crafting," she sniffed haughtily.

He shot her a skeptical look. "I could see you dancing before I could see you scrapbooking."

She frowned. "I'm not sure how offended I should be by that."

"Sorry. Hungover. My internal filter isn't working yet. What were you glittering?" Despite the throbbing headache, he was surprised that he had the energy to be curious.

"Holiday wreaths."

"Oh, God. I knew you were one of those obsessive Christmas romantics," he accused.

"Lighten up, Grinch. It's for a fundraiser. I fell asleep at the table on some dumb glitter explosion bow. Woke up looking like I'd gotten in a fight with TinkerBell."

"It's not a bad look on you."

Her eyes narrowed in his direction. "You're imagining me in pasties right now. Aren't you?"

He sucked in a breath of sharp winter air and choked.

"Wow. I was just kidding," Sammy laughed.

"I was thinking about... how I need to find someone named

Rainbow so I can get out of this sparkly holiday hallucination."
He'd most definitely been imagining her in pasties.

"Rainbow Berkowicz?" she asked with an arch of her eyebrows.

"Is there more than one Rainbow in this town?"

"You'd be surprised."

"No. I don't think I would," he countered.

"She's bank president. Are you trying to get a meeting with her?" She started for the fence and he followed.

"Not trying. Succeeding," he insisted. "One meeting with this Rainbow person and I'll be whining about being hungover on a cross-country flight."

"That's the spirit," Sammy said. Then she wrinkled her perky nose. "Except she's not taking any meetings until after the holidays."

"That's ridiculous. No one runs their business that way," he scoffed as he fell into step with her.

She shrugged. "Her mother-in-law is coming into town for the holidays and it takes Rainbow a few days before and after the visit to prepare and recover."

"Are you related? Does she live with you?"

She laughed. "No. Why?"

"I find it disconcerting that you know that much about someone you don't live with."

"Welcome to Blue Moon, where everybody knows everything about everyone else," she quipped.

"It sounds unhealthy. I don't even know the first names of everyone in my department at work," he told her. "I've only met three of the neighbors in my building."

"That's depressing," she said, strolling toward the fence with her hands in her vest pockets.

"That's not depressing. That's normal. It's called having privacy."

"Or is it called being too wrapped up in your own agenda to bother getting to know anyone?" she asked. "Around here, we care about each other. We lend hands and bake casseroles and do favors."

He smirked. "You sound like a docent at a visitors center."

"Would a docent wear pasties under her vest?" The sound of her unzipping that vest and the ludicrous possibility that she *wasn't* teasing him distracted him enough that he nearly impaled himself on a fence post. The air left his lungs on a grunt.

"Serves you right," Sammy teased. She climbed up on the fence and swung her leg over the top. "Can you get out this way or do you need me to open a gate for you?"

He would prefer walking through a gate *like an adult*. But he felt certain that the sparkly doctor would judge him for it. "I can handle climbing a fence," he scoffed.

Gripping the top rail with his mittened hands, he dug the stunted toe of his boot into the chicken wire above a fence rail and climbed up next to her. Gingerly, so as not to crush his balls, he swung one leg over.

She winked. "Look at you being all farmy."

"Farmy. Just what I want all the ladies—" Something floppy flew at his face, knocking him off balance. "Shit!"

He tipped sideways, mittens clawing uselessly at the wood. The last thing he saw was a wide-eyed Sammy reaching for him. He felt her hands close around his biceps, but he was twice her size, and gravity was already working its magic.

The blue sky and white snow swapped as they toppled off the fence. He twisted at the last second, shifting so his body hit the ground first.

She landed on his chest with the sound of a bagpipe deflating.

Ryan gave serious consideration to just giving up and lying

there. Staying down for the count. Waving the white flag. Then he realized that an attractive woman was straddling his hips, and life seemed a little less stupid.

"Are you okay?" Eyes bluer than the sky above peered down at him. Efficient hands patted his arms and torso. From this angle, he could see even more glitter along her throat and wondered what her skin would taste like there. "Did you break anything?"

"Don't know. Have to wait 'til I thaw out," he wheezed. He closed his hands around her arms. "Are you okay?"

Snow clung to her, making her look like a mischievous snow angel. "I'm fine. You broke my fall." She shifted her weight, forcing him to think very inappropriate thoughts as her crotch slid over his.

"What the hell was that?" he asked, hoping the snow bath he was taking would calm the raging erection before she accidentally discovered it under the sweet curves of her ass.

"Chicken," she said.

He thought for a split second that she was calling him a chicken, wondered if that meant she wanted him to roll her over and kiss the hell out of her. Then the googly-eyed, mangy beast he'd stupidly felt sorry for mere moments ago wandered past clucking.

It paused next to his face and pecked at his puffball.

"I think she likes you."

"I'd like her better if she came with fries and a dipping sauce," he said, batting the chicken away.

"Are you sure you're all right?" she asked him. "I mean, your grouchiness is intact, but I'm worried about your spleen."

He'd be hard-pressed to come up with a less "all right" moment in his life.

"I'm fine," he gritted the words out.

"Good. I'd hate to derail my entire morning by running you

to the emergency department." Without warning, she shifted her weight back and down. Accidentally sliding over the exact wrong—or right—spot.

He gripped her hips hard to keep her from moving. But he wasn't fast enough. He caught the exact moment she realized he was hard under her when those eyes went wide. The friction and the perfect O her mouth formed didn't help his predicament. His stupid dick flexed shamelessly under her.

"Don't. Move," he growled, squeezing her hips harder when she opened her mouth to speak. "Just... be quiet and give me a minute."

Rolling her lips together, she froze in place and avoided looking directly at him. He squeezed his eyes shut and tried to think of unsexy things. Like spreadsheets and googly-eyed chickens.

"So, silver lining. Your equipment still works," Sammy said cheerfully. "Big life stressors like getting fired can mess with erections—"

"For the love of God, Sam. Stop. Talking. About. My. Cock," he enunciated.

"Right. Sorry."

It took longer than a minute before he was certain he'd regained enough control not to throw her under his body and thrust against her like a mindless beast.

"Okay," he said finally and lifted her carefully off him. She didn't run away like she should have. Instead, she leaned down and offered him a hand up.

When he was back on his feet, she stayed where she was, his hand still in hers. But her eyes were on his crotch.

"Sam," he said finally.

"Huh? What?" she asked, tearing her gaze away from the hard-on he was trying to will away.

"What do we do now?" he asked.

"What do you want to do?" she asked. Her voice was breathy which didn't help Operation Exorcise Erection at all. At least her dazed attention made the situation a few degrees less embarrassing. He was an adult with superb self-control. He didn't go around getting inappropriate hard-ons.

"About the chicken," he said, pointing to the derpy bird pecking at a fence post.

"Oh. *Oh!* Right. The chicken." She took a big step back and almost went ass up over a tractor tire in the yard, but he caught her by the shoulders.

He felt just the tiniest bit better. "Are you sure *you're* okay? You seem distracted."

"Oh, shut up," she said. "Help me get the bird."

They caught the damn chicken and returned her to the pasture. On the walk back to the house, Sammy lectured him on how to get the birds and the sheep into the barn before dark and what to feed them.

"I don't know why you're telling me this," he said. "I'll be on a plane tonight."

"On the off-chance that you're still here, you'll save me a trip tonight," she said, humoring him. "This must not be a big emergency if you can resolve it that fast," she noted.

"I'm confident it's a misunderstanding that can be easily straightened out." *No small-town bank stood a chance against his expertise. At least, not as long as his blood flow returned to his head.*

She looked skeptical. "Yeah, well, do me a favor and text me if you do get on a plane so I can make arrangements for our farm friends here."

"Fine."

They made it back to the house without any further farm animal attacks or erections. While Sammy scrawled her phone number on one of his uncle's many sticky notes, Ryan unwedged his feet from the too-small boots and put on his other pair of non-ruined loafers.

"Good luck with your hangover and finding Rainbow," Sammy said.

"Good luck with whatever it is you're doing today," Ryan said, holding the front door open for her. It felt oddly domestic, seeing her off to work in the morning. He found that weird and unsettling.

She stopped on the front porch and offered him a hand. "It was truly an experience meeting you, Ryan."

He accepted her hand and shook it slowly. "On that, we agree. I'd appreciate if you didn't mention... any of this to my uncle when he gets back."

"So you don't want me to tell Carson about the sheep abandonment and the drunken nudity and the erec—"

"Goodbye, Sparkle," he interrupted, giving her a nudge toward the steps. She laughed all the way to her SUV.

He climbed behind the wheel of his clown car trying not to analyze the vague feeling of dissatisfaction settling in his gut. *Maybe it was his spleen? He'd get it checked in Seattle, he decided.*

He didn't have time to be hungover or worry about vague feelings of uneasiness or pretty, overly thoughtful veterinarians. Ryan had a bank president to intimidate, a farm to save, and a plane ticket to book. With a renewed sense of energy, he stabbed the vehicle's start button.

Nothing happened. The tiny, useless engine didn't even attempt to turn over.

He stabbed it again. "Oh, come the fuck on," he growled.

He heard the toot of a horn and looked up. Sammy waved as she started to pull away.

"Wait!" The window wouldn't lower and the interior of the car was so small when he tried to wave his arms to stop her, he cracked his elbow on the glass. "Ow! Dammit!"

He wrestled the seatbelt off, threw open the door, and sprinted after her arms waving over his head. "Come back!"

His right foot went through the thin crust of snow and found the icy, mud puddle beneath. He sank in up to his ankle.

"Oh, come the fuck on!" he snarled, kicking snow and mud into the air. "I really liked these shoes."

"Problem?"

He whirled around and found Sammy staring at him from the window of her SUV.

~

BLUE MOON COMMUNITY Facebook Gossip Group

Lavender Fullmer: Veterinarian Sammy Ames was spotted pulling into Old Man Carson's farm very early this morning to pay a visit to his very single, very good-looking great-nephew!

10

$\mathcal{R}$yan let out a low growl from the seat next to her and shoved his phone back into his pocket.

"I told you the bank wouldn't be open yet," Sammy reminded him, turning Eartha Kitt's "Santa Baby" back up on the radio.

He rubbed his temples. "It's not that. The message said the bank president isn't taking meetings until after the holidays."

"I believe I also told you that."

"You don't have to be so smug about it," he said.

"It's a small town. We don't get a lot of banking emergencies here," she reminded him. "Besides, you can run into her downtown easier than setting up a meeting."

He grunted, then punched up the heat on the seat warmer. "What would it take for you to turn off the Christmas carols?" he asked.

"More than you have," she said cheerfully. "Are you always this grumpy or is it circumstances?"

"Just because I don't run around with a stupid grin on my face all day every day doesn't mean I'm grumpy."

"So always this grumpy," she deduced. "Sure you're up for

riding shotgun? I've got a lot of stops to make." She'd already had a full day scheduled down to the minute before adding a crabby passenger into the mix.

"Whatever. Just get me in the vicinity of Rainbow Berkowicz today. I can find a way back to the farm," Ryan insisted.

"What exactly *do* you need with Rainbow?" she asked, her curiosity piqued. Whatever it was, it was enough to get the man to fly across the country during a personal crisis, but the situation was one he felt could be wrapped up in a single meeting.

Ryan fiddled with the air vents on the dashboard, pointing the warm air at his face. "It's a family matter."

She glanced over at him. "What kind of family matter involves your uncle and Rainbow Berkowicz? As far as I know, they settled their Bingo Night dispute."

"Look, Sparkle. Just because you're used to your backwoods neighbors talking about every ridiculous detail of their days doesn't mean I have to gossip about my family's problems."

"Message received," Sammy said. "Unrelated. Just because some backwoods neighbor generously offered to drive you into town doesn't mean you get to be a dick no matter how hungover, or annoyed, or used to being an ass you are. So you will be polite and respectful to me and anyone else we come in contact with today. Got it?"

His sigh was weary. "Got it. I'm sorry. I'm not usually this much of an asshole."

"I don't believe that."

"I guess I can't blame you," he admitted.

"You can tell a lot about a person by how they handle the rough patches in life. It's easy to pretend to be a good human when things are going well. But if you start kicking kittens when things go south, odds are you've always been a kitten-kicker underneath it all."

"I've never once kicked a kitten," he said dryly. "I did punch a parakeet once. But he was asking for it."

She shot him a look. "I'm sorry. Did you just make a *joke*?"

"I'm one of those funny grouches," he insisted.

And just like that, Ryan labeled himself her own personal catnip. Broody hot guys were attractive for obvious reasons. But throw in a sense of humor, and that upped the probability of getting into Sammy's pants by a thousand points or so.

They rode in silence for a few minutes, past winter white fields and farmhouses with Christmas stars on silos. The early morning skies were already turning that wide-open blue. The beauty of Blue Moon sometimes snuck up and sucker-punched her.

"Thank you for the ride, Sparkle," Ryan said as if the words pained him. "Despite my assholery, I do appreciate it. You're nicer than I deserve."

Nope. No. No. No. She didn't need him to be hot, grumpy, funny, and *sincere.*

"You're welcome," she said. "You can buy me a coffee."

"I suppose it's the least I can do."

"It actually is," she said with a smirk.

The opening bars of Dolly Parton's "Hard Candy Christmas" were abruptly cut off by a text alert. Sammy's SUV came with the handy option to read text messages aloud when she was behind the wheel.

"*Text message from Summer Pierce,*" the robotic voice enunciated. "*Hey, girl. Any chance I can get four wreaths with buffalo plaid bows? I need them for a photo shoot. Praying hands. Praying hands. Smiley face.*"

"Well, *that's* not annoying," Ryan announced.

"Here's a fun fact," Sammy said with forced brightness, as a bead of sweat worked its way down her back at the very distinct possibility that she wasn't going to finish all the wreathes.

"Those electric cars only work when you remember to plug them in."

He let out a long-suffering sigh, which cheered her up. "Thanks for the tip," he said dryly.

"Huh. That's funny. I could *almost* say the same," she mused, recalling his excellent erection.

"No one likes a funny veterinarian," he said dryly.

She grinned.

The smoldery glare he sent in her direction had her insides doing funny things. Maybe it had been a little too long since her last roll in the hay. Long enough that it had been a literal roll in the hay in much warmer weather.

Dammit. That's why this hungover grouch was playing her hormones like a world-class pianist. It had been too long. It was irresponsible to overlook good old-fashioned sex as self-care.

She wondered how long it had been for Ryan. Her gaze slid across the console to his lap.

"Eyes on the road, doc." He sounded a little too smug for a guy wearing hand-knit rainbow mittens and matching hat.

Entering the town limits, she pushed aside thoughts of Ryan's penis. The winter holidays had indeed exploded everywhere in Blue Moon. The Horowitz family's inflatable Jewish star perched directly across the seat from the Ravenwoods' Yule tree. On the corner was the Methodist Church's nativity scene.

In a matter of minutes, Sammy maneuvered into a parking spot in front of McCafferty's Farm Supply. "First stop," she told him, shutting off the engine.

"I can't believe businesses are even open this early," he complained, eyeing the three-story white clapboard building. The big glass windows were painted with a pastoral winter scene beneath the words Happy Holidays.

"Come on," she said, releasing her seatbelt. "We've only got a couple of minutes."

"To do what?"

"To get you outfitted."

~

"I DON'T NEED NEW CLOTHES," Ryan complained as Sammy shoved a heavy work coat on top of the mound of clothing he already held. "I'm not going to be here long enough—"

"Long enough to what? Get frostbite? Because I'm not going to be responsible for your favorite calculator fingers freezing and falling off."

"I realize you've had more medical training than I have but I still don't think that's how frostbite works."

"Go try this stuff on," she said, shoving him toward the dressing rooms. Her tight schedule was getting tighter by the minute. But she couldn't in good conscience let him go stomping around farms in damp jeans and nice loafers.

While he changed, she ran upstairs to check out the new thermal layers. A snarky donkey had taken a bite out of the sleeve of her favorite top last week. She grabbed two new tops, one in serviceable white and one dotted with mistletoe— because why not?—and headed back downstairs with her finds.

It wasn't her fault that Ryan chose the dressing room with the saggiest curtain. Or that she just happened to have an excellent view from the stairs. At least, that's what she told herself when she was stopped in her tracks to take in the view of the hungover accountant's naked torso.

If she added up last night and this morning, she'd seen almost every square inch of the man without clothing. She'd also managed to *feel* several rigid inches of him.

"See anything you like, dear?"

Sammy jumped and nearly lost her footing on the stairs.

The thermal shirts and their clothes hangers flew over the railing down to the first floor.

Mrs. McCafferty was a short, round woman with no-nonsense gray hair, a wardrobe of flannel shirts in every color, and shrewd green eyes behind wire-rimmed spectacles. She ate gossip for breakfast, lunch, and dinner.

She peered down at Sammy from a few steps above.

"Morning, Mrs. McCafferty," Sammy said, avoiding the woman's question. She didn't need it spread all over town that she'd been caught slobbering over a half-dressed stranger in the middle of the store. "Are you ready for the Solstice—" The small talk died on her lips with the whoosh of the curtain being drawn back.

"Well? How god-awful do I look?" Ryan stood in front of the dressing room in insulated work boots, fleece-lined jeans, and a thick thermal shirt under a heavy work jacket. His hair was disheveled from the rainbow vomit hat, and that rugged stubble that had sprouted on his jaw overnight made him look... *good*.

Better than good. Downright sexy.

She swallowed. "You look... warm," she decided.

Mrs. McCafferty gave a pointed throat clearing. "Ahem!"

Sammy descended with the shop owner on her heels. "Ryan, this is Mrs. McCafferty. She owns the store. Mrs. McCafferty, this is Carson's great-nephew," Sammy said, making the introductions and trying not to stare too hard at Ryan's chest or crotch or jawline.

"Your uncle is a pain in my ass," Mrs. McCafferty announced.

"That sounds about right," Ryan agreed.

"But I love him like a brother. Well, maybe like a distant third cousin."

"He's a lovable pain in the ass," he said.

Sammy checked her watch. "Can you put these on my

account?" she asked, holding up the thermals. "And could you ring up the clothes while Ryan wears them? We've got to be at Hershel's by eight."

"Not a problem," Mrs. McCafferty said, ushering them to the pine counter. "I'll get you out of here in just a jiffy."

"How long exactly is a jiffy?" Ryan whispered in her ear.

Sammy jumped at the heat of his breath on her neck. Fortunately the helpful storekeeper chose that moment to drag him into position to get at the price tag on his coat.

While the woman was pulling Ryan this way and that to scan tags, Sammy grabbed a cap with fleece-lined ear flaps. It was only slightly lower on the ridiculous scale than his rainbow puffball hat, but it would perform the dual jobs of keeping his ears warm and distracting her from his overall yumminess.

"Do you happen to know where Rainbow Berkowicz is this morning?" Sammy asked the woman, plucking a pair of gloves from the display and producing her credit card.

Ryan elbowed her out of the way and dug through his old jeans for his wallet.

"It's my treat," she insisted, wedging herself between him and the counter.

"No." He manhandled her like a sack of feed and moved her aside. That wasn't supposed to be hot. But her libido didn't seem to mind.

"I can write this off as a business expense," she tried again, appealing to his practical side.

"Nice try. Still no. You already made me breakfast."

Across the counter, Mrs. McCafferty's eyes flicked to Sammy's face. *Shit.*

The gossip radar had been activated. Ryan had no idea he'd just bashed open a hornet's nest.

"I stopped by this morning to show him how to pasture the sheep and chickens," she explained quickly. She felt beads of sweat breaking out on her forehead. The front door opened, and Ernest Washington walked in, rubbing his hands together to ward of the chill.

Great. Another witness.

The entire town was going to be gossiping about Sammy's one-night stand with Old Man Carson's nephew by lunchtime.

"She's too nice," Ryan complained to Mrs. McCafferty, completely unaware that his audience was taking actual notes on a yellow legal pad as he spoke. "If a man was rude to you and so drunk he took his pants off in front of you not once but twice, would you make him breakfast?"

Mrs. McCafferty wrote down "No Pants" and underlined it twice.

Sammy stepped between him and the counter once again and shot him her best death stare. "Stop. Talking. Now," she hissed.

Mrs. McCafferty leaned around her to give Ryan a once-over and an answer. "That depends. Does he look like you?"

Ryan gave an amused snort.

The store phone rang, and Mrs. McCafferty reached for it. "McCafferty Farm Supply," she said, accepting Ryan's credit card. She didn't look like she was in any hurry to finish the transaction. The longer they stayed in the store, the later they'd be for her first appointment, and the more fodder the Blue Moon gossip group would compile.

Sammy took matters into her own hands and started stuffing Ryan's old clothes into a bag.

"IRS Collections Department?" Mrs. McCafferty said shrilly. "What do you mean... Hang on... You're saying I owe the IRS *how much*?" The woman's face turned an unhealthy shade of tomato.

Thinking quickly, Sammy grabbed the legal pad off the counter and fanned Mrs. McCafferty with it.

"I didn't get any notices in the mail!" She was yelling now, and Ernest Washington wasn't even bothering to pretend to browse. "You'll accept a credit card?" Mrs. McCafferty looked wildly about.

Ryan reached across the counter and gestured for her to hand over the phone. "I'm an accountant," he said with authority.

She dropped the receiver in his hand like it was a hot potato.

"This is Mr. McCafferty," Ryan said gruffly into the phone. Both Sammy and Mrs. McCafferty shared a look. "What's all this about the IRS Collections Department?"

As he listened, a hard gleam lit his eyes. It was a good look on him.

"I see. And to whom am I speaking? Detective Smith. Uh-huh." He listened for a few moments longer. "Let me stop you there, Detective Smith. Here's the thing. The IRS doesn't call people. It doesn't try to collect delinquent taxes over the phone. And it most definitely doesn't call and demand a credit card number. Judging from the background noise on your end, you're in a scammer call center."

Sammy and Mrs. McCafferty shared twin gasps. Ernest inched his way closer presumably to eavesdrop more efficiently.

"Here's what's going to happen," Ryan said. "You're going to lose this number and every other number in your database. You're going to hang up, walk out of that call center, and quit trying to scam people out of their hard-earned money."

Sammy looked on, enthralled. Mrs. McCafferty had hearts in her eyes.

"Or what? I'm so glad you asked," he continued. "You messed with an unemployed accountant with a lot of time on his hands. I am the Liam Neeson of accounting. I am going to hunt you down, Smith. I'm going to find you and dedicate my life to destroying yours."

He leaned an elbow on the counter casually as if he were asking for directions instead of doling out threats.

"I'll hire investigators to follow you. They'll show your wife pictures of your mistress. Your mistress pictures of your wife. I'll get you fired from every job you land. I'll ruin every scheme you attempt. I'll sue you, your boss, your boss's boss, your grandmother. Then I'll turn the Justice Department on you. By the time I'm done with you, your entire family will wish you'd never been born. Now hang up the phone, get an actual job, and earn your own money, assface."

Sammy was impressed... and maybe a little aroused.

He handed the receiver back to Mrs. McCafferty. "The IRS never calls you," Ryan explained. "They're understaffed, and with the tax code changes, they don't have time to do anything besides send collection notices in the mail. If you run into something like this again, tell them to send all documentation to your attorney."

Mrs. McCafferty looked up at him like he was Santa *and* Jesus. "Thank you," she whispered. "Thank you so much. I would have given him my credit card number, my Netflix password, whatever they asked for."

"You can't be too careful these days," he cautioned. "The rest of the world isn't as..." Ryan's gaze met Sammy's, "... friendly as Blue Moon."

Mrs. McCafferty slapped his unswiped credit card down on the wood and shoved the bag of clothes at him. "On the house."

"That's not necessary," he said, looking almost embarrassed.

"I insist," she said, beaming at him. "Consider it the hero's discount."

He looked like he was going to argue so Sammy stepped on his foot.

"Oh, uh. Then thank you," he said gruffly.

"Thank *you*." Mrs. McCafferty giggled.

"We have to go," Sammy said, before the "No, no. Thank *you*" game could continue. She dragged Ryan toward the door. "See you at the Solstice!"

"Yes, the Solstice," Mrs. McCafferty said. "Don't forget. I want a wreath with a red velvet bow and bells."

"Red velvet bow and bells," Sammy promised over her shoulder.

"Oh! One more thing," the shopkeeper called after them. "If you two are looking for Rainbow, I heard she's meeting the Solstice Recycling Committee at the cafe this morning."

"Thank you," Ryan called as he was dragged through the door.

"The Liam Neeson of accounting? That was impressive," Sammy said, sliding behind the wheel.

"Felt pretty good," he admitted, stabbing the seat warmer button. "I still don't see why I needed new clothes or why that woman insisted on *giving* them to me."

And just like that, Grumpy Ryan was back.

"Oh, you'll see," Sammy said as she backed out of the parking space and headed north. "Now put on your hat and gloves like a good boy."

He crammed the hat on his head and frowned at his reflection in the visor mirror. "Don't you people have normal, black ski hats?" He flopped the ear flaps up and then down again.

She bit back a laugh. "What's the fun in that?"

"Not everything has to be fun," he pointed out.

It was hard to take him seriously with ear flaps. "I bet you had fun once, and it was awful," Sammy teased.

"As a matter of fact," he harrumphed.

She laughed. "So, how do you feel about cows?"

"Cows? Why? Are we stopping for burgers?"

She smirked and cranked up the Christmas carols.

To: The esteemed members of the Beautification Committee
    Subject: Calendar stand shifts

Dearest Committee Members,

    As you know, in addition to our ongoing Operation Frolicking Condor, we will be selling our tasteful nude fundraiser calendars during the Winter Solstice and Multicultural Holiday Celebration. Due to the popularity of our calendar, we would like to have three committee members staffing the booth at all times.

    Attached please find a shift sign-up sheet and digital photos from the calendar to share on your social media accounts.

    Yours truly,
    Bruce Oakleigh

11

---

*H*ershel Dairy sprawled out over 120 acres of rolling fields and pastures ten miles north of Blue Moon. Fifty pampered dairy cows called the acreage and huge green barn home.

"This does not look like a coffee shop," Ryan observed.

"Good news. Your hangover hasn't blinded you," Sammy announced as she pulled up to the immaculate dairy barn. "This is a work stop. I've got a herd check on dairy cows. You can wait here or you're welcome to join me," she told him.

"Yeah. I'll wait," he drawled.

"I'll be about an hour," she told him with a sunny smile then exited the vehicle.

He swore under his breath and climbed out.

She waved a greeting to owner and operator Mavis Bilkie as the woman pulled up in a tractor going twice the speed it should have been. She was wearing coveralls and an elf ears headband over an orange ski cap.

"Why does she get a normal hat and I have to look like Cousin Eddie?" he groused.

"My guess is karma. That's Mavis," Sammy shouted over the chug of the engine.

"What are we doing with Mavis?" he yelled back.

"Herd check."

"What the hell is a herd check?"

The engine cut off, and Mavis slid to the ground before Sammy could explain.

"Good to see you, doc. Ready for the Solstice?" the woman asked. "I've got my heart set on a nice, traditional wreath with one of them plaid bows."

"You can count on it," Sammy lied through her teeth. She'd woken up at her table with a glitter bow stuck to her face and a cat with the front page of *The Monthly Moon* glued to its tail. She was in no position to be promising anyone anything.

Thirty-nine wreaths in two days? *Eeesh. Things weren't looking good.*

"You replace Demarcus?" Mavis asked, eyeing Ryan.

"No one can replace Demarcus," Sammy assured her. "He's in Buffalo for Hanukkah with his wife's family. This is Ryan. Carson Shufflebottom's great-nephew. He's tagging along with me today."

"Nice to meet ya, Ryan," Mavis said, offering him a dirty hand.

"A pleasure," he said. To the man's credit, he shook the offered hand without flinching or sarcasm.

"Let me get my bag, and we'll get started," Sammy said.

FIFTY-EIGHT MINUTES LATER, she closed the cover on her iPad, the final herd stats recorded. "Ladies are looking good," she reported to Mavis. "Tennessee's gait is a lot better this week, and the wait and see with Vermont worked. No antibiotics needed."

The farmer swiped a hand across her brow, miming sweat. "Thank God for that."

"You've got a healthy herd here. Keep up the good work, and I'll see you in two weeks."

"Thanks, doc. I'll see you at the Solstice," Mavis called. "Ryan, it was a treat."

"Thanks again for the tour, Mavis," he said, sounding almost cheerful. "You've got a hell of an operation here."

"Was it my imagination, or did you actually enjoy yourself?" Sammy asked when they climbed back into the SUV.

He'd asked a hundred questions about the dairy business. Animals as capital, day-to-day maintenance, streams of income. Mavis had been delighted with the interest in her livelihood from the rugged-looking accountant.

"Definitely your imagination," he said, checking his phone. He let out a surly sigh and shoved his phone back in his pocket.

"Nothing from your firm?" she guessed.

"It's stupid," he said, staring out the window. "I feel like the guy who got dumped on prom night and sits on his front porch hoping she'll change her mind and show up."

"It's not stupid if you love your job," she told him, shifting into drive.

"I do. Did," he corrected, picking up the to-go mug and sniffing the cold coffee. "Though, judging from how you stuck your entire arm inside that poor cow, not as much as you."

"Every day, I feel like I'm doing what I was meant to do."

He shot her a look like he was trying to tease apart the meaning of her words. "Really?"

"Didn't you?" she asked.

He frowned, considering the question. "I thought being good at something and being well-compensated for it was as good as it got. But I suppose I never considered saving corporations millions of dollars a calling."

"The way I looked sticking my arm up a cow's rectum is how you looked yelling at that IRS phone scammer," she pointed out.

"I didn't get to do much yelling at scammers in my job. It was more dealing with internal accounting departments, managing bookkeepers, interpreting volumes of tax code, and attending a lot of meetings that could have been emails."

"But there was *something* you loved about it. Otherwise you wouldn't care so much."

"Maybe," he hedged, brooding out the window.

"Let's go find you a Rainbow Berkowicz," she decided. "While Mavis gave you the tour of her financials, I called the coffee shop. Rainbow is there right now."

"Oh, thank God. Coffee."

Sammy smiled as she accelerated toward town while Trans-Siberian Orchestra poured from the speakers. She'd deliver Ryan to Rainbow, grab a fresh cup of coffee for the road, and be back almost on schedule.

"*Text message from Mom,*" the stereo reported. "*The dates you suggested for Christmas won't work for us. I have the third weekend in January open.*"

She sighed and felt Ryan's gaze on her.

"Your mother bailed on Christmas with you?" he asked.

"At this point, it's kind of a family tradition. She's one of those perpetually busy, over-scheduled people. She likes it that way."

"What do you do for Christmas?"

"I sleep late. Have wine for breakfast and hang out in my pajamas all day. It's kind of great." It really was. But she had to admit that sometimes she wished she had someone to eat cookies with on the couch. "What about you?"

He blew out a breath. "I try to survive a Sosa-Shufflebottom Christmas. I fly to Philly and split my time between my dad's place and my mom's. It's chaos with siblings, cousins, aunts, uncles. Everyone's yelling just to be heard over everyone else's yelling."

"That doesn't sound *that* terrible."

"It's always too hot because there's thirty exhausted adults stuffed into a room. My cousin Margo's kids run around biting each other and knocking over furniture. She's got six of them and decided to raise them free range."

"What does that mean? Do they live outside?"

"Worse. Their parents don't use the word 'no'." He shuddered. "Do you know what it's like trying to get through a meal with six kids who have never heard the word?"

"Okay, sounding slightly more awful," Sammy conceded.

"My mom sneaks into the pantry to drink wine straight from the bottle. By the time I leave in the afternoon for my dad's, she's shit-faced and eating chocolate chips by the five-pound bag. For my dad's side of the family, we go to his sister's house. She breeds these tiny fluffy dogs that never stop barking. Her entire house smells like dog pee, and everything is covered in fur."

"Fun."

"It gets better. Last year, my cousin Albert showed up to surprise his mom and introduce her to his boyfriend. Aunt Maude ripped the wooden baby Jesus out of the nativity scene on her mantel and threw it at them. Apparently, she'd told everyone that Albert wasn't coming home for the holidays because he was going into the priesthood in South Dakota."

"Oh, no."

"My dad flipped off Maude, and my siblings and I stole two apple pies on the way out. We took Albert and Ricardo to a bar, ate the pies, and drank until Christmas was over. They're getting married next fall."

She blinked. "Wow."

"I'd already decided to skip the whole thing this year. So, yeah, your Christmas for one sounds far superior. As soon as I get this Carson crisis taken care of, I'm flying home and taking a page out of your book."

~

OVER CAFFEINATED WAS A COLORFUL, cozy storefront on Main Street. Sammy and Ryan were welcomed at the door by a rush of heat and the smell of freshly ground coffee beans. The window display was a Christmas tree made entirely from gold, silver, and green to-go mugs, looped with tree lights.

"Which one is Rainbow?" Ryan asked, eyeing the cafe's clientele as he stuffed the gloves in his pocket.

Sammy craned her neck and spotted Enid Macklemore and Mervin Lauter at a table in the corner. They were wearing tie-dye Solstice Recycling Committee sweatshirts. Enid had an advanced degree in something hard to pronounce from MIT and was the oldest dog walker in Blue Moon. Mervin was a bit of a YouTube sensation, posting Dad advice videos on everything from how to change your locks to how to edge your flowerbeds.

There was a third mug sitting in front of an empty chair.

"I don't see her. She might be in the restroom or maybe she stepped out for a phone call."

"I guess I can buy you that cup of coffee before she comes back," he offered.

She studied the menu behind the counter. "Ooh! Christmas cookie latte. Yes, please."

Ryan snorted. "Why don't you just eat an entire bowl of sugar instead?"

She gave him a long look then shook her head. "Nope. I can't do it," she said.

"Can't do what?" he demanded.

"I can't take you seriously with those ear flaps."

He whipped off his hat and ran his hand through his hair. "*Now* can I be judgmental?"

"You can be whatever you want as long as you're buying me a Christmas cookie latte." She nudged him toward the counter. "I'll keep an eye on the Recycling Committee."

Grudgingly, he headed to the register to order.

Sammy unwound her scarf and unzipped her vest. She had just started for the table in front of the window when a redheaded blur appeared in front of her.

"Is that Sheep Guy?" demanded Eva Cardona, the sheriff's bride, baby-mama-to-be, and Sammy's newest friend. She wore a white winter coat over rumpled rainbow pajama pants. Her cheeks were a dewy pink from either the cold or the pregnancy. Judging by the curls escaping her messy top knot, it had been several days since she'd washed her hair.

"Shh!" Sammy hissed, looking around to make sure Ryan wasn't within earshot. "Yes, that's him. What are you doing here? I thought you had words to write today?"

"I was procrastinating, of course, by visiting my incredibly handsome husband at the station when Minnie Murkle told us you and Sheep Guy were going to be here." She peered around Sammy. "Wow. He's really good-looking. I mean like *really*."

"I'm aware," Sammy said in exasperation. "How did Minnie know we were coming here?"

Eva was still ogling Ryan. "The gossip group. How else? Wow. I'm digging the broody, stubble look," she said with approval.

Sammy closed her eyes. *Ugh. The damn gossip group.* Blue Moon was so committed to keeping up on the latest gossip they had created a group on Facebook to spread news and rumors faster.

"His car wouldn't start this morning. I gave him a ride into town to help him track down Rainbow."

"Oh, she already left," Eva said, oblivious to the fact that she'd just peed all over Sammy's get-back-on-track parade. "Said she had an important errand to run before lunch at Dad's restaurant."

Eva's father, Franklin, ran the Italian place in town. His bread was to die for, and his hugs were as legendary as his Hawaiian shirt collection.

"Damn it," Sammy grumbled. "Do you know what time she's heading there?"

"Twelve thirty. It's a business ladies' lunch. They usually linger over wine and cannoli for at least an hour after they're done with their meals," Eva said. "Ooh! Incoming."

"Here's your Instant Diabetes," Ryan said, handing Sammy a pretty gold to-go mug.

Touched, she accepted the mug. "You got upsold."

"I get ten percent off every order when I bring this in," he said, holding up his own green mug.

"Isn't your departure imminent? You're not going to be around to collect the discount," she reminded him.

He shrugged. "Yeah, well. They got me with the whole 'proceeds benefit the Quiet Hour' thing."

Sammy and Eva both grinned up at him.

The Quiet Hour was a committee of adults and kids that organized early admission to town events for families with sensory issues. Aurora and her brother Evan had come up with the idea after befriending new Mooners Rubin and Claudia, who were both on the autism spectrum.

"It's a great cause," Sammy agreed.

"I thought it was a decent idea," Ryan admitted. "My sister has autism. She loved Christmas lights when she was a kid, but had a hard time with the crowds."

"Have sex with him now," Eva coughed into her hand.

"This is my friend Eva," Sammy said glaring daggers at the woman who was sizing Ryan up like he was the hero in one of her novels. "She'd stay and introduce herself but she has to go away right now."

"Oh, no. I have all the time in the world," Eva said, grinning evilly. "It's *so* nice to meet you, Ryan."

"Don't you need to deliver your husband's coffee?" Sammy stared pointedly at the cup in Eva's hand.

Ryan frowned. "You don't by chance have a daughter who hangs out in liquor stores? She's about this tall," Ryan said, holding up a hand.

"Ah, you met my niece Aurora. She belongs to my sister, Gia."

"Strong family resemblance," Ryan said, eyeing Eva's pajama pants.

"There is, isn't there? Now, tell me, when you seduce a woman, are you a flowers-and-wine kind of guy or do you get more creative?"

Sammy clamped a hand over her friend's mouth. "Please excuse my inappropriate friend. Eva is a romance novelist, and she's definitely leaving."

"I don't do flowers and wine," Ryan said, looking amused. "I find it more helpful to solve a problem. Like get her car detailed or do something for her that she hasn't had time to do. Pick up dry cleaning. Make dinner. Shred old documents."

Eva pried Sammy's hand off her mouth. "Hmm, useful romance. Interesting," she mused. "I may want to pick your brain about that more, Ryan."

"Too bad he's leaving town," Sammy said, doing a terrible job at feigning disappointment as she steered Eva toward the door.

"Well, if you'll excuse me," the redhead said, grinning mischievously, "I've got a coffee to drop off for my real-life hero and a surly fictional one waiting for me on the page."

"Happy writing," Sammy said, propelling her out the door.

"Oh! I almost forgot," Eva called from the sidewalk. "Donovan and I would *love* a wreath with a navy bow and gold balls."

Sammy was going to need a workshop of elves to help her with the damn wreaths. "Navy. Gold balls. Got it," she said weakly.

"It was lovely meeting you, Ryan. I have a feeling we'll be seeing each other again," she said before disappearing down the sidewalk.

"You have interesting friends," Ryan observed. "Did you find Rainbow?"

She winced. "Here and gone unfortunately. But I do have a lead on where she'll be at lunch."

Ryan sighed. "Dammit."

Sammy patted his shoulder. "It's a small town. We're bound to run into her sooner or later."

"I'm starting to think there is no Rainbow. Like this entire town is in on some cosmic joke and I'm the only one who hasn't heard the punchline yet."

"Relax," Sammy said. "There's no conspiracy or convoluted inside joke. Why don't you call the bank on the way to the next stop and see if there's anyone else there you could meet with. You might luck out and get on someone's calendar today."

"Fine," he said grudgingly as he held the door open for her.

She started the vehicle and turned on his seat warmer while he paced on the sidewalk, phone pressed to his ear. Judging by the pantomime of drop-kicking his phone into the street, she guessed it wasn't going well.

"Good news?" she joked when he got in.

Ryan tossed his phone over his shoulder into the back seat. "Great news," he said, the words dripping with sarcasm. "Apparently Rainbow Berkowicz is the only bank employee who can help me. No one else is authorized to talk about it."

Which meant she was most definitely still stuck with him. They both sighed. He turned to glare at her. "I don't know what you're sighing about. You get a delightful companion for your morning and I'm the one hung out to dry."

"I don't think you know what 'delightful' means," she pointed out. "Besides, it's not a contest to see who is most inconvenienced."

"Well, if it were, I'd win since I flew across the fucking country."

"Yeah, yeah. Christmas in Blue Moon. Worst day ever. Buckle up, grump."

He dragged on his seatbelt and clutched his coffee. "What's the next stop? More baby goats to examine? Perhaps a problematic pony?"

"Nice try. Next up is llamas."

He blinked. "Llamas?"

"Llamas."

~

Blue Moon Community Facebook Gossip Group

Marsha McCafferty: Old Man Carson's nephew is the Liam Neeson of accountants! He just saved me from an IRS scam! If you see him around town, give him a hug, buy him a drink, and ask him for accounting advice!

12

_____

"lamas are stupid animals. Why do they even exist?" Ryan groused, shoving Sammy into the passenger seat.

"They're actually domesticated South American pack animals that can carry up to thirty percent of their own body weight. And I am perfectly capable of driving," Sammy chirped. He found her enthusiasm while she bled from a wound on her arm irritating.

"Stop being so cheerful. You're injured. You were violently attacked," he insisted, opening the glove box and digging out a wad of fast food napkins. He pressed them to her forearm, where only moments ago, one of the disgusting beasts in the backyard of the green cottage had sunk its huge teeth into her.

"Bet you're glad now that I made you get new clothes," she mused. He glanced down. They were both covered in green, frothy liquid. It smelled like fresh-cut grass and bile.

Ryan's New Plan
  1. Track down Rainbow.
  2. Solve Carson's problem.

3. Shower for at least an hour.

4. Nap.

5. Book plane ticket home.

6. Never get within twenty feet of a stupid llama again.

He applied more pressure. "You sure know how to show a guy a good time, Sparkle."

She snorted. "You've never spent a morning getting spit on by bad-tempered llamas before? You are missing out, my friend."

"I refuse to believe it's still morning. I feel like I've been awake for a week straight. Does it hurt?"

The woman had taken him to a relatively normal-looking house on the outskirts of town. The lots were bigger, but there was a sidewalk out front, for Christ's sake. That was supposed to mean civilization. Not near-death experiences with farm animals.

Apparently, Blue Moon had no town ordinance about housing violent, flesh-eating woolly mammoths, since Charisma Champion with the Cher hair and gypsy stylings— he didn't need a palm reading, thank you very much—had two of them in her backyard. Oh, sure, they'd *looked* harmless. Who would be afraid of a giant pipe cleaner with legs? But those two-inch long buck teeth were capable of inflicting serious damage.

The male, Fernando, had waited until Sammy was paying attention to the girl, Abba, before trotting over and sinking his yellow fangs into her forearm.

"It was a love bite," Sammy scoffed. "Besides, you're the one who got kicked."

When Sammy and Charisma hadn't appeared properly concerned over the blood spurting from the wound, Ryan had yelled. Then grabbed Fernando the Beast's bridle, looked it in its stupid, glassy eyes, and told it if it ever bit anyone again, he'd fly across the country and give the stupid thing a mohawk with hedge clippers.

Fernando had backed off, prancing across the yard to glare at him from the safety of the shed. But Abba had taken offense to Ryan insulting her boyfriend and kicked him right in the thigh. Those dainty little devil hooves carried a wallop. His leg was still throbbing. And then the spitting had happened.

"She's lucky I didn't decide to kick and spit back," he muttered. "Where's your first aid kit?"

Sammy pointed to the back seat. He limped around and found it in a neatly organized duffel bag tucked between a change of clothes, extra medical supplies, and a stash of protein bars. Ryan approved the orderly provisions. To some men, all it took to get turned on was a low-cut shirt and a pair of big... eyes. He certainly had nothing against those things. But he was more attracted to someone if she had labels in her pantry or a color-coded filing system. Or, apparently, a neatly organized go-bag.

Ripping open an alcohol swab, he returned to her.

She grinned up at him. It felt like he was staring directly into the sun. Thawing something inside him that felt like it had been frozen for a long time. Because what kind of an idiot stared directly into the sun?

"What?" he asked gruffly.

"You were very heroic prying Fernando's jaws open. For a big city guy, you sure catch on quick to small-town farm life. Ouch! Bedside manner, buddy," she complained when he swapped blood-soaked napkin for alcohol sting.

"Don't be a baby, Sparkle. It's your fault you have a job where you get bitten for a living. I don't like the idea of you doing this on your own."

"My vet tech is on vacation. He's usually the one Fernando bites. Besides, it keeps things interesting." She hissed out a breath through her teeth as he cleaned the wound. "I bet there are parts of your job that seem masochistic to an outsider."

"Paper trails," he said, shredding the packaging of a gauze pad and placing it firmly over the wound.

"Paper trails?"

"I love taking fifty pounds of paperwork and digging through it to find answers."

Hell, he didn't just love it. He *lived* for it. Knowing that everything he needed was boxed up in front of him and all he had to do was methodically work his way through each and every scrap of paper? It was gratifying in a "what kind of weirdo enjoys this?" kind of way.

So was being this close to her. In this light, her eyes were an almost depthless sky blue.

The llama kick must have dislodged something in his brain. He had never given a woman's eye color more than a passing thought.

They were looking at each other. Measuring each other. Gazes locked. Breath synced. He studied every inch of her face for the reason for his interest. Was it the smattering of freckles across her nose? The dimple in her chin? That mouth of hers?

Or was it the way she looked at him, *really* looked at him? As if she were peeling back the layers of responsible accountant down into areas that hadn't seen the light in years.

It was terrifying. Annoying. Exhilarating. And for some reason, the endless morning didn't feel quite so cold anymore.

With a heroic effort, he dragged his attention back to the task at hand. But he let his fingers linger longer than necessary on the tape as he smoothed it over the gauze.

"You're an interesting guy, Ryan. Where'd you get so good at first aid?"

He couldn't tell if it was his imagination or not that was making her sound a little breathy. Was it possible she was as affected by the proximity as he was? Of course not. Women didn't get breathless over the responsible, good-ish guy. He was the smart choice, not the "swept off her feet, love defies all logic" pick.

He was too grouchy. Worse, he worshipped organization, planning, efficiency. None of those ranked on the romance meter with women or led to the aforementioned sweeping of feet.

"I was nominated emergency director for my floor in the office," he told her. "We have—had—three floors in a building downtown. Each floor has a director trained to take charge in the event of an emergency."

"You're so responsible," she said with that bright smile that made it impossible for him to look away from her mouth.

"I can be irresponsible if I want to be," he insisted.

That was probably a lie. He always paid his property taxes within twenty-four hours of receiving the notice. He kept an up-to-date pantry inventory that made grocery shopping for the eight meals he regularly rotated through on his menu a breeze. Monday was dry cleaning drop-off day because it was cheaper than Fridays. Thursdays, he ran his robot vacuum cleaner. Saturday was leg day at the gym so his co-workers wouldn't see him limping around the office the next day.

Sure, he'd never forget a birthday or an anniversary. But he also wasn't the bad boy who would push a woman up against a wall to kiss her without being 100 percent certain that's what she wanted first.

Great. He was boring himself again.

Not that he was trying to impress the wounded Sammy. It wasn't like he had a reason to. He wasn't going to be here long enough to start a relationship or even some bizarre, short-term friendship.

"I'm sure you can," she said, patting his arm.

Patronizing, smug, pretty pain in his ass.

"Dr. Sammy! Ryan!"

They both looked up as Charisma trotted down the driveway toward them. "You forgot your biscotti!"

"I forgot? Silly me. Thanks," Sammy said with forced brightness as she accepted the folded bakery box. Something in those guileless blue eyes told Ryan she had definitely not forgotten.

"I packed an extra box for you, Ryan. Consider it an apology for the spitting and the kicking and a thank you for the recommendations on llama insurance," she said, whipping a two-foot-long section of dark hair over her shoulder. He wondered if she noticed that it wrapped around the mailbox post behind her.

"It's not necessary. Happens all the time," he said.

Sammy snorted, then covered it with a cough.

"I insist!" Charisma said, shoving the second flimsy cardboard closer to his nostrils. To prevent her from inserting the biscotti directly into his nasal cavity, he accepted the box.

"Thank you," he said.

"You are so welcome. And Sammy, don't forget. I'd like a wreath with pine cones, jingle bells, and fake snow."

"You got it," Sammy said, sounding even more strained.

"Now, if you'll excuse me, I need to get back to my baking. Ta-ta!"

"Toodle-oo," Ryan said.

Sammy elbowed him.

"Ow. What?" He rubbed his ribs

"Toodle-oo? Seriously?"

"I was speaking her language."

With an eye roll, she swung her legs into the vehicle.

"Where to next?" he asked, sliding the seat back a good eight inches and opening his box of biscotti.

She consulted her watch. "We should be able to catch Rainbow at Villa Harvest restaurant. And I wouldn't do that if I were you," she warned as he plucked a chocolate-covered chunk out of the box.

"Why?" he asked.

"Charisma is gluten-free and vegan. And a terrible baker."

"I'm starving. How bad could it be?" he scoffed.

"Don't say I didn't warn you."

He bit into the baked good and had immediate regrets. "Dear God. Is that concrete? Did she bake concrete?" It was gritty and crunchy. And the brown stuff was most definitely *not* chocolate. "Why does the chocolate taste so bad?"

"She makes it with black beans, prunes, and cocoa powder," Sammy said, grinning.

"This is worse than the hangover. I might actually vomit in your car," he said.

She dove for the glove box and pulled out the last of the napkins. "Here."

He spit out the masticated disaster, then scraped his tongue clean. "No one is that bad at baking. That kind of horror has to be on purpose. I think I taste rubber cement and construction paper. It's an act of aggression."

She was laughing at him. "I warned you."

"I thought it was hyperbole. Like 'watch out for Tina, she'll bore you to death with stories about her guinea pigs.' No one actually dies from a conversation with Tina. But this poison masquerading as biscotti should come with an FDA warning label."

She held up his coffee, looking amused. "Drink and try to forget it. And maybe next time you'll listen to me."

He washed down the remaining grittiness with a hit of coffee. "Please tell me Villa Harvest is a restaurant. I need something else in my mouth to block out the memory of that."

"It is. Since you were such a good sport about the spitting and kicking, I'll buy."

She directed him through town. Block after block of tidy houses with festive exteriors. He was getting a wrist cramp from acknowledging all the bundled-up pedestrians who insisted on waving at him like they knew him. It was a weird town full of weird people. But the friendly, kooky kind of weird. Not the starting-a-militia-in-the-backyard kind of weird.

Sammy was looking at him again like she was considering something. He wondered if she was going to ask him for tax advice.

"You're definitely leaving soon, right?" she said, biting her bottom lip.

"First chance I get."

"And you won't be back?"

"Nothing could drag me back to this holiday hellmouth," he promised.

"Interesting," she mused. "I imagine losing a job like that can do a number on a guy's stress level."

"What are you getting at?" he asked with suspicion.

"I was thinking. Since you're obviously attracted to me, and since I don't find you physically repulsive, we could have sex."

A fine mist of coffee coated the dashboard.

"Jesus, Sam," he choked. "Warn a guy before you're about to proposition him." He pulled over in front of a rambling Victorian home with porches and windows everywhere.

"Good sex is a great stress reliever." She said it like she was lecturing a high school health class. "As long as you're still getting on that plane, things wouldn't have the chance to get awkward."

Carefully he put the coffee back in the cup holder and picked up the wad of napkins. He smeared coffee and half-chewed concrete around on the dashboard as he drove. "Let me get this straight. You're offering to have a one-night stand with me so I can blow off some steam? How altruistic of you."

She lifted a shoulder. "Okay. Fine. So maybe it would *also* scratch an overdue itch of mine. It's a win-win. As long as you put forth a solid effort in bed, of course. You do, don't you?"

He stopped swiping at the windshield. "What am I supposed to say to that?"

"You're supposed to say something like 'I'm freaking great in bed, Sammy. I'll leave you walking like a bowlegged cowboy.' Or maybe 'I'm extremely thorough in bed.'"

He opened his mouth to say something, anything. But words failed him.

He was bombarded with images of a naked Sammy writhing under him, looking at him with those blue eyes gone glassy. There was no chance of him not getting hard. It was a foregone biological conclusion.

The breath he'd been holding left his lungs slowly like a deflating balloon. His silence had stretched on too long. Now it was weird. He was making it weird. Well, she'd made it weird first with her "hey, wanna have awesome sex with me?" query.

She made it sound so easy. So uncomplicated.

But in his world, sex didn't sneak up on him. It was worked toward, planned for, elegantly executed. There were preparations. Condoms. Manscaping. Wearing the deodorant that he'd been too hungover this morning to remember. Showering off llama spit was a new one, but it ranked right up there with the condoms. And that was only *after* he and the woman in question had thoroughly vetted each other.

Sure. He was a man, but dammit, sex was a big deal. His erection throbbed its agreement.

She shot him a glance. "You've been silent for almost three minutes."

"I'm processing," he said through gritted teeth.

"Are you telling me you've never been propositioned before?"

She sounded incredulous and some distant part of his brain that hadn't been broken by "Hey, wanna bang?" felt flattered.

"Not like *this*," he insisted. "I haven't had sex that wasn't attached to a date since college."

If he wanted to be a stickler about the facts, he hadn't had sex that hadn't come after three to five dates since college. Even in college, he'd never experienced an actual one-night stand. Sure, he'd had offers—most memorably Kimara Leigh, a smart, sarcastic prelaw major with a minor in poetry. It had been the minor that scared him off. Well, technically, it had been his fifty questions about where she saw herself in five years and whether she would be comfortable with public school for any future children if she decided to have them that had scared *her* off.

He couldn't help it. There were consequences to decisions. Condoms broke. Accidental babies were conceived. Being the practical, responsible guy he was, Ryan had made sure to only sleep with women with whom he felt he could successfully co-parent.

"Look, it's not a marriage proposal. You make me laugh and you're still pretty okay-looking even in stupid hats. Plus, you look like you could blow off some steam," she said, eyeing his crotch.

If she didn't stop looking at him like that, he would be in danger of forgetting all about the deodorant and llama spit and accidental babies.

"Think about it. Could be fun. I'm great at it, by the way," she said, stretching her legs out. "It's probably all the medical school."

He swore under his breath and shifted in his seat. His hard-on throbbed painfully against the confines of the zipper. He needed to rethink the whole going commando thing. "While I appreciate the offer," he said through gritted teeth, "if there is a God, I'll be on a red-eye flight home tonight. Tomorrow at the latest."

She shrugged. Casually. As if the invitation and his RSVP were of no consequence. He wasn't sure what was going to explode first—his left eye or his penis.

"Well, if you *are* still here tonight, the invitation stands," Sammy told him. "Take the left up there."

13

*I*f there was a God, Rainbow Berkowicz would be dining on chicken Alfredo. Ryan and his mysterious emergency would become *her* problem. And Sammy could grab one of Franklin's amazeballs chicken parm breadstick sandwiches to go and pretend she'd never met Grumpy Ryan Sosa.

She'd offered up a logical win-win with no discernible downside, and he'd acted like she'd asked him to French kiss a rattlesnake. It was hard not to take that personally. Hard not to be supremely embarrassed.

She'd taken the man's morning wood too seriously, attributing it to him actually being attracted to her, when in all likelihood, it had just been a biological response to someone with a vagina sitting on top of someone with a penis.

So she wasn't five-foot-ten-inches tall with waist-length blonde hair.

So she wasn't a dark-eyed beauty who looked like she had secrets that needed unlocking.

And yeah, maybe she was covered with llama spit and smelled like dairy cows. But it wasn't like she'd insisted that he had to take his pants off right that second on the side of the road.

None of that meant that she wasn't attractive "in her own way."

However, he'd still turned her down without even considering the possibility. *Ouch.*

Villa Harvest was a pretty gold stucco building with fanciful trellis work on the exterior and a Tuscan-inspired patio for warm weather months. Inside, Blue Moon residents ignored carb counts and thoroughly enjoyed memorable dishes and friendly service.

"Can we go in there like this?" Ryan asked, looking down at his stained coat.

She pointed at the front door where two farmers kicked manure off their boots before strolling inside in their overalls and decades-old baseball caps. "I think we'll be fine," she said and climbed out of the SUV before he could say anything else. Or before she could punch him for saying anything else.

He jogged to catch up and reached around her to open the door.

"Thanks," she said, plastering a phony smile on her face.

His eyes narrowed. "What's wrong?" he demanded as they stepped into the small vestibule. Balmy heat blew down over them from the ceiling.

"Nothing," she said, reaching for the inner door.

He stopped her with a hand on her shoulder, spinning her around. "That. That right there," he said, drilling a finger into her shoulder, "is why women end up miserable in relationships."

"What are you babbling about?" *Okay, so she knew exactly what he was talking about.*

"Something's wrong. Some mysterious offense took place in

the last five minutes, and when a well-meaning guy asks about it, you tell him, 'Nothing.'"

"Mysterious offense?" her voice rose. He'd insulted her with a knee-jerk repulsion to her suggestion and then acted like it was a *perfectly natural reaction*. She was definitely going to punch him.

Fortunately for Ryan's face, the interior door opened. "Hey, Doc. Hey, Ryan," Calvin Finestra, Blue Moon's resident contractor, greeted them as he exited the restaurant.

"Hey, Calvin," Sammy said, trying her best to calm herself down.

"Don't forget to give me a call after the first of the year, and we can start drawing up plans for some of those renovations," Calvin reminded her.

"Will do," she promised.

"See you at the Solstice," he called as he exited the building.

Ryan frowned. "How does everyone know my name?"

Perhaps word of his astronomical ego preceded the man? "It's the Facebook gossip group," she explained. "You don't want to know. Let's see if Rainbow is here so you can solve your mystery, and I can get back to my regularly scheduled day."

She didn't wait for him to agree. Instead, she marched through the delectable scents of garlic and fresh-baked bread, making a beeline for the host stand. It was manned by Emma Vulkov, Franklin's third daughter. Emma had short red hair and no tolerance for nonsense. Like her youngest sister, Eva, she too was newly married and pregnant. Unlike Eva, she was dressed in stylish leather leggings and a cowl neck sweater that matched the green of her eyes.

"Hey, Emma. What are you doing here? Don't you have another restaurant to run?" Sammy asked. Emma was a West Coast transplant brought in by Jax Pierce to manage John Pierce Brews.

Emma grinned at her, and Sammy noticed her gaze travel to Ryan. "Oh, you know restaurants. It's my day off at the brewery, but the hostess called in sick and Niko's in New York for a photoshoot. Plus, Dad promised me a free lunch, so here I am. Table for two?"

"Actually, we're looking for Rainbow," Sammy told her. Her stomach growled, complaining that she wasn't prioritizing chicken parm over getting rid of Ryan.

Emma gave a toss of her coppery blunt bob and glanced around the dining room. "You know what? I think you just missed her. She was here with her women's entrepreneur group, but she headed out just a few minutes ago."

"What? Why? Where is she? Where did she go?" Sammy demanded.

Emma's eyes widened, and Sammy dialed it back a notch. "Uh. I don't know. She didn't say. Is it an emergency?"

"Yes," Sammy said.

"No," Ryan said at the same time. "We'll take that table for two."

Emma smiled up at him. "You must be the famous Ryan."

Sammy decided her next project would be to take that gossip group and infect it with a virus that would prevent anyone in it from ever typing her name again.

"I am," Ryan said. "I'd shake your hand, but you don't want to know what happened at our last stop."

Emma laughed and picked up two menus. "Knowing Sammy, I can only imagine. Follow me. A spot in front of the fireplace just opened up."

Sammy frowned at the Reserved sign Emma plucked off a cozy table directly in front of the stone hearth. Wood snapped and crackled comfortingly as orange flames warmed the space. A half-wall lined with plants and wine bottles created a kind of separation from the rest of the tables. It was prime dining room real estate for a romantic, intimate meal. *Lucky her.*

"Is there another table available?" she asked, hoping for something noisy near the door for a quick escape.

"Don't listen to her. This is perfect," Ryan said firmly as he warmed his hands near the fireplace.

"It was a canceled reservation," Emma explained. "Make yourselves comfortable and consider the stuffed mushroom caps. They're incredible." She left them to an awkward silence.

"I'm going to go wash my hands," Sammy announced and headed to the restroom.

She took her time, washing her hands until they were red, then stripping off her hat and fluffing her hair. Not that it mattered what her hair looked like. Her lunch date wasn't interested. Besides, the hat was just going to go right back on.

When she returned to the table, she found Ryan deep in discussion with Franklin Merrill, the huggable owner. He was a burly man in his sixties with broad shoulders and a squishy center. In deference to the holidays, the man had traded in his trademark Hawaiian shirts for ugly Christmas sweaters.

"So you're saying I'd be better off depreciating the new pizza oven with a one hundred fifty or two hundred percent method than the straight line?" Franklin asked.

"Restaurant equipment like ovens lose more value faster. So it makes more sense to depreciate it that way," Ryan said. His gaze flicked to Sammy.

"Dr. Sammy!" Franklin said. He dropped the basket of bread and butter he was holding on the table and enveloped her in a warm hug. He was a champion hugger, Sammy thought as she squeezed him back.

"How's Mr. Snuffles?" she asked, referencing Franklin and Phoebe's adopted sinus-infection-prone pug.

"A disaster as always," Franklin announced, pulling her chair out for her. "I'm just kidding. That last sinus infection cleared up right away. The grandkids have been teaching him some tricks, but he only lasts ten minutes or so before he needs to recover with a two-hour nap. What are you two up to?"

"We've been tracking Rainbow Berkowicz," Sammy said, pouncing on the basket of bread. Breakfast had been approximately one hundred years ago, and the one thing guaranteed to soothe her wounded pride was delicious carbs.

"You just missed her," Franklin said. He paused to wave at a table of knitters sitting in the window, downing espressos and cannoli with abandon. "But she'll be at the ribbon-cutting this afternoon for Mason Smith's office."

Sammy stuffed a slice of bread in her mouth and closed her eyes. A few measly hours. She could deal with Ryan for that amount of time... if she had bread and chicken parm—maybe she'd do the lunch entree instead of the sandwich since they were dining in. That thought cheered her.

"I'd better get back in the kitchen," Franklin said. "Fennel and Orion are fighting over preschool options."

"Wait a minute. Did I miss some big adoption news?" Sammy asked.

"No. They're just being proactive," Franklin said with a wink. "Enjoy your lunches."

"Back to your offer," Ryan said, the second the man was out of earshot.

Sammy groaned inwardly. "Are you still thinking about that? Forget it. Let's not waste any more time on that topic." She was going to do her best to forget she'd ever been stupid enough to make the offer.

"Hello, and welcome to Villa Harvest. Are we trying the mushroom caps today?" Fennel, the server, clutched his notepad to his chest with brave dignity while casting glares at his chef husband in the open kitchen.

For his part, Orion banged the pots and pans on the stove around with excessive force. Sammy sympathized.

They placed their orders as Fennel's lower lip trembled then handed the menus over.

"You're pissed at me because I turned you down," Ryan said, the second Fennel disappeared through the kitchen doorway.

"Ryan, for the love of fresh-baked bread. Let's stop talking about it. I offered, and you declined," she said, picking up a second slice of bread and slathering it with butter. She had a very specific routine at Villa Harvest. First, she always arrived too hungry. Which then required her to eat too much bread before her meal came. Which in turn forced her to box up half her entree so she could eat the leftovers later. It was a flawless system.

"Things don't get resolved by pretending they never happened," he said loudly over the yelling—some in Portuguese—coming from the kitchen. The pot banging grew louder.

She slapped Ryan's hand away from the butter. He could stomp on her self-esteem, but that didn't mean she had to surrender her butter. "There's nothing to resolve. And even if there were, you're leaving, so it doesn't matter."

His eyes narrowed as he studied her. "I don't like leaving problems unsolved."

"You didn't say anything I wasn't expecting. Let's leave it alone."

"Fine," he said, snatching the butter away from her and slathering it on a fluffy piece of rosemary and olive oil bread.

The yelling in the kitchen stopped.

She swallowed the huge bite of bread along with her own anger.

"Your appetizer is here," Fennel sang, dropping a mustard yellow platter of mushroom caps in front of them. With a flourish, he placed two small green plates on the table, blew them a kiss, and vanished.

"I guess they made up," Ryan observed. "Like *adults*."

"I guess so," she said, too busy diving for the mushrooms to rise to the bait.

Like a sneak, he waited until she'd shoveled her half of the appetizer onto her plate.

"Mmm," she moaned around a mouthful of butter and garlic.

"All I'm saying is I take sex very seriously," he said. "Decisions that I take seriously require time and consideration."

"For Pete's sake, man. Shut up," she said. She lunged across the table and shoved an entire mushroom cap into his mouth. "You're not interested. I get it. Let it go."

He opened his mouth like he was going to argue but was interrupted by a figure dressed all in black popping up over the other side of the half-wall.

"Holy shit," Ryan choked, chewing rapidly.

"Sammy! I hope you're saving me a wreath with naughty Santas," Mrs. Nordemann announced with a flourish of her faux fur cape.

"Where did you come from? A trap door?" Ryan asked, peering over the wall.

Their visitor chuckled. "You must be Ryan. I've heard so much about your dry wit."

"From who?" Sammy and Ryan said together. He gave her a good glare, and she shrugged back.

"You two are a hoot! I'll leave you to your date," she sang.

"Not a date," he said.

"*Definitely* not a date," Sammy agreed.

"What's that supposed to mean?" Ryan demanded.

Mrs. Nordemann reached into her cape pocket and fished out

her phone. She plunked her reading glasses down on her nose and peered at the screen. "I'll just... ah, yes. There it is." She pointed it at them, and Sammy heard the distinct sound of a camera shutter.

"Did you just take a picture of us?" Ryan asked.

"Don't be silly," the woman trilled, still frowning at her screen. Her thumbs moved at a snail pace.

Sammy checked her watch. It took almost a full minute before Mrs. Nordemann hit the last keystroke and triumphantly returned the phone to her pocket. "Well, I'm sure I'll be seeing more of you two."

"Why is everyone so interested in us?" Ryan asked.

She shook her head. "It's a small-town thing. Don't worry about it. As long as a goth princess doesn't show up next, we're fine." There was no way the Beautification Committee was involved in Ryan losing his job, flying across the country, and finding himself in need of a ride. They were sneaky, but more Pink Panther than James Bond when it came to efficiency.

"You mean that goth princess or a different one?" Ryan pointed behind her.

"Damn it," she hissed as she spotted Mason helping Ellery shrug into her floor-length ebony trench coat. "Don't make eye contact."

"Too late," he said around a bite of mushroom cap.

"Sammy! Ryan! I didn't know you'd be here for lunch," Ellery said cheerfully. Her face looked even paler with the glossy purple lipstick and thick charcoal eyeshadow. She wore a black turtleneck and over it a tiered necklace made up of dozens of tiny daggers.

"Hi, Ellery. Hey, Mason," Sammy said wearily. "Have you two met Ryan?"

"We were in the same aisle at the liquor store last night," Mason said.

"I snuck Masey away for lunch before the big event this afternoon," Ellery said, linking her arm through her husband's.

Mason Smith was a khaki-starching, number-crunching, risk-avoiding man in his mid-thirties. He'd been brought to Blue Moon under false pretenses constructed by the Beautification Committee and somehow managed to fall head over heels in love with the gothic paralegal. They married on Halloween in the midst of an astrological apocalypse.

"My hubby's an accountant," Ellery told Ryan. "The grand opening of his firm is happening today."

"What kind of accounting?" Ryan asked.

"Mostly small business," Mason said. "Apparently, a lot of Mooners thought paying taxes was voluntary," Mason said.

"Why does that not surprise me?" Ryan mused.

Sammy resisted the urge to kick him under the table.

"It's my favorite ex-boyfriend and his lovely wife," Emma said, strolling up with a stack of dessert menus in her hands. "Are you ready for the big ceremony?"

Ryan appeared to be watching the conversation with concern and vague interest, like a man sitting down to watch his first episode of *Real Housewives*.

"Yes," Mason said, with a shy head bob.

He was a man of few words.

Ellery beamed at her husband with abject adoration.

"Mason and I used to date when I lived on the West Coast," Emma explained to Ryan. "There's a few of us transplants here in town."

"You must miss it," Ryan guessed.

Mason and Emma exchanged a grin. "Not really," the accountant said.

"Blue Moon has its own special appeal," Emma agreed.

"What are you guys up to?" Sammy asked, crossing her arms.

"Up to? I'm just enjoying lunch with my handsome hubby," Ellery said innocently.

"And I'm just greeting my dad's patrons," Emma promised, looking at Sammy like *she* was the crazy one. "I wasn't even supposed to be here today."

"I don't like what this smells like," Sammy insisted.

"What does it smell like?" Ryan interjected, sniffing the last mushroom cap.

"Are you feeling okay, Sammy?" Ellery asked. "You've had a busy couple of days. Do you need help with your wreaths? We're all so excited about supporting Down on the Farm."

"Thanks, but I'm fine," Sammy said. She didn't need help. She could still do it all. As long as she got rid of Ryan and double-timed her errands, she could get back on track in time for the Solstice. *Probably.*

"Lunchtime," Fennel announced, arriving with a tray of steaming hot entrees.

"We'll let you two get back to your meal," Emma said.

"Don't forget! We want a wreath with cute little skulls on the bow," Ellery said, blowing them a kiss as she and Mason headed for the door.

❧

BLUE MOON COMMUNITY *Facebook Gossip Group*
This month's meeting of the Blue Moon Astrologers Group has been postponed until next month's full moon. This is not to be confused with the Blue Moon Astronomers Pot Luck, which will still occur at Destiny Wheedlemeyer's house on the 27th.

14

---

*M*uttering something about running an errand, Sammy dumped Ryan at the curb half a block down from the crowd of people. The woman was clearly not over the thing they weren't going to mention ever again.

He'd tried to explain, but she'd shot him down. As far as he was concerned, it was her own fault for being pissed off.

His conscience was clear. *Mostly. Besides. He had more important things than a pissed off veterinarian to worry about.*

Assuming he'd find the elusive Rainbow Berkowicz with the small crowd of outdoorsy folk down the block, he headed in that direction.

Ryan's New List
    1. Stop thinking about Sammy's now-rescinded offer.
    2. Find Rainbow Berkowicz.
    3. Get his hands on all pertinent paperwork.
    4. Figure out the solution or loophole and exploit the hell out of it.
    5. Be on a plane by midnight tonight.

Everyone was bundled up against the cold in bright coats

and a neon nightmare of hats and scarves. They were milling about, trying to hold glasses of champagne and napkins of appetizers with mittened hands.

The conversations he overheard seemed too lively, too friendly for this to be a work thing.

The professional events he'd attended—before his unceremonious firing—consisted of small social circles predicting dramatic exits of co-workers and spreading rumors like contagion. The backstabbing and sabotage some of the staff used to get ahead. He hadn't cared for that part of it. He also had never shown up for a work event covered in llama spit before.

He recognized Mayor Pierce in a narrow alleyway next to the building. The man was in a suit and wool coat, making time with a petite redhead in leggings and a white fleecy jacket that reminded him of Stan.

Ryan hoped that Stan was having fun in the snowy pasture.

The woman looked up at Beckett with the kind of adoration in her eyes that had something weird and burny happening in Ryan's chest. When the mayor pinned the redhead to the brick and started kissing the hell out of her, Ryan decided to find someone who wasn't busy making out to point him in the direction of an evil bank president.

He spotted Mason standing on the curb, seemingly oblivious to the clucking and fussing of people around him. He looked up at the building, a ghost of a smile and something that looked a bit like pride on his face.

It was a two-story brick storefront with a large, plate glass window with fresh lettering that said Blue Moon Accounting. The brick had been painted a deep navy, the door a cheerful purple, a color combination he wouldn't have approved on paper. But in person, it seemed almost charming.

Deciding he didn't want to interrupt Mason's moment, he tapped a woman wearing a Karen's Plumbing jacket on the shoulder. "Can you tell me where to find Rainbow Berkowicz?" he asked. She'd probably left to go to the dog groomers or headed out of town for a 10-day Panama Canal cruise. Or more likely, she'd never existed and he'd hallucinated this entire trip.

"Oh, sure. She's inside."

He blinked, momentarily shocked. "Uh. Thank you," Ryan said. He'd been burned too many times to feel actual relief. He'd save that until he laid eyes on the woman.

From his vantage point on the sidewalk, he saw Beckett had finished his make out session and was heading inside. Ryan tried to make his way through the crowd as politely as possible to follow, but it was difficult when half a dozen strangers greeted him by name and asked how he was liking Blue Moon.

He finally managed to extricate himself from an overly chatty woman in a Save the Bay shirt and entered the building.

The door opened into a small, bright reception area. He'd expected coffins and skulls. But apparently Mason's wife, Ellery, hadn't had a hand in the decorating. The walls were a warm vanilla. Plants in glossy white pots sat on a glass shelf in the big front window. A stately bookshelf held new volumes of tax law and New York small business accounting standards. Club chairs in a supple, aged leather—probably pleather given the leanings of the town, Ryan guessed—waited for clients.

There was a coffee bar on a counter fashioned out of what looked like an airplane wing. Coffee mugs with sayings like Accounting Ninja and It's Accrual World hung from hooks on the wall.

He spotted the redhead from the alley restocking appetizers while discussing the merits of hot yoga with a man in bell-bottom overalls.

Skirting around them, he followed the sound of voices.

Next to the reception desk—more metal like the coffee bar—was a wall of cubbies, big enough to hold binders and packages or thick packets of financial reports. Beyond the desk was a small glassed-in conference room and restroom divided by a short hallway. He liked the vibe of the space. It felt... friendly, healthy. There was no sea of cubicles. No stifling lack of natural light. Basically the exact opposite of his offices in Seattle. And for the first time he considered the fact that maybe it wasn't the worst thing in the world to be looking for a new challenge.

The first office was already furnished with a desk, workstation, and built-ins. There was a large photo of Ellery in a white wedding dress on the wall. The voices were coming from across the hall. It was another office, this one unfurnished but with a glass door that led outside to a small patio area.

Beckett was in discussion with Bruce the bearded Santa guy he remembered from the liquor store. A middle-aged woman in a crap brown business suit frowned at them and paced the carpet while she listened. In the corner, a woman with a very shiny gray beehive wrung her hands.

"I tried to tell you last night," Santa Bruce said with the distinct note of a whine in his voice.

The mayor was staring at the floor, hands on hips. Ryan knew that stance. It was the "give me patience before I murder someone" posture.

"What do you mean the state auditor found discrepancies in the paperwork, Bruce?" Beckett said, rubbing the back of his neck and staring at the ceiling. Another not good sign.

"Well, it's not so much a discrepancy. It's more that they haven't received any of the paperwork."

The woman in brown ceased her pacing immediately. "Why the hell not, Bruce?" she bellowed.

"Well, you see, Amethyst was handling the bookkeeping for me. The day-to-day transactions. Except I got her a subscription to this thing called Hulu for her birthday—"

"I fell down what's called a 'rabbit hole,'" Beehive chimed in.

"Did you know there are seven seasons of *Buffy the Vampire Slayer* on Hulu?"

"You're saying instead of handling the town's reporting to the state, you watched seven seasons of a TV show instead?" Beckett asked. His voice was very calm.

"To be fair, Mr. Mayor, it wasn't just *any* TV show. It was *Buffy*," Bruce said.

"Uh-oh."

Ryan jumped at the whisper and found the redhead standing next to him. "That's Beckett's 'you're in huge trouble' voice. What's going on?"

"From the sound of it, Mrs. Beehive was supposed to be keeping track of the reporting to the state and instead spent six months watching *Buffy the Vampire Slayer*."

"Oooh! Team Spike," the redhead said.

"Amethyst, this is beyond irresponsible," snapped the woman in brown. "The state auditor will be here on the twenty-fourth. How are we supposed to get everything in order by then?"

"It's my fault," the bearded man said, hands fluttering. "I never should have gotten her Hulu. I should have just gotten her a blouse or a beanbag."

Amethyst began to wail in a manner completely undignified for someone wearing a lace turtleneck and pearls.

"This is really not good, right?" the redhead asked Ryan.

"It's pretty bad." Barring a miracle, the town was likely good and fucked. A state auditor would have no problem levying fines and wreaking havoc on the municipality. Funding would be frozen during an investigation.

"I'm Gia, by the way," she whispered.

"Ryan," he said, shaking the hand she offered. "I met your husband and daughter at the liquor store last night and your sisters today."

Gia grinned. "Did Aurora try to give you peppermint schnapps?"

He shook his head. "Tequila."

"Beckett, we need to deal with this now," the woman in brown announced. "Maybe a town meeting. We can ask for volunteers. Anyone with QuickBooks or bookkeeping experience. Hell, anyone with a computer and a scanner."

The mayor sighed heavily. "Rainbow is right."

"That's Rainbow Berkowicz?" Ryan asked.

"That's her," Gia said before stepping forward and knocking on the open door. "Sorry to interrupt. But it's time to cut a ribbon with a comedically large pair of scissors."

HE HAD to wait until after the ribbon-cutting, after getting wrangled into the group photo next to Mason in front of the building. But Ryan finally got Rainbow alone.

She was aggressively puffing on a clove cigarette on the concrete patio outside the empty office.

"Rainbow Berkowicz?"

"Who wants to know?" she grumbled.

"I'm Ryan, Carson Shufflebottom's great-nephew."

Rainbow blew out a cloud of smoke. "What does that nincompoop's great-nephew want with me?"

"I need a few minutes of your time to discuss the foreclosure on Carson's farm."

"Unfortunately, I'm in the midst of a crisis. But you're welcome to schedule a meeting after Christmas."

"That's convenient, seeing as how you're foreclosing on my uncle's farm on Christmas Eve."

She peered at him through a villainous cloud of smoke. "I assure you, there is nothing convenient about a foreclosure. We take our loans very seriously. Unfortunately, your uncle didn't do the same."

"I need to see a copy of the loan and an accounting of the overdue balance, late fees, and accrued interest." he insisted.

"Ha!" she scoffed. "Then you better start digging through your uncle's files. Though I don't see why you need to bother since Carson doesn't seem concerned."

"Carson is helping a family member after a surgery," Ryan said stiffly.

"Cry me a river," she puffed. "If the man cared about saving his farm, he would have paid his debt and he would have stayed in town to fight for it."

"You expect me to dig through decades of a man's personal finances when you could have an employee hit email or print?" The woman was diabolical.

Her smile was Machiavellian. "Unfortunately for you, the bank's system is offline for maintenance for the next twenty-four hours. But Carson already has all of it. Still insists on paper statements. The man never throws anything away. A smart accountant like you should find exactly what he's looking for in no time."

She clamped the cigarette in her teeth like a bad guy with a cigar.

He thought of the leaning stack of shoeboxes on the couch. The note. *Everything you need is here.*

"You mean to tell me that not only are you refusing to take a meeting with me, no one else in your bank has room on their calendars to talk to me, and the 'system' is down so you can't prove that there is a debt to be paid?"

"That's exactly what I'm telling you," Rainbow said smugly.

"I'm not buying it."

She shrugged. "Prove it."

He kissed #5 on his list goodbye. There would be no plane ticket tonight. He had a small-town bank to destroy.

"Fine. But be warned, I'm not going to allow you to foreclose on the man the day before Christmas," Ryan said darkly.

"Then I suppose you'd better get busy," she said, with an unsettling wink and a cloud of blue smoke in his face.

Ryan coughed.

"You'll be hearing from me very soon," he promised.

"Looking forward to it," she said. Her cackling laugh turned to a fit of coughing behind him as he followed the alley to the street.

Rainbow Berkowicz had no idea who she was dealing with. If anyone was up to the challenge of finding the loophole in four hundred pounds of garbage, it was Ryan Freaking Sosa.

～

BLUE MOON COMMUNITY *Facebook Gossip Group*

Pete McDougall: New-in-town nephew of Carson Shufflebottom makes a public appearance without gal pal Sammy Ames. Is there trouble in paradise? Was there never any paradise in the first place?

15

"*D*id you rob a craft store?" Ryan asked in horror when he climbed into Sammy's SUV.

She glanced in the rearview mirror. Her back seat was filled with ribbons, bows, reels of fine wire, festive tablecloths, and a host of other items buried beneath the rest. "Har har. It's for the wreaths."

"I have to admit, I'm a little disappointed the glitter really was craft-related," he said.

She punched him in the arm. "Stop picturing me in pasties!"

"You're the one who was all, 'Hey, let's have some hot sex tonight.'"

"That was *after* you almost impaled me with your hard-on and *before* you declined my invitation."

"I thought we weren't talking about that," Ryan reminded her.

"Oh, shut up. Did you find Rainbow and book your flight home?" she asked, pulling away from the curb.

She had just enough time to dump the man back at his uncle's place before hitting her last stop of the day. Then if she neglected her paperwork and stayed up until midnight, she might feasibly finish some of the wreaths.

"I found her," he said, sounding annoyed. "But the situation is more complicated than I thought. So no flight home tonight."

"Great! I'll drop you off at Carson's. And you can feed the chickens and the sheep tonight."

"You don't have to sound so cheerful about it," he complained.

"*Text message from Joey Pierce. Can you come by early? Jax has writer's block and I need to take advantage of him this afternoon,*" the robotic voice recited.

"Dammit," she groaned.

"Do all your clients share their sex lives with you?" Ryan asked.

"Most of them. Can you handle one more stop?"

"Fine as long as nothing there bites you or spits on me," he said.

"You can wait in the car," Sammy decided.

"*Text message from Eden. If you need to get laid and that Fake Mistletoe Kisser isn't man enough to do it, I'll find someone who is! Flame emoji. Eggplant emoji.*"

"Oh. My. God." Sammy patted her pockets one-handed for her phone. She'd texted her friends after dropping Ryan off at the ribbon cutting to catch them up on her humiliation.

He snorted next to her. "Typical. 'No, Ryan. I'm not pissed off at you. Nothing's wrong. Let's not talk about it,'" he said, mimicking her in a falsetto.

"*Text message from Layla. Find one for me too. I'm overdue for an oil change.*"

"Bluetooth is so stupid!" Sammy wailed, poking the touchscreen in the dash looking for some kind of off button.

"*Text message from Eva. Describe the angle of your hips when you were astride the grumpy steed on the ground. Asking for a friend who needs a sexy build-up scene in her romance novel."*

"I *knew* you were pissed off that I turned you down," Ryan said triumphantly.

"Yeah. Fine. Congratulations, dick."

"*Text message from Eden. Davis has a second cousin named Dirk who just got out of a long relationship. Waiting to confirm penis size."*

"Who the hell is named Dirk?" Ryan demanded.

"What do you care?" Sammy gave up the search for her phone and turned off the sound system.

"I don't."

"Good," she said.

"Great," he shot back.

They were silent for a few moments. "I'm not pissed because you said no," she said finally. "I'm annoyed because you insinuated that the offer was gross."

"I did no such thing!" His expression was one of horror between his ear flaps.

"You spit out your coffee and practically gagged at the thought," she reminded him.

"Sam." He closed his eyes and heaved a sigh. "As I tried to explain to you, my reaction had nothing to do with my physical attraction to you, which *obviously* exists."

"Yeah. Whatever. Let's go back to not talking about this," she said, tightening her grip on the wheel and heading out of town toward Pierce Acres.

"No. Not, 'Whatever,'" he insisted. "I'm not the friendliest guy to begin with. But you surprised me. And I was—am —hungover."

"I hope for their sake no one ever tries to throw you a surprise party."

"All of the Sosas hate surprises. My sister's mother-in-law threw her a surprise baby shower and my sister showed up unshowered in gym shorts and her husband's dirty t-shirt thinking she was there to help reorganize a closet."

Sammy winced. "Ouch."

"I'm human. Okay? I like to know what's coming and when I fail to anticipate it, it takes me a minute to catch up."

"A minute?" she said dryly.

"Fine. A minute or a month. Sometimes I say dumb shit when I'm caught off guard and thinking about you naked."

"Can we not talk about this?"

"Pull over," he said.

"Why?"

"Just pull the damn car over, Sparkle."

She heaved her most dramatic sigh and pulled off the road next to a copse of leafless trees. Melted snow gushed out of a drainage pipe next to the road, sounding like a waterfall.

"You surprised me, Sam. Shocked the hell out of me," he admitted. "I didn't know how to react, and inappropriate, stupid, snarky humor is my fallback. And you're an idiot if you think I'm not attracted to you or that I wasn't tempted by the offer."

"You're not great at apologizing," she observed.

He rolled his eyes. "I'm not *apologizing*. I'm *explaining*. I didn't do anything that requires an apology. If anyone should apologize, it's you."

"Fine. I'm sorry for asking if you'd be interested in having sex with me."

He slapped a hand on her knee and gripped it hard. "You are infuriating! Don't apologize for offering a man a night of no-strings sex. Apologize for pretending nothing was wrong and not even trying to understand my answer."

"If I apologize, will you shut up about this?"

"Not until you hear what I'm trying to tell you. I've never dabbled with casual sex before. I take it very seriously. Decisions that I take seriously require time and consideration. So remove your head from your ass and hear me, Sam."

"Wow. Okay there, Prince Charming."

"I like the build-up. Okay? The flirtation. I like getting to know someone before I stick body parts inside them. I also like being able to focus one hundred percent on sticking body parts inside them to the best of my abilities. Not worried about getting fired or whatever trouble my great-uncle got himself into. Or wondering exactly how you—someone who is still practically a stranger to me—would like me to stick those body parts inside you."

"I'm just throwing this out there for any future propositions you receive," she began. "You could try *asking* your partner how they like sex."

"I'm not a fan of learning as I go. I like to have the ground-work laid and a clear idea of how to reach my objectives. And yes, I realize how unsexy that sounds. But I don't like to fail. I'd rather calculate the specifics of a woman's desires and be able to guarantee her the necessary number of orgasms."

"Oh," she managed. *Unspontaneous sex had never sounded sexier to Sammy.*

"So no matter how much I'd like to stick a few body parts in you—spoiler alert: a lot—I don't know you well enough to antic-ipate what you need and if my mind is on something else, I'm not going to deliver the best. And since my attention is going in seventeen different directions, I'm not sure I could even deliver fifty percent. You deserve a hell of a lot more than fifty percent, Sam."

She looked at him for a long beat, reading the blunt, annoyed sincerity in his expression. The tension drained from her neck and shoulders.

"Okay," she said.

"Look, if the circumstances were different—"

She covered the hand that rested on her leg with hers. "I said okay. And I mean it. At least, this time. Thanks for clarifying that you don't find me repulsive."

"You're a doctor, for fuck's sake. What the hell do you think an erection means? I've been walking around with one—hungover, by the way—all damn day."

She bit her lip. "Really?"

"You're starting to piss me off, Sparkle."

"Same goes, Grumpy Ryan," she said. But she was smiling when she said it. "Can we get on with our day?"

"One more thing," he said.

She didn't see it coming. Not from Mr. I Plan Out Everything. Ryan fisted a hand in her vest and yanked her toward him. Her seatbelt gave just enough for their mouths to collide and tangle over the console.

His lips were hard. She imagined it was from all the excessive brooding. Felt him pouring his frustration into the kiss, stealing the air from her lungs. It was too much and not enough. So she shoved her fingers into his hair and gripped. His hat fell off into his lap. She opened her mouth to say something, but his tongue stormed inside, rendering her speechless.

There was nothing gentle or romantic about the way his mouth moved over hers. It was a no-nonsense assault. A battle she didn't feel the least bit sorry over losing.

The only thing she knew for sure in that moment was the fact that Ryan Sosa was one hell of a kisser. Abruptly, he released her, dropping her back into her seat. She felt boneless and so very warm.

"Wow," she whispered.

He jammed the hat she'd dislodged back on his head, then adjusted his erection in his jeans. "Now we can go," he said, sounding more surly than when they were fighting.

"Wow," she whispered again, not sure if she'd regained control of her limbs yet.

The knock on her window scared the hell out of her.

"Holy shit!" she yelped.

"Car trouble, doc?" Sheriff Cardona peered into the vehicle, looking concerned.

Sammy felt her cheeks turn fuchsia.

16

_____

"I can't believe we got caught making out by the sheriff," Sammy said as she turned left onto a paved lane lined with white fencing. "What are we? Teenagers?"

"Oh, good. You've regained the powers of speech." Ryan smirked. He felt pretty damn good about his performance. Granted, he'd only meant to shut her up for a minute. But the way her mouth moved under his, those sexy little moans she made at the back of her throat, getting carried away had been the only choice.

"Yeah, you can joke about it because you don't have to see the sheriff every damn day for the rest of your life. It's a good thing he's not in the gossip group."

Snow-covered pastureland rolled out to the left, woods to the right. It was picture-perfect. Even to a grouch like him.

Ahead, smoke rose from the stone chimney of a large timber cabin. On the front porch, a pack of baby goats clamored at one of the front windows.

"What is it with this town and goats?" he asked.

"Those are the same goats," she told him. "That window is

Jax's office. He's a screenwriter. They're waiting for him to finish writing for the day."

Goat Guy. Ryan remembered his knee-jerk reaction of annoyance to the flirtatious goat herder. Well, Goat Guy hadn't just kissed the hell out of Dr. Sammy Ames. *He* had.

The huge barn rose out of the snow, buttoned up at the seams. No hint of disrepair here. There were a few horses under blankets dotting the white pastures.

"Is it safe for them to be out in the cold?" he asked, pulling his gloves out of his pockets.

"Most farm animals are hardier than you'd give them credit for. Fresh air's good for them."

"What are we doing here?" he asked.

"Pregnant mare check," she said, cutting the engine and dragging on her gloves. "Can you be nice in there, or do I need to lock you in the car? Between the farm, the riding school, and the breeding program, Pierce Acres is my biggest client. And if you piss off Joey, I'll have to grovel for you and I won't like that."

"I can be nice," he insisted. *Probably.*

"Try hard," Sammy prompted.

"Fine. I, uh, like your scarf," he said, desperately latching on to something that wouldn't be misconstrued as a double entendre or piss her off again. He wondered if she had any idea just how distracting she was, with those full pink lips that still had the "just kissed" look to them. Her eyes, a darker shade of lavender now, were wide and still just a little glassy. He wanted to kiss her all over again. To unzip that vest and fill his hands with her while he tasted her mouth.

She glanced down at the soft, green fabric around her neck and looked embarrassed. "Oh. Thanks."

"Now what?" he asked, exasperated and very, very hard.

"Well, fun fact. Your cousin gave it to me."

He was appalled. No, more than appalled. He was downright

horrified. "You hung on to a ratty scarf that some douchebag gave you fifteen years ago? You don't *actually* think you're in love with him, do you?"

"What? God, no! It was a nice memory and a great scarf. Jeez! And you said you liked it!"

On closer inspection, maybe it had been a great scarf at one time. Now it was missing more fringe than it had. There was a distinct bite mark in the hem. Probably llama. "Yeah, well, you put me on the spot, and I lied. I don't like it. It's a shitty scarf, and you should get rid of it."

"I'm confused, is this you being nice?" she quipped.

"Get out of the car, Sam," he growled.

They exited the vehicle. And Ryan took a deep breath of winter air. Despite his frustrations—sexual and otherwise—with Sammy, he felt like they were finally back on an even keel. She was happy. His hangover was almost gone. He had a starting point for Carson's problem. He'd had the best Italian meal of his life. And he'd kissed a woman breathless.

It could *almost* be labeled a good day.

Sammy led the way into the barn. As he stepped inside, he marveled that it was his second barn in one day. *What the hell was happening to his life?*

Inside, it was warmer than he expected. Cleaner too. Practically livable. It smelled better than the dairy barn, which, to be fair, hadn't been terrible either. But this sweet aroma was almost good. The scents of hay and horse and sawdust tangled together to create something interesting. If there were a horse barn candle, he'd consider buying it for his condo.

He thought of the scents of his own workplace. Fresh paper, stale coffee, the ghosts of cologne and furniture polish that lingered behind in the conference rooms. It didn't smell like *life*. Not like this.

The order of it all piqued his interest too. He appreciated the organization that was evident. There was an entire room of horse-riding equipment—a tack room, according to the sign next to the door—all shined and hung. Glossy black wheelbarrows and no-nonsense tools dripped dry on the stone floor. The hose that had cleaned them was coiled neatly on the mount on the wall.

Horse heads, huge yet dignified, poked out of stalls and eyed them as they passed. A big, black steed stared imperiously at them then gave the stall gate a hard gouge with his front hoof.

"Watch out for this guy," Sammy warned with a grin. "He's a biter."

"I know nothing about horseflesh, but that's one hell of a horse," he said, eyeing the beast.

"This is Apollo, the resident stud. He's a royal pain in the ass, but I love him. Don't I, big guy?"

Ryan flinched when she gave the stallion a scratch under the chin, expecting the horse to snap off a few of her fingers. Instead, he tolerated the affection for a few seconds before pretending to try to take a bite out of her shoulder.

But Dr. Sammy was a professional and accustomed to the trickery. She danced out of the horse's reach. It was all for show, he realized. A flirtation between stubborn and loving souls. The stallion practically had hearts in his eyes when he tossed his head arrogantly and looked away from Sammy.

"Come on," she said, waving. "The office is this way."

They turned a corner and found a small office with an open door and a glass window that overlooked the indoor riding ring.

"Bullshit," barked the woman refilling a mug of coffee in the office. She was long-legged like one of the fine specimens of horse in the stalls. Her dark hair was stick straight and pulled back in a long tail through a dirty ball cap. She wore those tight riding pants that horse people preferred, knee-high boots, and a heavy sweatshirt.

"It's not bullshit," the girl behind the desk argued. "You called the distributor a mercenary dictator and threatened to feed him his own balls last month."

"I have a feeling you'll like Joey," Sammy predicted before knocking on the door frame. "You pissing off distributors again?"

Joey snorted over the rim of her coffee cup. "No one would have to get pissed off if people did their damn jobs in the first place and weren't so damn sensitive about perfectly reasonable criticism."

Sammy was right. Ryan felt an immediate kinship with the woman. He bet she hated Christmas movies, too.

"I keep telling her she should let me take over the ordering so we wouldn't have to switch suppliers every few months," the girl said.

"I agree with Reva," Sammy said, leaning against the door. "You might need to finally accept that you suck at peopling and dump that responsibility on someone who doesn't make grown men cry at least once a week."

"You both can kiss my ass," Joey said with a toss of her long tail of hair. The movement reminded Ryan of Apollo's disdainful head toss.

"But you'll think about it," Sammy predicted.

Joey grunted. "Maybe."

Sammy winked at Reva, who looked smugly triumphant.

"Who are you?" Joey asked suddenly, her eyes narrowing in on him.

"This is Carson's great-nephew Ryan. Ryan, this is Joey Pierce and her daughter Reva."

Given the narrow age range between the women, Ryan guessed that biology hadn't played a part in the parent-child relationship.

"What are you doing here?" Joey asked.

She was the first person to ask him that. Everyone else

seemed to already know. "I'm handling a family matter for my uncle," he said.

"Your uncle's family matter involves my stables?"

"It's a long story," Sammy cut in. "Ryan's car wouldn't start, so he's playing vet tech today in exchange for a chauffeur."

"Hmm," Joey mused. She sounded like she didn't quite buy the explanation.

Sammy glared at the woman. "Don't tell me you've been in the gossip group."

"*I* haven't," Joey said defensively. "But that one over there maybe mentioned something about you two and your romantic romp around town." She nodded in Reva's direction.

"Romantic romp?" Ryan scoffed. "Doesn't anyone here have anything better to do with their time than gossip?"

"Not really," Joey and Sammy said together.

Reva grimaced. "You know. I think I hear something... somewhere that's not here. Bye!" Hiding a grin, she jumped up from the desk and hurried out the door. "Nice to meet you, Ryan!"

"You, too," he called after her.

"Well, let's look at a horse uterus, shall we?" Sammy said, rubbing her palms together.

"Now, thanks to Apollo and Calypso, the farm's biggest moneymaker is the breeding program," Joey explained to Ryan.

"And you're still running the riding school and boarding horses?" he quizzed her. The streams of income available to a farm with some creativity and capital were fascinating.

"Yep. Speaking of which," she said, peering over Sammy's shoulder at the ultrasound image on the iPad, "your girl could use a ride. I wasn't able to get her out yesterday."

Sammy blew out a breath through her teeth and hit send on

the images. "I planned to today," she admitted, "but we're tight on time."

Ryan felt a sting of guilt. If there was one thing he understood, it was responsibility. And the fact that he was keeping Sammy from one of hers irked him. Should some poor horse suffer just because he was in a hurry to go get paper cuts while digging through a disorganized mound of paperwork?

"I have time," he announced.

Sammy looked at him with a "you're sweet but" expression. "I'd need at least forty-five minutes. I know you have things to do."

"I can wait," he insisted.

"Why wait?" Joey piped up. "You ever been on a horse before?"

"Me?" Ryan looked over his shoulder to see if Joey was addressing someone else. "Hell no. I don't like sitting on animals. It feels too Napoleonic."

17

"I still don't understand how it happened," Ryan complained. "I very distinctly remember saying no."

Sammy turned in her saddle and grinned back at him as he plodded along on Shakira, a dappled gray horse with a bristly mane. She was a school mount for beginners. Ryan looked both uncomfortably out of his element and just a little delighted about it. It was adorable.

"Joey is very determined. It's always safer to just go with whatever she wants you to do."

"I seem to recall you were also rather convincing," he said dryly.

"I did no such convincing," she argued, swinging away from the fence line to cut down the middle of the field.

"You underestimate the power of those big, blue eyes, Sparkle."

She shifted and looked at him again. His ear flaps were down, the reins clenched in a death grip in one hand—a stickler for the rules. He looked both ridiculous and yet still unsettlingly attractive. "Are you flirting with me?"

"I don't flirt. I'm simply stating a truth."

"Well, it *sounds* like flirting," she pointed out.

"It's not my fault if you take it that way."

Sammy shook her head and returned her focus to the ride. She reached down and patted the neck of sweet Magnolia. Maggie was a blue roan Tennessee Walking Horse. Sweet and dainty, she had an enviable stride. She also was a skittish mount. With a little more time, a little more love, she'd find her confidence again.

Sammy loved a snowy ride. The thick quiet broken only by the crisp crunch of hooves. The trail of prints the only imperfection in the otherwise intact blanket still covering the ground. The creak of the saddle. The rock of the gentle horse beneath her. The way the sun and sky and snow built a picture so vibrant she couldn't stare directly at it.

"How do I catch up to you?" Ryan called from behind.

"Give her a little kick with your heels and click your mouth."

It took him three times, and his mouth click was more like a kiss, but he managed to bring his mount next to hers and looked pretty pleased about it.

"Nice job, cowboy."

"Thank you, ma'am."

A young boy in a snowsuit and bright orange hat burst out of the back door of the barn, a scruffy gray-and-white dog in a sweater on his heels.

"That's Caleb and Waffles," Sammy explained, returning the wave the boy sent her as he ran for what looked like the beginning of an army of snow people lining up against the pasture fence. "Both adopted by Jax and Joey. Reva too. They're good people. They built their own family." She respected that about them.

"Are all your friends married?" he asked.

"Married or in committed relationships. Layla and I are the lone holdouts in our little circle," she said. "You?"

"Mostly married. The ones who haven't divorced already are struggling their way through the early years of kids," he said with a shake of his head. "People just don't get it. Marriage isn't some romantic thing that happens to you—it's a decision you make based on your current and predicted compatibility."

"Be careful, your accountant is showing," she teased. "You're a very practical man."

Ryan shrugged his broad shoulders then had to steady his balance. "Why waste each other's time with grandiose ideas of mortgages and minivans and basketball practice if all those goals are built on the idea that one of you has to change to make it happen?"

She pressed her lips together and thought about it. "You're not wrong," she admitted. "But is there a place for romance or is it just a business partnership?"

"Romance is like the big family vacation every year. The thing you look forward to while you're doing the hard work. The hard work is what makes that vacation possible. The hard work that you've put into the relationship is what allows you to enjoy the reward of the romance. It works that way. But it never works the other way. How long can someone live off of flowers and candy and surprise Christmas morning proposals if your partner uses baby talk in bed or consistently runs up her credit cards over the limit?"

"Those are some very specific examples," she noted with a grin. He was unsettlingly cute when he got carried away lecturing. "But what you're saying makes sense. It's a shaky foundation to start an entire relationship based on what you think you can turn the other person into. It's much smarter to prioritize compatibility."

He shot her a searching look. "Are you just saying that so I don't feel like some Cupid-stomping robot?"

She laughed. "I'm not. But—"

"I knew that was coming," he groused.

"Compatibility is important," she conceded. "But there's also something to be said for finding someone who challenges you, who makes you a better version of yourself. If you went by compatibility alone, wouldn't you just end up with Lady Ryan?"

"What's wrong with Lady Ryan?"

"Do you want to wake up next to someone as grumpy as you are for the rest of your life?"

"God, no," he shuddered. "But why can't I just go out there and find Less Grumpy Lady Ryan?"

"I'll tell you why," she said, warming to the topic. "Because you need to be challenged with a puzzle, a mystery. We all do to a point, but you especially. There's a special kind of chemistry between people when there's interest. When you don't already understand every motivation. When you're surprised by a reaction and feel the need to dig into it and get to the bottom."

"Hmm."

"Hmm 'interesting point' or hmm 'shut up'?" she asked.

"Hmm, somewhere in the middle," he decided. Ryan carefully leaned forward and patted Shakira on the neck.

She knew better than to ask him if he was having fun. Instead of admitting it, he'd provide a list of criticisms for the experience before even attempting to decide if there were any positives. But somewhere, deep down, Grumpy Ryan was having a nice time.

"You know, the last twenty-four hours have felt like an out-of-body experience," he said.

"Every once in a while, we all need one of those," she sympathized.

"Will Magnolia come to live with you when you finish your barn?" Ryan asked, changing the subject.

"She will. As long as I have another horse. She came from a big riding stable operation in Pennsylvania. An unstable ex-husband broke into the barn and shot the trainer. The trainer survived, the bad guy went to jail, but Magnolia here was traumatized. The students and staff couldn't seat her anymore and put her up for sale. I fell in love with her the second I saw her online, and I think she liked me at first sight. She's doing really well here."

"How do you deal with it?" he asked with a frown aimed between his mount's ears.

"Deal with what?"

"The cruelty. The neglect. You're not a DEA agent busting up drug rings. You're an animal lover caring for animals that are in pain or traumatized. Some you can't save."

She pulled up on the reins and brought Magnolia to a halt before exhaling a stream of silvery breath to the sky.

The view from the ridge of the hill was a picture-perfect winter scene. Fields rolled out gently before them. A small pond where the Pierce men were rumored to skinny dip on occasion turned almost turquoise under the afternoon sky. Patches of woods and sentry lines of pine trees popped green against the white and blue.

"It's not easy," she admitted. "It can be crushing to try to save a starving calf, to see the fear in a horse's eyes when you try to approach it after years under bad hands. To know you can't save them all or give them all the life they actually deserve."

"I hate that for you," he said with a quiet vehemence that she found oddly comforting.

"Thank you," she said, not daring to look at him. "But the key is to find the good and to hold on to it with both hands. I'm there when a calf takes its first breath in the spring. I get to watch sheep unburdened of their winter wool dance around the pasture in the spring. I fix baby goats' legs so they can keep up with their siblings. I celebrate every birth, every recovery with the family."

"That means you also mourn every loss with them," he pointed out astutely.

"Ah, but there's no good without the bad, Ryan. No life without death. No celebration without mourning."

"But someday, you'll watch Magnolia take her last breath," he said. Not cruelly. Almost like he was warning her, like he was afraid she hadn't protected herself enough from the eventuality.

She reached out and laid her gloved hand on his. "I know. But when she does, I'll know that I gave her the best possible life I could between our meeting and our parting."

He wrapped his fingers around her fist. "You have to know how terrifying that concept is to me."

"Maybe that's why you think you can look for a life partner and not the love of your life."

"I like certainties. Guarantees."

"You don't get a lot of those in real life," she said with sympathy. "This land? It was tended by John Pierce. Phoebe's first husband and father to the Pierce brothers. This was a dilapidated, broken-down farm when he took it over. He grew crops, raised a family, taught the whole town a lot about respecting the land and each other. To honor him, his family carried on with his legacy. They took what he'd built and found ways to make it their own. Carter works the land. Beckett's the natural-born leader. And Jax has the artistic soul. Phoebe remarried, but she still lives on the land she and John worked together. Just because he's gone doesn't mean they all don't still love him."

Sammy thought about John on that long-ago Winter Solstice, beaming at her in that flannel coat. "For a long time, I thought it was your cousin who talked me into being a vet, but I think the credit is really due to John Pierce. We all leave fingerprints on each other. His mattered so much to so many people. I want mine to matter too."

"Some fingerprints shouldn't be left behind," Ryan said

softly. His grip on her hand tightened, and she wondered who had left their fingerprints on him.

"No, they shouldn't," she agreed. "Maybe that's why we gravitate toward people and animals with the right kind of prints."

They sat shoulder-to-shoulder on their mounts and took in the panorama.

"This doesn't suck," he said finally.

She laughed. It was as good as a gold star from the man. "We should head back. You've got an emergency to tackle, and I've got wreaths to make."

He looked earnestly into her eyes. "If I were smarter, I'd have taken you up on your offer."

"You *are* smarter. You'd have to be different, and I don't want that. I kind of like you the way you are."

"Surly and unfiltered?"

"Brooding and realistic," she decided. "I hope you find your partner, Ryan."

"I hope you find the love of your life, Sam."

She stifled a sigh. "Let's get back before you freeze your West Coast ass to the saddle. Think you're up for a trot?"

"Most definitely not."

Ten minutes later at a slow and awkward trot, the stone barn on the hill came into view. "That's John Pierce Brews," she said, slowing her mount.

"Part of the legacy?" Ryan asked.

"When Jax came home from LA, it was with two aims: to win back Joey and to start the brewery. He knocked them both out of the park... eventually."

"She looks like she'd put up a good fight."

"You're not wrong. Rumor has it the first time Jax saw her when he came home, he kissed the crap out of her and she slapped him so hard, people in town heard it," Sammy said.

Ryan snorted in amusement.

A shrill whistle cut through the air, and she spotted her former crush and current client Carter Pierce bundled up against the cold next to his pickup truck. Summer's blonde head popped up on the other side of the hood. They both waved and Sammy returned the greeting.

"That's Carter Pierce and his wife, Summer. And their twins," she added with affection when two toddlers practically tumbled out of the back seat.

"Older brother to goat guy and the mayor, right?"

She glanced at him, surprised. "You sure get around a lot for a guy who can't wait to get out of here."

~

BLUE MOON COMMUNITY Facebook Gossip Group

Frieda Blevins: Spotted! Veterinarian Sammy Ames canoodling with sexy stranger at Villa Harvest! Is love in the air for our single Sammy?

Bill FitzSimmons: Has anyone seen my Velcro pants? I can't remember the last place I ripped them off.

18

Sunday, December 22

*R*yan rolled out the kinks in his shoulders and slid the chair back from the kitchen table to survey the progress. It was late morning. His eyes were bleary. His ass was sore from sitting on a goddamn horse the day before.

In between fantasies of what would have happened had he taken Dr. Sammy Ames up on her offer, he'd eaten half of a vegetable korma casserole he'd found in Carson's freezer for breakfast and methodically picked his way through nearly every single shoebox, ruthlessly organizing, scanning, and tallying as he went.

His weapons of choice were a laptop with spreadsheets, highlighters—yellow for important, red for essential—a three-hole punch, and a now-empty pot of coffee.

Great-Uncle Carson had saved every grocery store receipt from 1983. He'd also used his tractor loan statements to write out shopping lists.

Organizing as he went, Ryan banded the receipts together and put them back in the shoebox now labeled Potentially Sentimental Paperwork. Property tax paperwork went into one binder. Farm equipment statements and manuals went into another. There were seven years of recent tax filings rolled up and secured with blue rubber bands. He'd found nothing of interest in the taxes. No mention of mortgage interest. No late fees or back taxes due.

He'd moved on to the paper statements from Blue Moon Bank. Opening each one, scanning it with an app on his phone and uploading them to the cloud before stashing the originals in yet another binder. He raised his eyebrows at the current account balances. He'd assumed that his elderly great-uncle living in a shabby farmhouse eating casseroles supplied by his neighbors was living Social Security check to Social Security check.

However, the six figures in CDs and $50,000 in savings told a different story.

Something wasn't adding up.

It didn't make sense that the man had saved coupons for dish detergent for the better part of two decades but hadn't managed to hang on to loan documents or any of the ensuing late notices. Of course, he'd recently claimed to be flying through an air tunnel on his way to a fetlock surgery so it was possible, Ryan mused.

If his uncle wasn't of sound mind, there might be a valid argument for buying more time for the balloon payment or having the lender held up to a review.

On an impulse, he picked up his phone and dialed his mother. While it rang, he popped the lid off another shoebox. Inside was a treasure trove of old photos.

"Ryan!" she said. "You made me think it was Tuesday."

Lisa Sosa kept a strict schedule of weekly phone calls. Ryan and his sister Tina were Tuesdays.

"Sorry," he said. "I'm face-deep in Uncle Carson's paperwork. How sharp would you say he is?"

"Well, we only talk once a week on Sundays," his mom began. "But honestly, Ryan, the man is more with it than I am."

That was saying a lot. Lisa Sosa's walk-in closet was organized by season, color, and last time worn.

He picked up a black-and-white photo with crimped edging. Uncle Carson and Aunt Midge stood on the steps of a courthouse. Carson had a flower tucked into the front pocket of his overalls. Midge's dress flared out over a petticoat. She was clutching a small bouquet of daisies. They were beaming at each other like they couldn't wait to start the adventure.

"I'm finding cash in his accounts, every piece of paper he's touched in the last forty years, and nothing but a vague letter from the bank about an overdue balance on a loan and a foreclosure."

"Do you want me to try to get him on the phone? Maybe he can clear some of this up," Lisa offered.

"Couldn't hurt. He hasn't responded to any of the voicemails I left him. Maybe you'll have better luck." He picked up the next photo. A group shot from one of the Shufflebottom family reunions. Ryan was perched on his father's shoulders. In the next, the cousins, all twenty of them, had formed a sloppy class picture-style pose on the grass.

There he was again, eight years old, hanging upside down by his knees from the jungle gym on the playground. His skinny arms dangled toward the ground. Where had his parents been? He was lucky he hadn't fallen and landed on his head. That was a spinal injury waiting to happen.

To make himself feel better, Ryan turned the photo around so Young Ryan was right side up. His hair stood on end, but the grin on his face looked much like the one on Carson's on his wedding day.

When had he stopped smiling upside down and started worrying about spinal injuries?

"So, how much trouble is Carson in? Do I need to take up a collection from the cousins?" she asked.

"I'm still not sure. The bank is giving me the runaround, but I'll figure something out."

"Oh dear. Well, I hope you're at least getting a chance to enjoy the holiday festivities. It's been a few decades since I've been there, but I recall the whole town going all out."

"That hasn't changed," he said.

"Speaking of the holidays, I was talking to your father at dinner yesterday," his mom was saying.

"Hang on. What? You and Dad had dinner?"

"Of course. We have dinner every week."

"*Why*?" He couldn't quite contain the shock. His parents divorce had been contentious, ugly... *devastating*. He had no idea they were capable of speaking cordially to each other let alone having dinner together.

Lisa laughed. "Oh, I don't know. Maybe because we share five children and four grandkids? We have to catch each other up in case one of us got news the other one didn't hear yet."

"How long has this been going on?"

"Honey, where have you been? We've been having dinner for years."

Years?

"I guess I just didn't realize how much things had changed." In Ryan's reality, when he'd gone off to college, his parents had still been arguing over visitation and holidays and sports uniforms. He had never returned home for anything other than short visits, dividing his time between his parents' homes.

Was it possible his perception had frozen in place while reality had actually moved on?

"Anyway, we were talking about your sister and wondering if she and Jeff are going to move now that baby number three is on the way."

"Marcie's pregnant?" He tried to remember the last time he and his oldest sister had talked. There'd been that missed call a few weeks back. But he'd been in the middle of a merger and too busy to talk. Hang on. The merger had been months ago, not weeks. But he'd never returned her call.

His mom laughed like he'd told a joke. "Of course she's pregnant. She's due in February. It's another girl, and they can't decide on a name yet. You know Jeff and his terrible taste in names."

Did he? He wasn't sure he could pick Jeff out of a line-up if his sister wasn't standing next to the man.

"Anyway, are you going to be able to make it home for Christmas since you're still on the East Coast or have you used up all your measly vacation time on Uncle Carson?"

He winced. Misleading his mom hadn't exactly been intentional, but when she'd called with the emergency he didn't feel mentally up to confessing that he'd been fired and was, for the first time in his life, adrift. "I don't think so, Mom. I have to get back soon."

His mom sighed. "Well, I'm not going to pretend I'm not disappointed. But I understand. I suppose Marsha wants to spend Christmas with you. How is she doing? You haven't mentioned her in quite a while. Where does her family live?"

Ryan pinched the bridge of his nose between his fingers. "Marsha and I broke up." *Last year.*

"Oh no! I'm so sorry. Did you tell me? Your dad and I were just saying you hadn't brought her up in a while. We both just assumed you'd been busy."

He had been. But too busy to mention that he'd broken up with the woman a year ago? Too busy to know his oldest sister was expecting another baby? Too busy to know that his parents had become friends?

"I rode a horse yesterday." He blurted the words out.

"On purpose?"

It seemed he and his mother had managed to shock the hell out of each other in the span of one phone call.

"It wasn't my idea. But yes. On purpose."

"I'm impressed. Who convinced you to overcome your Napoleon thing?"

"I accidentally spent yesterday with a veterinarian. She took me to a dairy farm, I got kicked by a llama, and then we rounded out the day on horseback after looking at a horse's uterus."

It was eerily silent on his mother's end of the call for thirty seconds, and then she started laughing. "I haven't heard a more un-Ryan-like sentence come out of your mouth in years. It sounds like your vacation is turning out to be pretty memorable."

He winced then opened his mouth to tell her. To say the words. But they got stuck somewhere in the throat region. "Yeah," he said weakly.

"Anyway, I need to go. Let me know if you need me to rally the troops for Carson, my good, low-maintenance son. I owe you for taking time away from work to handle this. I know how busy you are."

"It's, uh, not a problem," he said lamely. "I'll talk to you on Tuesday."

He stared at the phone for a long beat after disconnecting. Then looked at the remaining shoeboxes.

At home, when he'd needed to puzzle over something, he'd walk a few blocks. Perhaps a stroll around the farm would help him clear his head.

He dressed in as many layers as he could without immobilizing his limbs and headed outside.

He wandered down the lane to the road where he spent a few long minutes admiring the expansive sky. Infinite blue today with a few thready clouds.

There was something about the paperwork niggling at the back of his mind. He paced down the lane, avoiding puddles from the melting snow.

"Baaaa!"

"Mother of God!" he yelped.

Stan the sheep was waiting expectantly at the pasture gate, his white wool camouflaging him against the backdrop of snow.

"I already fed you breakfast," Ryan told the sheep.

Stan stared at him mournfully.

"What? I don't speak sheep."

"Baaaa!" Stan jogged toward the gate, then back again to Ryan.

"Do you want out?" he asked.

The sheep trotted back to the gate.

"I don't know, man. What if you run away? It's fucking cold, and I don't feel like chasing your ass around again."

"Baaaa!"

Stan sounded sad and desperate. Lonely even. Ryan could empathize. "Fine. But if you run away, it's on you. Got it?" Stan's tail wagged. Knowing he was probably making a big, rookie farmer mistake, Ryan unlatched the gate and opened it. Stan barreled through, but instead of continuing his sprint to freedom, the sheep rubbed his head on Ryan's bruised thigh.

"Are you wiping your nose on me or is this some kind of barnyard hug?" he asked.

"Baaa!" Stan's tail wiggled in delight, and he pranced toward the back door of the farmhouse.

"Hey. Wait up," he called.

He didn't know what the etiquette was for hosting farm animals inside the house. But he also didn't feel like freezing his ass off outside anymore. Deciding that the sheep and the house were someone else's long-term problems, Ryan opened the door.

Stan happily wandered into the kitchen.

Maybe the sheep just didn't want to be alone? Ryan couldn't blame him.

Alone is exactly what he would be as soon as he boarded that plane for home. Back to his dove-gray condo with a few tasteful paintings, a small collection of books that he never seemed to get around to reading, and a bed that he slept in alone.

Without a job to dedicate his life to, just what in the hell did he have?

He couldn't blame the partners. The only thing worse than the idea that he was complicit in the fraud was the truth: that he'd been too stupid to see it. He *should* have seen it. The evasiveness, the runaround. He hadn't dug deep enough. He'd been too busy building portfolios to build relationships with clients.

"Want some casserole?" he asked the sheep.

"Baaaa!" The sheep nudged the empty plate on the living room floor and looked at him expectantly.

Ryan glanced up from the binder in his lap and shook his head. "I don't know, man. I don't think you need to have any more vegetable korma."

Pouting, Stan wandered over to the blanket Ryan had put in front of the electric fireplace and flopped down.

Ryan glanced back down at the binder. So far, the only document inside was the notice from the bank on the incense-scented letterhead. Several re-reads of the letter hadn't produced any new information. He held it up to the light for one last scan. He studied it carefully, reading each word for the bingo. At the top, partially obscured by the bank's peace sign logo, he spotted something interesting.

"Aha!"

Finally, a break. It was a barely legible loan number. *This* he could work with. He cracked his knuckles, prayed his access hadn't been revoked, and logged into his firm's network.

∼

BLUE MOON COMMUNITY Facebook Gossip Group

Blue Moon Sheriff's Department: Nikolai Vulkov and wife Emma caught making out behind Fitness Freak Gym by Deputy Layla Gunnarson. Their $20 fine will go into the Indecent Exposure Fund, which purchases and distributes new winter clothing for those in need.

19

"Hang on. He turned you down for no-strings sex because he didn't have enough time to analyze the decision?" Layla's eyes narrowed over her slice of spinach tofu pizza.

Peace of Pizza was in its mid-lunch rush. But Sammy, Layla, and Eden had managed to snag a table near the open kitchen where Bobby, the popular dreadlocked pizza maven, was belting out Billie Holiday and expertly rotating pies in and out of the oven.

"Basically," Sammy answered, spearing a piece of tomato out of her salad. "And that he was concerned he had too much on his mind to perform well."

"No man is *that* practical," Eden insisted, sawing through her stromboli with gusto.

"You haven't met Ryan," Sammy countered. He was probably already on a plane, heading out of her life forever.

Their conversation cut off abruptly as Nikolai Vulkov, tall, gorgeous, reformed ladies man stepped inside from the cold. His gray wool coat flapped behind him in the wind.

"Ladies," he said with a wink.

"Hey, Niko," Sammy said. "How was the shoot?" Niko was a fashion photographer with a glossy portfolio of luxury brand clients.

"It went well enough that we got all the shots in one day instead of two. Which means Baxter and I get to surprise my beautiful, hormonal wife with the buffalo chicken special she's been craving since 3 a.m."

Sammy glanced through the glass where Baxter the yellow lab wore a plaid Christmas sweater and chewed on his reindeer antler headband.

"She's a lucky woman," Eden told him.

"Not as lucky as I am," he insisted.

"Your order's ready to go, Niko," Bobby called from behind the counter.

Every woman in the place watched as Niko paid, collected the dog, and left. A collective sigh of female appreciation rose up as he disappeared from sight.

"I don't trust this guy," Layla announced.

"Who? Niko?" Sammy asked.

"No. Ryan. Anyone would be honored to be invited into your pants," her friend insisted.

Sammy's gaze roamed the restaurant. Bobby had swapped out the regular orange lava lamps on the tables for the red and green ones. Sparkly cutouts of dreidels and Yule logs hung from the ceiling, drifting on alternating breezes from the pizza oven and front door.

"I think he meant what they all mean," she said with a sigh.

She'd stayed up too late the night before, watching wreath-decorating videos on YouTube and massacring bows and pinecones. Then she'd spent another few sleepless hours replaying Ryan's side-of-the-road kiss. His insightful conversation on horseback. His curt "Thanks for everything, Sparkle" when she'd dropped him off at Carson's. Sometime around two a.m., she'd tiptoed into the gossip group on Facebook and cursed herself for looking so eager and hopeful in every one of the nine pictures her neighbors had managed to sneak of her and Ryan together.

Please like me, her eyes seemed to say in each picture.

"What do you think they all mean?" Eden asked.

"That I'm good enough to drive them around, or cook them breakfast, or babysit their little sister. But not good enough to take to prom or date. Or in this case, have a steamy one-night stand." She was feeling sorry for herself. It made her want to slap herself in the face. There was no room in her schedule for a pity party and no tolerance for being annoying.

Eden and Layla exchanged a look.

"What?" Sammy asked.

"Sammy, I say this with love." Eden patted her hand on the table. "That is the most asinine thing I've ever heard you say. And that's including the time we were loaded on cheap rum, and you thought you saw Oprah in the ladies' restroom at the skating rink."

Technically, it had been a poster of Oprah.

"You're making it sound like you get rejected all the time," Layla said, steering them back on topic.

"I *do*," she insisted.

"Do not," Eden argued.

"Men look at me, and they see a little sister or a tomboy or a woman who puts her arms up cow asses. I wouldn't expect you two to get it."

"Us two?" Layla's eyebrows raised as she took a bite of cheesy pizza.

"They look at you two and see beautiful, interesting sex goddesses. Men trip over their pants to have sex with you."

"Technically that was only because Davis had a concussion and his balance was off," Eden pointed out.

"And I haven't gotten laid in—" The door of the restaurant opened and Huckleberry Cullen, the blond, built high school guidance counselor stepped inside. "A while," Layla finished, seemingly very interested in her plate.

Eden dropped her utensils. "Permission to enact my Voice of Reason rights."

"Permission granted," Layla said, pretending not to notice Huckleberry's head nod in her direction. Sammy's curiosity would have piqued but she was too busy feeling like crap.

Eden interlaced her fingers on the table. "You're feeling sorry for yourself and looking for stories that reinforce the 'men aren't tripping over their pants to bang me' narrative. But in reality, we all know what's going on."

"Oh, really? *All* of us?" Sammy scoffed. "Please, enlighten me."

"She's going to make me say it," Eden complained to Layla.

"She needs to hear it," the blonde said, crossing her arms over her ample chest.

This sounded like a conversation the two of them had been having for a long time. An inside joke that Sammy was left out of... or worse, was the punchline of.

"Dr. Samantha Ames," Eden began, "what exactly do you think makes you less attractive?"

"Because I smell like manure for fifty percent of my working hours and I don't look like either of you."

Eden's smile was dangerous.

"That's such a crock of shit," Layla complained.

"I don't expect anyone who looks like you two to understand." Sammy sniffed.

"I unclog guest toilets for a living," Eden said.

Her friend managed the Lunar Inn on the outskirts of town and spent her days making guests feel pampered and appreciated. Sure there were probably a few plumbing emergencies, but there was also a glamour to hospitality. "Yeah, but you look amazing while you're doing it."

"Aww, thanks." Eden gave her short dark hair a fluff. Her earrings, sexy filigree dangles, sparkled at her ears.

"Listen, Whiny Pants," Layla said, pointing her pizza crust menacingly at Sammy. "Last week, remember when I had that weird rash all over my face from Rupert Shermanski's god-awful organic moisturizer?"

Layla's perfect Swedish features had been covered with scaly hives. "I do recall something along those lines," Sammy said.

"While rashy and on the job, Colby and I went through a drive-thru for tacos. I farted twice in the car. Once so bad we had to roll the windows down, and he *still* asked me out." Colby was Blue Moon's other deputy. He was also too young to be taken seriously.

"You're still gorgeous when you're rashy and gassy," Sammy pointed out. "Plus you have great boobs."

"You do," Eden agreed.

Layla grabbed her girls and hoisted them up. "Thanks."

There was a commotion at the back of the restaurant, and Sammy saw Huck bending down to pick up a potato chip display he'd knocked over.

"My point is, if you're gorgeous, you can fart on anyone you want and they'll still ask you out," Sammy explained.

"I farted *near* him. Not *on* him," Layla clarified. "But if you don't open your ears and do some listening, I will fart on you."

"You need to lay off the dairy," Sammy warned.

"We're getting off track," Eden said. "What my flatulent friend here is trying to say is that just like us, you're beautiful, smart, sexy, funny, witty, and all of those other bangable adjectives. *But...*"

The but caught Sammy's attention.

"But what?"

"Your effort goes in the wrong place," Layla said.

"Huh?"

"Look at Layla's boobs," Eden said. All three of them paused to admire Layla's rack. "Now, she's wearing a to-die-for, high-end, sexy push-up bra under that deputy's uniform. And why is that, Deputy? Why are you wearing an underwire for your shift?"

Layla shrugged as if the answer were obvious. "Because when my boobs look good, I feel good."

"And what happens when you feel good?" Eden asked.

"My Awesome Sexy Factor goes through the roof. When I feel sexy, I exude sexy. When I feel good, people want to be around me. And not just the ones with penises. Same goes for our on-trend, vampy friend here," she said, pointing at Eden.

"A good-quality mascara and leggings that make my ass look like a gift from the heavens are not required for toilet scrubbing or scone baking or vineyard walking," Eden informed her. "But when I put a little effort into myself, when I pull on the perfect cleavage sweater or try a new eyeliner, or get eight hours of sleep, I feel like the best version of myself."

They both looked at her expectantly.

"All I'm hearing is you saying if I get better bras and slap on some makeup, maybe I can find a guy," Sammy said sullenly.

"Honey, that is not what these beautiful young women are saying," Bobby said, stopping next to the table, one hand on a curvy hip. "You gotta take care of you first. If you're running all over town taking care of everybody else, who's taking care of you?"

"Is this a conversation the whole town has about me?" Sammy wondered.

"Just the Dr. Sammy Roundtable," Eden smarted off.

"We're up to forty-two members," Layla said.

"Meetings are every other Tuesday," Bobby teased.

"You run yourself all over town working and elbowing your way to the front of the line to volunteer for every damn thing. What's left for you? When's the last time you did something for you like blow-dried your hair?" Layla asked.

"Or got a facial?" Bobby suggested.

"Or sat in front of your fireplace with a big ol' glass of wine and a sexy book?" Eden added.

"Or ate an entire tray of brownies?"

"Exhausted people aren't sexy. They're not the life of the party," Liz, the town florist, chimed in from the table next to them. "They're too tired to have fun."

Sammy felt a little stunned.

"It's a good news-bad news kind of thing," Eden told her.

"Good News: You're hot AF, dummy," Layla said fondly.

"Bad News: You're the one who needs to make the effort," Eden said. "Until you start taking care of yourself and remembering what a brilliant, beautiful badass you are—"

"Awesome alliteration," Bobby cut in.

"Thank you, Bobby," Eden said with a quick grin. "Until you start taking care of yourself, no one else is going to excavate under the layers of exhaustion and pathological helpfulness and self-neglect to find your sexy center."

The women at the tables around them broke out into spontaneous applause. Eden and Layla leaned back in their chairs, wisdom dispensed.

"Raise your vibe, honey, and watch the world fall at your feet," Bobby told her.

Sure. She'd just schedule in longer showers and some online shopping sprees in between calving seasons and vaccinations and renovations to the farm. Maybe take up paragliding or pottery. Didn't they understand? There was no time left over in the day for herself.

But she was too damn tired to say just that.

The shop door opened on a burst of cold. With it came one stubbled, scowling Ryan Sosa. He was wearing glasses today. They made him look like a rugged, crabby poet.

Sammy felt her vagina flutter in appreciation. *He was still here! Still gorgeous! Still grumpy! And he was looking right at her.*

"Yeah, that's the look of a man who finds you repulsive," Eden whispered, picking up a menu and fanning herself with it.

"Shut. Up," Sammy hissed. God. She was a mess. She wished she would have actually washed her hair instead of just cramming a hat on her head that morning.

"Here he comes," Layla sang under her breath.

"I can see that," Sammy growled.

"Sparkle," Ryan said, a hint of a smile playing on his lips.

Eden kicked her under the table. "Ouch! Uh, hi. Ryan," she said. "These are my sometimes friends, Eden and Layla."

"Ah. Those friends. Did you ever get confirmation on Dirk?" he asked Eden.

Eden choked on her soda. Layla snorted. "Maybe this guy's not such a dumbass after all?"

"Maybe I'm not," he agreed.

"You're still here?" Sammy asked a little too loudly. "I thought you'd be long gone by now."

"I thought so too," he said, oblivious to the fact that Bobby was making a heart symbol with her fingers behind the counter. "I may have underestimated the complexity of my uncle's filing system."

"Well, I need to get back to the inn," Eden said, pointedly looking at her bare wrist.

"And I just got a call from dispatch," Layla lied.

"No, no, no. Nope. Not this time," Sammy said, standing abruptly. "This time, *I'm* leaving." She dragged on her coat, which today smelled like a chicken farm. "Thanks for the lunch and the lecture."

Turning to Ryan, she looked him up and down one more time. God, he was so stupidly gorgeous. "Good luck with whatever it is you're doing," she said to him. "And goodbye again."

She marched out the door, head held high.

Blue Moon Emergency Text Alert: All citizens with any level of accounting experience are encouraged to attend tonight's emergency town meeting at Take Two Movie Theater. Please do not call Beckett Pierce's house or office to ask for details prior to the meeting.

20
___

So maybe she'd overreacted the smallest, teensiest bit, Sammy thought in the concession stand line. Take Two was the town's Art Deco movie theater that showed second-run movies. It was also commandeered as a venue for town meetings like the one tonight, which were arguably just as entertaining as the films.

The smell of fresh popcorn and gallons of organic butter tantalized her nose. Her stomach let out a plaintive groan. She'd left half her salad on the table at Peace of Pizza when she'd stormed out into the cold.

But that was the effect of a spiritual kick to the head. She wasn't thinking about normal, everyday things like lunch. She was suddenly staring down at the big picture of her life, seeing it from a different angle.

The emergency alert text message—which, since its inception, had only been used for non-emergency situations—about the "essential" and "urgent" town meeting had been received on her way home after spending over an hour getting a donkey to hold still so she could stitch up a wound on his leg.

With Layla, Eden, and Bobby's words echoing in her head, Sammy had taken an extra long shower and dusted off her rarely used hair dryer. She'd forgotten how decent she looked with a little product and five minutes of diffused drying. Her sleeker, shinier hair—as well as the mascara and lip gloss she'd found at the back of her vanity—had actually managed to put a little bounce in her step.

She got her popcorn and a water refill in the bottle she brought from home and stepped into the theater.

As expected, it was a madhouse. Half the town had come out of hibernation for the popcorn, Milk Duds, and mysterious crisis.

"Sammy!"

She turned and found the blonde, chic Summer Pierce waving from the middle of a row. Carter was next to her, looking mountain man chic in a flannel coat, ancient jeans, and a thermal shirt. His dark, full beard made him look more bad boy than good guy. Even after all these years, Sammy still felt the faint echo of her teenage crush on the man whenever he looked directly at her.

She slipped into their row. "Hey! Where are the kids?" she asked.

"Phoebe and Franklin have them for a sleepover in the bunk room," Summer said.

The house Phoebe and Franklin built on Pierce Acres had a bunk room built to house a dozen grandkids and the way those Pierce brothers were going, Grandma and Grandpa were going to need to build an addition.

"It's costing us a big, fat gift card to the Hershey Spa in Pennsylvania," Carter said, with a wink at his wife.

"Totally worth it," Summer said, slipping her arms around his waist. Sammy couldn't help but smile. The two of them radiated love and healing. Summer was a cancer survivor, and

Carter had come home from Afghanistan wounded. Together, they'd built something beautiful together.

Summer turned to greet her sister-in-law Gia Pierce, who had just arrived with Evan, Aurora, baby Lydia, and pregnant Eva in tow.

"Your girl, Magnolia, is doing well," Carter told Sammy. "She's starting to get her confidence back around the other horses."

Sammy's heart glowed a little bit thinking about the sweet mare soaking up Carter's attention. The man was one of the most restful people she knew. He had a soulful connection to the earth he cultivated. Animals—and people—gravitated to his calm. He reminded her so much of his father. "I can't thank you enough for working with her," she said.

"It's a pleasure. Really," he insisted.

"Your dad would be proud of you," she blurted out the words.

He cleared his throat gruffly. "Thanks, Sammy. I think he'd be pretty tickled to see you on the farm, too. He always said you had a better way with horses and people than your mom."

Sammy managed a laugh around the lump in her throat. Even all these years later, it was still hard to accept the fact that a good, kind man was gone forever. "I won't tell her if you don't," she promised.

Carter winked. "Deal."

Ellery clomped onto the stage in her Frankenstein boots. "Five minutes to show time," she announced into the microphone on the lectern.

Sammy took a seat and grabbed a handful of popcorn as she scoped out the attendees. She was happy she'd come. Sure, she could have used the time to finish another few wreaths, but seeing so many of her neighbors showing up for each other warmed her.

Taneisha Duval, the enviable beauty and women's record holder for the Blue Moon 5-Miler, was deep in conversation with Destiny Wheedlemeyer, a six-figure Etsy entrepreneur with a knitting store. A few rows from them, Kimoni Henderson and Kathy Wu had their heads together over what looked like a jar of moonshine.

Young, old. Black, white. Vegan, Paleo. Jewish, agnostic. Blue Moon managed to come together time and again in a brash, weird, wonderful celebration of similarities and differences.

She loved this damn town and everyone in it. Sometimes it snuck up on her and stole her breath.

"Is this seat taken?"

Sammy jumped, bobbling her popcorn. Ryan caught it and helped himself to a handful before returning the bag to her.

He was in his farm store jeans and a thermal shirt. Stubble darkened his jawline and his hair was carelessly tousled. The tiny echo of a girlhood crush on Carter Pierce was eclipsed by a rush of white, hot adult lust.

"What are you doing here?" she asked.

He took the empty seat next to her and stretched his long legs out in front of him. "I was making a run for office supplies and saw the crowd and the marquis. I've never been to a town meeting before and figured it might be entertaining."

"That sounds very unlike you," she pointed out, enjoying the nearness of him. He smelled like expensive shampoo, crisp winter air, and Sharpie marker.

He snagged the bag from her and helped himself to more popcorn. "You could say that about everything in the last forty-eight hours."

"I take it you don't have good news on Carson's situation since you're still here and not watching *Pitch Perfect 2* somewhere over the Dakotas right now?"

"Things are unfolding," he said cryptically, his knee nudging hers in the confined space. "What about you? You left the pizza place like your ass was on fire."

"My ass was fine. I just had things to do," she said.

"What did you do to your hair?" he asked, eyeing it.

On reflex, she patted the fluffy curls. "Uh. Washed it," she said.

"Looks nice," he said. He leaned in a little closer. "Smells nice too."

Her toes curled under in her boots, and her internal temperature rose five degrees at the compliment.

"Mind if I sit?" Mason Smith, Ellery's husband and town accountant, appeared next to Ryan.

"Help yourself," Ryan said. "Want some popcorn?"

"Trade you popcorn for whiskey," Mason offered, holding up a flask wrapped in black leather emblazoned with a skull.

"Deal," Ryan agreed.

Mason dug out a short stack of Dixie cups from his coat pocket and had just started to pour when the Darth Vader theme blasted from the theater's speakers.

Sammy smothered a laugh. Bruce Oakleigh felt that Mayor Beckett Pierce's entrance to town meetings needed to be more dignified. The soundtrack was constantly changing and always entertaining.

She stole a glance at Ryan. He looked more intrigued than perturbed and she wondered if he was getting over his disdain for small-town life.

"Cheers," Mason said, distributing cups to Sammy and Ryan.

"Cheers," they echoed.

As Sammy sipped a truly delicious peanut butter whiskey, Mayor Beckett Pierce, in a suit and a God-awful powdered wig, took the stage. He was followed by Rainbow Berkowicz, Bruce Oakleigh, Elvira Eustace, and Taneisha's mom, Julissa. All wearing similar wigs.

Ryan leaned into her space, and Sammy swooned a little on the inside. "What's with the wigs?" he asked, his breath tickling her ear.

"Trust me, you don't have the time for the full story."

He didn't pull all the way back, she noticed. In fact, he rested his arm on the back of her seat.

"I'm going to keep this short," Beckett said into the microphone. "I know everyone is busy with the holidays and the Solstice preparations. But it's been brought to my attention that a state auditor will be arriving on Christmas Eve to investigate Blue Moon."

A murmur went up in the crowd.

"What the hell does that mean?" Sammy asked.

"Oh, just wait," Ryan said in her ear. His nose brushed her ear lobe, and she almost dropped the popcorn on the floor.

She knocked back the remaining contents of her Dixie cup and sternly reminded herself that she was *not* going to climb into Grumpy Ryan's lap during a town meeting.

"Due to unforeseen circumstances," Beckett said, "our reporting to the state was... disrupted."

She wasn't sure if she imagined it or if Beckett really was glaring at Bruce.

Mason poured another round. "We're all going to need this," he whispered.

Flask Mason was pretty fun, she thought.

"The state is missing the records of how Blue Moon used its funding from June through December this year, and a thorough investigation will commence immediately. I take full responsibility for the situation, but I need your help in mitigating the damage."

"Why is Bruce sweating like a hairy guy in a sauna?" Sammy asked.

"Because it's his fault," Ryan told her.

"No!" Bruce exploded out of his seat, his wig slipping over an eye and an ear. "I can't let you take responsibility for my unforgivable error, Mr. Mayor."

"How do you know what's happening?" she asked Ryan with suspicion.

He shrugged and helped himself to more popcorn in her lap. "It's a small town. Everyone knows everything."

Bruce elbowed Beckett out of the way and took control of the microphone.

Amethyst buried her face in her hands in the front row, and Sammy wasn't sure if it was from embarrassment or something worse.

"People of Blue Moon, I have a confession to make. I, Town Supervisor Bruce Oakleigh, head of the Beautification Committee, strayed from my committed relationship."

The indrawn gasps of so many Blue Mooners created a breeze in the theater.

"Yes. It's true. I was swayed by a newer, shinier temptation."

"There is no way he's talking about a woman," Sammy said.

"Five bucks says he took his car to a different car wash and can't live with the guilt," Carter guessed.

"You're both wrong," Ryan informed them.

Bruce moved on, wig still crooked, expression still penitent. "You see, after years of being loyal cable customers, I made the decision to try... a streaming service." He paused as if waiting for more gasps from the crowd.

"It takes him a while to get to his point. You might want to recap it for us," Sammy suggested to Ryan.

"He tasked Amethyst with keeping the records and filing the paperwork for the state," he began.

"Then he bought her a Hulu subscription for her birthday," Gia added from the row in front of them. "Nice to see you again, Ryan."

"Hey, Gia," he said.

"How do you guys know each other?" Sammy asked, wondering if she'd stumbled into some kind of alternate reality.

"We're old friends," Gia whispered.

"So Amethyst went on some massive TV show binge-watch," Ryan said, picking up the thread again.

"*Buffy the Vampire Slayer*," Mason supplied. "Cheers."

"Cheers. Team Spike," Sammy whispered, downing the contents of her Dixie cup.

"Hard agree," Gia said.

"Mama, who's Spike?" Aurora asked in a loud whisper.

"I'll tell you when you're a teenager," Gia promised.

"Aww, man." The little girl's lower lip poked out in a pout.

Beckett returned to the podium and said something in Bruce's ear.

"I'm being told by our valiant mayor that I should get to my point," Bruce announced. "The state didn't receive our reporting because we never completed it. There is no reporting to send. So the state is sending an auditor. It's very likely that our funding will be revoked, our homes will be foreclosed upon, our property taxes will skyrocket, our children will grow up tooth-less with no education, and we'll be forced to sell our wigs on eBay."

On a dramatic wail, Bruce buried his face in his hands.

"He seems really attached to those wigs," Ryan observed.

The theater was deathly silent for five whole seconds before the rumblings started.

"I've got a spare kidney we could sell," someone offered.

"What about a bake sale?" Charisma Carpenter shouted.

"What if we kidnap the auditor—"

"No! There will be no kidnapping or abducting or organ harvesting," Beckett said into the microphone.

He handed Bruce over to a very annoyed-looking Rainbow

Berkowicz, who patted the sobbing man on the head and looked at her watch.

Fitz, in a cropped wooly sweater that showed an unfortunate amount of belly hair, jumped up from his seat. "Does this mean the apocalypse is back on?"

"That guy has a bunker," Ryan whispered to Sammy.

"He also terrorizes bachelorette parties as an exotic dancer. How do you know all this?" she asked.

He shrugged and helped himself to more of her popcorn. "I get around."

"No," Beckett announced into the microphone. "The apocalypse is not back on."

"What apocalypse?" Ryan asked.

"We had a teeny tiny issue with Uranus in October," she told him.

He frowned. "Whose anus?"

"I wore Gene Simmons Kiss makeup to my wedding," Mason interjected.

"Joey got bangs. Eva got pregnant. Half the town ended up incarcerated in the high school gym," Sammy said. "It was a whole thing."

Ryan leaned in closer this time. His knee pressing firmly against hers, lips just a millimeter from the tender skin of her ear lobe. She went from mildly concerned about current events to frantically concerned with the thrumming pulse that had started between her thighs. "You're fucking with me aren't you?" he whispered against her ear.

"You wish," she shot back.

21

*R*yan couldn't decide if she was joking or not. Then decided it didn't matter because in Blue Moon, anything was possible. But he liked the way the topic made her eyes light up, her lips curve.

Great. Now he was thinking about her mouth again. Which made him think about their kiss yesterday. Which made him think of what else they could have been doing in addition to more kissing. Which made him hard. Again.

"What does all this mean?" called a tall man with an Afro in the back.

"Yeah. Are our kids really gonna be toothless?" asked a woman in a tie-dye onesie from the second row.

"Explain like we're five," the teenager next to Gia suggested.

"Good call, Evan," Beckett said, pointing at the kid. He stalked over to the whiteboard and picked up a marker. "This is Blue Moon," he said, drawing a circle.

A man with a fanny pack and camera with a telephoto lens jumped up onto the stage and started blasting Beckett with blinding flashes.

"That don't look like the town limits," someone yelled from the balcony.

"Pretend," Beckett said dryly. He ignored the paparazzo and drew a second, bigger circle. "This is the state."

"How's come Blue Moon isn't *in* the state?" a guy in a straw hat and a Grateful Dead sweatshirt asked.

"Just go with it," Beckett suggested with what Ryan felt was unwarranted patience. "Every year, the state gives our town money to help fund things like our schools, fire department, police, public buildings."

The photographer shoved his camera into Beckett's face and snapped half a dozen shots in rapid succession.

"Like an allowance," the big, bearded guy on Sammy's right supplied.

Carter Pierce. Ryan recalled seeing him from a distance... on the back of a horse yesterday.

"Exactly like an allowance," Beckett said, blinking rapidly. He reached out blindly for the whiteboard, accidentally swiping his dry-erase marker over the camera lens and photographer's face.

"Hey! Freedom of the press!" the guy yelled.

"That's Anthony Berkowicz," Sammy said, leaning in to his side. Her hair smelled like cinnamon. "He's Rainbow and Gordon's son and editor of *The Monthly Moon*."

"The what?" Ryan knew exactly what *The Monthly Moon* was, but he liked how it felt to have her leaning against him.

"Town newspaper," she whispered back.

"I vote that we use our allowance to install heated sidewalks," a skinny teenager with pink hair and wearing a Nirvana shirt called out.

"I second the motion!"

"That's not how this works," Beckett said in exasperation. "The state tells us how we're allowed to spend our allowance."

"That doesn't seem fair," shouted a woman from the far side of the theater. "I'm tired of shoveling. I vote for heated sidewalks."

With an exaggerated sigh, Gia stood up and handed Sammy her wiggly toddler. "Hold this, please," she said, then climbed onto her seat. She stuck her fingers in her mouth and whistled shrilly.

The crowd quieted.

"Listen up, people!" Gia addressed the crowd. "Heated sidewalks mean no school district. No fire trucks. No public library or town parks. So if you want to put all the teachers and support staff out of jobs, drive around potholes that can swallow your Volkswagen, and put out your own fires, by all means, demand heated sidewalks."

"This is like a soap opera," Ryan said, leaning in to catch another whiff of Sammy's hair.

"Yeah, but like a telenovela," she said, jiggling the kid on her knee. The baby or toddler—Ryan wasn't sure what the age cutoff was—giggled.

"Do you still want heated sidewalks?" Gia yelled.

"I guess we can go back to shoveling," someone said.

"Good. Then let's take a deep, cleansing breath together," Gia insisted.

"Yoga teacher," Sammy whispered.

Around them, the audience inhaled noisily and then exhaled, creating an indoor gale-force wind. Blue Moon had an impressive collective lung capacity.

"Good," Gia said, giving them a curt nod. "Now let's sit down, shut our faces, and listen to my very handsome husband as he tells us what this means and how he's going to get us out of it."

There was scattered applause as Gia regained her seat. Someone in the sound booth played a few bars of "Respect" by Aretha Franklin.

"Hang in there with me for just another minute, folks," Beckett begged. "The state is sending an auditor to Blue Moon." He drew a stick figure.

"How come the auditor has three legs?"

"Maybe that's not a leg."

Beckett erased the third leg and soldiered on. "If we can't prove that we spent our allowance in the places the state said we could, we will lose all of that funding for next year and we may be responsible for paying this year's funding back to the state."

"That sounds bad," someone called.

"Yes. It is very, very, very bad," Beckett verified. He drew a big frowny face on the whiteboard.

"Mama, that's just like the sticker I get at school for talking too much," Aurora whisper-yelled to Gia.

The mayor returned to the lectern. "I promise you we are going to do everything we can to make sure that doesn't happen. We're asking for any volunteers with accounting or small business experience to help us go through six months of town transactions to reconstruct the reporting we're missing. Be advised, this is a massive undertaking," Beckett cautioned.

"When is the auditor coming?" asked a woman in a long caftan.

Beckett looked like he was going to be sick. "The auditor will be here at eight a.m. Christmas Eve."

The murmurs in the crowd cranked up to full volume.

"That's the day after tomorrow," Sammy groaned. "Exactly how bad is very, very, very bad?"

"Even worse than you think," Ryan said. "The town risks losing all future state funding. Property taxes will sky-rocket to cover the difference. People won't be able to afford to own real estate. Which means foreclosures, a mass exodus. And that's not even touching on potential jail time if Blue Moon can't prove the town didn't commit fraud or embezzle the money."

"We're fucked," Carter Pierce muttered under his breath.

Aurora's red head swiveled around and eyed her uncle. "I heard that, Uncle Carter," she whispered. He reached forward and tugged a fire-red curl.

"If you have the experience we're looking for and you have time you're willing to donate, we will be eternally grateful," Beckett said. "Please see Rainbow Berkowicz after the meeting, which ends now."

Bruce popped back up at the microphone, blowing his nose noisily into a handkerchief. "I would like to issue a public apology to the fair and just people of Blue Moon. Amethyst and I plan to throw ourselves on the mercy of the court—"

"This isn't a court, Bruce," Beckett said, wrestling the microphone back. "You can apologize later when we don't have a Solstice to celebrate and six months of financial records to recreate. Thanks, everyone, for your time. If you can volunteer, please see Rainbow."

Ryan had every intention of seeing Rainbow, he thought grimly.

Beckett made a gesture toward the back of the theater. The spotlight dimmed and the microphone's audio cut as Bruce launched into another convoluted bid for forgiveness.

Ryan saw Sammy eyeing the line that was already forming. "I should volunteer," she said half to herself.

"Do you have accounting experience?" he asked.

"Not exactly. Phoebe Pierce handles my books."

"Then I suggest you leave it to the experts."

"Who? Mason?" She nodded at the aisle where Mason was surrounded by a crowd five people deep in all directions. Everyone was volleying rapid-fire questions at him.

"If you get involved in that mess, you'll regret it," he advised.

"That's not how things are done around here," she said, blue eyes narrowing. "We don't just turn our backs. We help each other out."

"Relax, Sparkle. I have a feeling the perfect solution will present itself," he assured her.

She raised a skeptical eyebrow. "Since when are you Mr. Positivity?"

"Me? I'm just a guy trying to save a farm and get on a plane."

"You know something, don't you?"

He most certainly did. But he couldn't afford to tip his hand just yet.

"Excuse us." Carter the Beard was standing. "We're heading out."

The gorgeous blonde next to him grinned. "This was the fastest meeting in history. We've still got an hour on the clock with the babysitting grandparents."

"Ah," Sammy said. "Have fun, you two."

Sammy got to her feet, and Ryan did the same so the couple could step into the aisle and haul ass toward the door.

"Does everyone in this town have libidos in overdrive?" Ryan wondered.

"Sure looks that way," Sammy said wistfully.

She glanced back at the table where a long line had formed. The Berkowicz guy was dancing around the people with his camera, asking them to "look concerned." Ryan was willing to bet his entire portfolio of CDs that ninety percent of the Mooners in line did not have the experience necessary.

"I guess I should get home and get some work done," she said.

"I guess this is goodbye. Again," he said, sticking his hands in his pockets so he wouldn't try to touch her. Every time they said goodbye, he felt less enthused about the idea that he wouldn't see her again. Which, frankly, was annoying. He'd known her two days. Forty-eight hours. That wasn't enough time to miss someone.

"I feel like I keep saying goodbye, and you keep turning up anyway," she said, biting her lower lip.

He forced himself to look away from that tempting mouth. "Maybe we should stop saying goodbye then," he suggested.

She held out her hand to him. "In that case, I'll see you around, Ryan."

He took her hand and held it firmly in his own. "I can't wait," he said.

With a smile hovering on those kissable lips, she slid her hand free and walked down the aisle. He watched her all the way, hoping for one final look. He should have kissed her again. Might have seriously considered it if they hadn't been surrounded by an entire municipality.

Finally, once she'd reached the concession stand, Sammy paused and glanced over her shoulder. She found him in the crowd and gave a little wave. He blew out a breath and tried not to think about how much he was going to miss those blue eyes despite the fact that it made no sense.

When she was out of sight, he wandered over to the volunteer table and got in line. For once, he had nothing but time on his hands.

Which was convenient since he ended up waiting nearly twenty minutes. The woman in front of him, Kathy Wu, went into great detail about her qualifications due to an at-home vibrator business.

By the time he got to the front of the line, a sweaty Bruce Oakleigh was hovering behind Rainbow.

"Evan, put Kathy on the Only If Absolutely Necessary list," Rainbow said to the kid next to her. Gia and Beckett's oldest, Ryan guessed. He had an owlish, serious look.

"You got it. That brings us to forty-seven Only If Absolutely Necessaries and three Actually Know What They're Doing. And two of those weren't volunteers. They were nominated."

Rainbow rolled her eyes.

"Oh, thank goodness you're here, Ryan!" Sweaty Bruce exclaimed, mopping his brow with a hand-stitched Team Angel handkerchief. "Ryan will save us. He's a corporate accountant, you know, Rainbow."

"I am aware of Ryan's qualifications," she said testily. "What I don't understand is why he's here."

"Obviously he's here to help," Bruce scoffed.

"I'm not so sure about that," Rainbow said.

Evan glanced back and forth between them, then shrugged. "I'm gonna see if there's any popcorn left."

Rainbow steepled her fingers. "What can we do for you, Ryan?"

"I think the question should be what can I do for you?"

"What can you do for us? Tell us!" Bruce begged. He was leaning so far over the table that he was almost prone.

"I have experience related to your problem," Ryan announced.

"What kind of experience?" Rainbow asked as if she had zero interest in the conversation.

"Ever hear of the town Red Rock Bay in Washington state?" he asked.

"Nope." Rainbow sounded bored.

"I could Google it," Bruce offered, patting his pockets for his phone. "Do you want me to Google it?"

"You've never heard of Red Rock Bay because I stepped in at the eleventh hour and saved the town from a very public bankruptcy."

"Bruce, why don't you go get Amethyst some water," Rainbow suggested, leaning back in her chair.

"Yes. Good idea! Don't say anything important until I get back. Amethyst, my pearl! I'm coming," Bruce said, charging into the crowd.

"Let's step outside," Rainbow suggested, pulling on her coat.

Ryan followed her out the exit door. The alley was dark and frigid. He dragged on his hat while Rainbow lit another one of her clove cigarettes.

"Let's get down to brass tacks," she said.

"I came across some interesting information regarding my uncle's loan today," Ryan said.

"You did?" For a moment, she looked perplexed. "I mean. Oh, you did. What do you want?"

"I want a sit-down with you tomorrow to hash this out once and for all."

"In exchange for?"

"I can make this state auditor problem go away. At least long enough for you to come up with the proper documentation."

He had her interest now, he thought as she eyed him shrewdly.

"How do I know you're not full of shit?" she asked, blowing out a contemplative cloud of smoke.

Ryan flipped his ear flaps down. "Guess you'll just have to trust me."

"So I meet with you tomorrow, and you solve this auditor problem before Christmas Eve?"

"Yes." He held out a hand. "I'll see you at eight a.m."

"Four p.m.," she countered.

"Noon."

"Deal," she said, shaking his hand, her grip firm enough to rearrange several of the smaller finger bones.

"Rainbow?" Evan the kid appeared in the doorway. He was shoveling popcorn into his face. "Pond Birkbeck wants to know if clipping coupons counts as accounting experience."

"I'll see you at noon, Ryan," she said menacingly.

"Looking forward to it," Ryan said.

❧

The Monthly Moon:

Contrary to recent rumors, Mayor Beckett Pierce confirms there have been no official steps taken to shun Bruce and Amethyst Oakleigh. Mayor Pierce also confirms that as far as he knows "alien life forms have not been living among us."

The mayor refused to weigh in on whether or not the school district's More Fiber for Better Poops movement would be on the next town meeting's agenda. He suggested the Monthly Moon's journalist schedule an appointment and not just show up on his doorstep at 11 p.m. on a weeknight.

22

S ammy was in the middle of wiring a glittery jingle bell in place when there was a knock on her door. It was after nine on a cold-ass winter night. If it was some Mooner wanting to place a custom wreath order in person, there was a distinct possibility that she was going to lose her shit.

Tripping over a naked wreath, she stomped to her front door. "Ryan?" Sammy nearly dropped her glue gun onto a cat when she opened her front door and found him standing there looking handsome and broody. "What are you doing here?"

Was this a booty call? Please be a booty call!

"I'm amped up on battling it out with Rainbow Berkowicz," he announced from his place on her Merry Everything welcome mat. There was indeed an unpredictable sort of energy crackling off him.

If this *was* a booty call, he was going to have to deal with the fact that she'd only remembered to shave one armpit and had eaten six garlic-stuffed olives in place of an actual supper.

"Plus, I thought you might need food," he said, holding up two John Pierce Brews to-go bags. "Goat Guy hooked me up with soups, sandwiches, and a six-pack of something called Apocalypse Ale."

He'd brought her food she didn't have to cook after she'd worked straight through dinner. *Booty call on.*

"Wow. Okay," she said, standing aside so he could come in. "Thanks. Did you seriously get into a fight with Rainbow after the town meeting?"

He crossed the threshold and she felt his gaze as it traveled over her from the ratty hooded sweatshirt, over her Naughty or Nice pajama shorts, down to her candy cane knee socks.

Dammit. Well, at least her hair still looked good.

"Holy shit!" she yelped when a gigantic cotton ball appeared next to him in the doorway.

"Oh. You don't mind that I brought Stan, do you? He was bored and I'm pretty sure he's housebroken." The sheep wandered past her into the house.

"Uh. That's fine," she said, watching Stan trot into the living room. Holly, the almost-glue-gunned cat, skulked behind him, eyeing the sheep with suspicion.

"He's pretty good company," Ryan told her.

The man had developed a friendship with a sheep he let in the house. *Booty call off.*

"How did you find my place?" she asked, following him as he headed for her kitchen.

The man looked out of place in the tight space with its ancient apple wallpaper and dingy pine cabinets. She wished she would have gotten around to doing the dishes and vacuuming.

"I asked the bartender at the brewery. She knew. The llama lady from yesterday with the bad biscotti was there for dinner and gave me turn-by-turn directions. Jax said you're usually in bed by nine, but I knew you'd be up late making wreaths."

Sammy blinked. "Hang on. You told *how many* Mooners that you were coming over to my house tonight?"

"Just three," he said, clearly not understanding the ramifications.

She preferred not having to field well-meaning but inappropriate questions about her sex life in the produce aisle at the grocery store or under a cow's udder.

On cue, her phone alerted her to a new text message. She picked it up and silenced it. Before she had the chance to put it back down, three more texts buzzed in. In desperation, she stashed the phone inside a stack of wreaths on her table.

Great. The gossip group had been activated. Everyone would be speculating that she and Carson's nephew were getting it on when—depressingly enough—they were not.

"Interesting place," he said, eyeing her living space as he dumped the bags on the kitchen counter.

He wasn't catching her or her home on their best days.

"It's usually much cleaner than this," she told him. "I've been busy."

She'd bought the two-story farmhouse and its ten acres that summer. With the help of local contractor Calvin Finestra, Sammy had worked her way down a prioritized punch list to make the house—mostly—livable.

They'd upgraded both bathrooms, opened up the living and dining areas, and stripped the dizzying pink heart wallpaper out of her bedroom. But the cramped kitchen with its pine plank cabinets and faded candy apple red counter tops was one step up from eyesore. And then there was the upstairs. The second floor needed more TLC. But it would have to wait until later like everything else since the barn and pastures were next on her list. Then there was the adjoining parcel of land she had her eye on. But that was far, far into the nebulous future.

At least she'd sprung for new, grown-up furniture.

The long, white-washed oak dining table occupied the space between the kitchen and front door. It looked pretty great... when it wasn't smothered under an obscene amount of craft supplies. Four days of dishes were stacked in the tiny sink in the U-shaped kitchen. Stan was currently shoving his face in the load of week-old clean laundry that sat half-folded on the coffee table in the living room.

"Given your get-up, I was expecting a Christmas tree," he said, his gaze lingering on her legs.

The way he looked at her was downright sinful. Sheep be damned. *Booty call back on!*

"I always get my tree from Carson at the Solstice Celebration. I had no idea he wasn't going to sell them this year," she told him.

"What's in the totes?" He nodded toward the four red and green plastic totes stacked behind her couch.

"Christmas decorations." There were a lot of things she hadn't gotten around to lately.

"Whoa." Ryan's eyes widened as a gray cat popped out of a wreath on top of the table. It narrowed its yellow eyes at him and tore across the table before disappearing under the couch.

"That's McClane," she said, finding her voice. "The black one is Holly."

"On the way over here, I was trying to predict how many animals you'd have. So far, unless you have a herd of goats upstairs, I'm disappointed."

"Said the guy who brought a sheep with him!"

"He's basically the same thing as a dog," he argued, unpacking the food.

"No goats. *Yet,*" she said. "Three cats and some fish outside in the pond."

Willis waddled out from behind the armchair in the living room, a strip of plaid ribbon wrapped around his foot.

"Oh yeah. And a duck," she finished.

Stan gave Willis a wide berth when the duck waddled in his direction.

"I thought you'd have at least four dogs. And I was betting on a blind one and one with three legs," Ryan said while he rummaged through her cabinets.

"Willis has a limp courtesy of a groundhog trap if that helps. But my friend Layla—the deputy—takes all the stray dogs. Her schedule is a little friendlier to needy pets."

He set bowls, plates, and utensils on the counter and opened the containers.

It smelled heavenly. "What are you doing here, Ryan?" she asked finally.

"My parents have dinner together once a week without fighting," he announced, plating sandwich halves with an unexplained bitterness.

"Uh. How dare they?"

He strode to the table with a plate and bowl in hand. She sat when he indicated a chair.

"They divorced when I was a teenager and were still fighting when I left for college," he explained.

"Okay." Her stomach growled when he put a bowl of chicken noodle soup and a chicken salad sandwich in front of her. It was her favorite comfort food meal.

"My oldest sister called to tell me she was pregnant months ago," he continued as he headed back to the kitchen for his food. "I didn't pick up or remember to call her back."

"Ouch," Sammy said, picking up her spoon and watching him.

He sat next to her, looking frustrated. Restless.

"I poured all my energy into being the best accountant in the firm. It was stable, predictable. There was a map to be followed. The outcomes could be anticipated. And the rug *still* got pulled out from under me. I walked into that conference room having no idea it would be my last time. I didn't have a defense prepared. I had no clue there was anything to defend."

She winced for him. The man who hated surprises had been dealt the worst kind. And the hits just seemed to keep coming.

He picked up half of a ham and cheese on marbled rye bread and stared at it. "My parents didn't know I broke up with my ex-girlfriend a year ago even though I talk to my mother every Tuesday."

Sammy held up a hand. "Hang on. There's a lot to unpack in that sentence."

"What? That I'm anal enough to schedule phone calls with my mother but I don't bother telling her when I end a relationship or get fired? She thinks I took vacation time to be here, by the way."

She let out a surprised laugh. "Why does she think that?"

His shoulders jerked up and then dropped. "Because that's what I insinuated."

"It sounds like you've had an interesting day."

"I was sitting there, surrounded by an entire lifetime of someone else's paperwork and family photos, and I didn't know what to do next. I *always* know what to do next," he lectured, waving his spoon at her.

"You're not here because you think *I* know what the next step is, are you?" she asked. She couldn't even craft her way through a few dozen wreaths.

"No. I wanted to see you. Because since I walked into that conference room a week ago expecting to be made partner, I've had this ball of ice in my gut. The only time it goes away is when I'm with you."

Her internal squealing was deafening.

"Oh," she said on a breathy sigh.

He looked at her over a spoonful of soup. "That's it? 'Oh'?"

"I'm processing. Slowly. I'm a little sluggish at night. Besides, there are a million things you could mean by that statement."

"But you know I don't mean a million things," he said, very, very seriously.

She swallowed hard. "Maybe you could narrow it down for me?"

"I've never been around anyone so..." He glanced around them, at the tangle of ribbons and ornaments, the loops of grapevines, clippings of pine. "Chaotic," he decided.

Booty call off. She willed the hair on her legs to grow longer. "Gee, thanks."

"Someone so chaotic, who made me feel comfortable, safe, challenged, intrigued," he clarified.

Okay, so it wasn't an "I'd like to rip your pants off and satisfy you six ways to Sunday" kind of statement, but it wasn't an "ol' buddy, ol' pal" punch in the shoulder either.

"You're going sixty miles an hour from dawn to dusk, changing directions, reacting, adapting. You got me on a horse when I should have been eyeballs-deep in bank statements. No one distracts me from a puzzle," he said. "But it turns out that you're the more interesting puzzle."

Now that was pretty freaking romantic, Sammy decided. *Booty call back on.*

"You reminded me of something I'd forgotten a long, long time ago."

"What's that?" she asked, staring hard at his mouth.

"That sometimes it's okay to let go. That maybe I don't have to be in complete control of every facet of my life. Maybe it's okay if I let things happen."

"*I* reminded you of that?" she asked softly.

"You did."

She pursed her lips and considered. "Damn. I'm smart."

Stan wandered over to the table and nudged her with his nose. She gave him a scratch between the ears.

They ate in companionable silence, Sammy's brain turning over everything he'd said.

When he was done, Ryan pushed his plate back. "A week ago, I was doing everything I'd set out to do. I had the biggest client list in the firm. I was on track for partner. I had a down payment on a new, bigger condo. But I never saw this coming."

Sammy reached out and took his hand. "No amount of planning can protect you from everything. You can't anticipate every possibility."

He laughed. "That's for sure." Those gray eyes raised to meet hers. "I never saw you coming."

Booty. Call. On.

"So," he said, drumming his hands on the table. "Want some help with all this?" he asked, gesturing toward the holiday explosion.

"Wait. What?"

SHE COULDN'T FREAKING BELIEVE INSTEAD of tearing off her Christmas-themed boxers, the man was sitting at her table making bows.

"What are these?" Ryan asked, hefting a fat stack of papers he found under a wreath and Holly, the sleek black cat.

Sammy groaned, feeling her muscles tense just looking at them. "Those are grant applications," she said, untying the lopsided Happy Hanukkah bow for the third time.

"For your practice?" he asked, flipping through the pile of intimidation.

"For the non-profit farm sanctuary I'm starting," she said with a sigh. "That's what these damn wreaths are for. It's supposed to be the first official fundraiser for Down on the Farm."

"I'm going to need more information than that," he insisted, glancing up from the paperwork.

"Right now, livestock that local animal control departments liberate from unsafe situations is distributed to a network of foster farms. It's not an ideal situation since farmers are already busy enough without adding abused or neglected animals in need of medical care and attention into the mix."

"So you bought this place to start your own sanctuary," he assessed.

"Yeah. Down on the Farm will be a no-kill sanctuary for homeless farm animals. Think of it as a retirement community for livestock. I've got ten acres here. But I need the funds to fix up the barn and the fields. Then there's the food and medical care."

"Sounds expensive," he said, flipping through the applications.

"Expensive, but worthwhile. Right now, I do what I can by providing free vet care for the rescued animals. I also pay for feed and supplies out of my own pocket. But it's not enough."

"That's a shitty, irresponsible business model."

"Well, don't pull any punches or anything," Sammy complained.

"Explain to me why the hell these papers are sitting here blank while we waste time tying stupid bows."

"Because I committed to selling wreaths. Okay?" she said in exasperation. "We always have a wreath stand at the Solstice, and last year's wreath maker is on a barefoot tai chi sojourn across Canada. Do you want Blue Moon to go without trees *and* wreaths this year?"

"Blue Moon isn't my concern. You are," he said, frowning over the applications. "Sam, these grants would put a hell of a lot of money into your coffers. You're wasting time and energy on a useless fundraiser that won't net you any real capital."

"Look. I paid for the booth. I promised people wreaths. I'm going to deliver."

He opened his arms to encompass the table. "Then why am I the only one here?"

"I didn't ask for your help or your food delivery," she said stubbornly. *Booty call off.* She didn't need some armchair quarterback coming in here and critiquing her priorities.

"Did you ask for anyone else's?"

She gave up on the bow and crossed her arms. "No."

"So in Sparkle's Perfect World, you were going to work full-time—without your vet tech—make fifty fucking wreaths, set up and man a booth, *and* finish your grant applications by..." He glanced down at the paperwork. "Tomorrow at midnight."

Sammy pressed the heels of her hands to her eyes and slouched in her chair. She was probably grinding glitter into her corneas. "When you say it like that, it sounds stupid. And impossible."

"Why didn't you ask for help?"

She picked up the bow, determined not to be defeated again and mashed it into a knot. "I didn't think I needed it." Giving up on any semblance of perfection—or aptitude above kinder-garten-level bow tying—she knotted the wire with pliers. *There. Done.* She propped it against the wall with the other finished wreaths and tried to ignore just how droopy and crooked they all looked.

"Do you want to know what your problem is?" he asked.

"No."

"Your problem is you want to fix everyone else's problems," he said, ignoring her.

"How is *that* a bad thing?" she scoffed.

"Can you ask that when you have an Oy to the World ribbon

glued to your sweatshirt?"

She glanced down and ripped the length of ribbon off her chest.

"You are prioritizing other people's problems over your own. Other people's needs over your own," he pressed on, warming to the topic.

"I don't have problems," she insisted.

He gestured at the table, the spools of ribbon, the reels of wire, one glittery cat tail, and dozens of unfinished wreaths. "How is this disaster going to turn into startup capital? By committing to the wrong priorities, you're missing the big picture and endangering your future."

"I appreciate your criticism," she said dryly. "However, it's not helping me finish these wreaths."

"Cancel the booth, the fundraiser, and fill out the damn paperwork, Sam."

If her spine got any more rigid, she worried it might snap like a dry twig. "I made a commitment," she said defensively. "Maybe *you* go back on your word, but I don't."

"No need to get snippy."

"There's no guarantee that I'll land any of those grants," she reminded him. "But I am guaranteed to sell every one of these horrible wreaths. No matter how lopsided and sad they are, Mooners will buy them to support the cause."

Ryan sighed. "What's the price of one of these holiday monstrosities?" he asked, holding up a wreath buried under jingle bells. Glitter rained down on the table.

"Twenty-five bucks a pop," she announced defiantly.

"What are your margins?" he asked.

"Margins?" she repeated, feigning innocence.

"You know what margins are. Quit stalling so I can win this argument. How much did you invest in supplies, time, labor?"

She eyed the mess in front of them. "I don't know. But the

branches were free."

"Let's say you spent five dollars in supplies on each wreath."

That was probably on the low side, considering she'd already made three trips to the craft store, but Mr. Grumpy Number Cruncher didn't need to be made aware of that.

"Then there's the cost of the booth rental," he continued. "And the signage and whatever booth decor you got."

Crap. She'd forgotten about that.

She couldn't just throw a bunch of wreaths on the ground and take people's money. She needed a table. Tablecloths. Maybe one of those cute letter board signs that crafty people always seemed to have. And lights. The event was at night. How was anyone going to see the wreaths without lights?

"Not to mention your time shopping, making the product, setting up the booth, running it, tearing it down." He was on a roll and hadn't noticed the panic his words induced. "Do you hear that?" he asked, cupping a hand to his ear.

"I think it's your sheep snoring," Sammy guessed.

He made a whistling noise like a bomb falling until his palm hit the table, startling two cats, a duck, and a sheep. "That's your profit margin plummeting."

"You don't have to be so dramatic about it," she complained. Accountants didn't seem to be an empathetic lot.

"Your time would have been better spent applying for these grants. If you get just one of them, you'll be bringing in far more money than if you'd sold every one of these crooked circles for two hundred dollars apiece."

"If your intent is to make me feel like an idiot, it's working."

"Good," he said. "You're not an idiot, by the way. You're just making idiotic decisions."

She threw a jingle bell at him. It hit his forehead and bounced off. McClane scrambled out of his ribbon nest and pounced on it. Holly's glittery tail twitched as she watched.

"You're a mean accountant," Sammy announced.

"I'm telling you what you need to hear in a way that it's going to sink in. You don't need a hand holder. You need an ass kicker. If you want to be successful in this endeavor, you need to forget everyone else's problems and focus on helping yourself."

"Why does everyone keep saying that?"

"Because you're pathologically helpful. Instead of filling out grant applications that you have an excellent chance of getting, you volunteered to make and sell fifty wreaths, babysit a flock of deranged chickens, find a home for a stray sheep, and drive a hungover stranger around town for a day."

"Do you *really* think I have a shot at a grant?" she asked him, watching him closely.

"I do. And I find the fact that you'd waste time worrying about that annoying."

She found herself oddly comforted.

"Of course, if your business plan and financials are a wreck, that's an obstacle," he continued, ruining her temporary sense of comfort. "But the idea? The solution you're providing and the way you'll execute it? You deserve this money."

She looked down at her sparkly, sticky hands. At her half-finished, half-decorated house. At the man who wasn't actively trying to seduce her into a one-night stand. *What the hell was wrong with her?*

"I mean seriously. What the hell is wrong with you, Sam?"

"A whole lot of things apparently." Leading with the fact that she'd let a stack of papers intimidate her into backing down. Her attempt to avoid rejection meant she'd set back any hopes of getting the sanctuary on its feet by at least another year.

He reached out and took her hand. "Whatever you think you're proving by being the first in line to volunteer or the one to never say no isn't worth never getting what you want. Sometimes you have to say no to everyone else so you can say yes to what's important to you."

She blew out a breath. "Wow. You're good at this. I feel ashamed yet motivated to do something about it."

He squeezed her hand. "They don't call me the client whisperer for nothing."

He'd just chastised her, but one hand-hold and visions of booty calls danced in her head again.

"It's after eleven. Way past your bedtime," he said. He tossed his finished wreath onto the floor like a Frisbee. Willis the duck waddled over and climbed into it like a nest.

"So what do I do?"

Ryan stood. "You're going to go to bed and get some sleep."

The booty call gods were cruel.

Disappointed, dejected, and downtrodden, she followed him to the door. She clutched a roll of black velvet ribbon as an anchor. He shrugged into his coat and whistled for Stan. The sheep lazily trotted over, a cat on his heels. Ryan turned to face her. She stared down at their feet, not wanting to say goodbye to him yet again. Not wanting to be left alone to face the mess she'd created.

Then he was nudging her chin up. "Look at me, Sam." His voice had a rough edge to it that made her blood turn to liquid gold. He hissed in a breath when she did as he asked. "Don't look so sad. I don't like it."

She forced a hideous fake smile, and he laughed softly, still holding her chin in his hand. "I'll be back in the morning, early," he said.

She blinked. "Why?"

"Because you're going to call in reinforcements for the wreaths, and you and I are going to fill out those grant applications."

She grabbed him by the arms. "Are you serious? It's a lot of paperwork," she warned.

"Yes. We'll get it figured out. And we'll get it all done."

"What about Carson's thing? And your secret feud with Rainbow?"

"That's for me to worry about. Not you. Have the coffee going."

Without thinking, she threw her arms around him and held on tight. He went still against her and then slowly slid his arms around her. She pressed her face to his chest. His solid, comforting chest. There, wrapped in his arms, she felt safe and warm and not alone.

She peered up at him. "You're great at your job. Your firm is incredibly stupid not to see that."

"Thank you, Sam," he said gruffly. He tucked her hair behind her ear, letting his fingers linger on her neck. Her skin heated at each point of contact.

She couldn't look away from his eyes. They'd gone silver on her.

Don't think about kissing him.

Crap. Too late.

"Sam?"

"Yeah?"

"I know I just told you to start saying no to everyone, but…"

"But?" she prompted him, feeling lightheaded.

"But I need you to have one more 'yes' in you."

She couldn't catch her breath. Her senses were full of Ryan.

Stan the sheep got bored and wandered back to his place in front of the fire.

"What's the question?" she whispered. If he asked her to pick up his dry cleaning or sheepsit, she would die on the spot. Then she'd come back to life just to throw him and his sheep out of her house.

"Can I kiss you goodnight?"

23

_____

She nodded slowly. The answer he needed to his question.

"How do you like to be kissed, Sammy?" Ryan's voice was quiet, but the words felt like gravel in his throat.

The black ribbon slipped from her fingers, hitting the floor and unraveling as it rolled toward the wall.

She sighed into the space between their mouths. "I-I don't know. I liked how you kissed me before."

He slid his hands down her arms to her wrists, tugging her forward. When her toes brushed his shoes, she still wasn't close enough to his liking. So he lifted her to stand on top of his feet.

"What are you doing?" she asked.

"Research." And then his mouth was dipping to hers. Her lips, soft and full, yielded to his immediately. The seam between them widened as he traced the tip of his tongue over it. And then she was opening for him, surrendering to him.

He groaned as her tongue met his. The kiss was sweeter, headier than he could have imagined. He intended to pace himself. To sample, not devour. But she tasted like so many forbidden things, and he couldn't get enough. The stroke of his tongue against hers was possessive, aggressive. She let out another breathy sigh that did strange things to his pulse.

He was playing with fire. And though he thought he'd assessed the risk, the second she breathed his name, he knew he'd miscalculated.

Ryan's New List

1. Find out how this woman says his name when he's inside her.

Leaning down, he slid his hands under her and lifted. She wrapped those candy cane socks around his waist as he spun them around. The table was the closest available flat surface. He shoved crafting paraphernalia out of the way, sending some of it tumbling to the floor.

McClane the cat stalked off the table in a huff.

And then Ryan was placing her on the white oak and sliding his hands under her ancient sweatshirt.

"Yes?" he whispered against her mouth, fingers stroking the taut skin of her stomach.

"God, yes," she breathed. Her fingers dove into his hair and tugged hard.

He found the edge of a cropped tank top just under her breasts. And just as he was ready to glide his hands under the cotton and over the softest, smoothest skin he'd ever encountered, Sammy pulled back.

"Wait. You don't do one-night stands," she reminded him.

"I seem to be doing a lot of things I don't do." His palms inched higher as he kissed her again.

She moaned, and his hard-on began to pulse painfully behind his zipper.

"Wait," she said again, breaking away from his mouth. "I don't want to force you into anything."

"Stop being honorable and take advantage of me, Sparkle," he growled.

"Well, if you insist." With one hand on the back of his neck, she reached for the fly of his jeans.

She managed to pop the button before he kissed her again. As his tongue swept into her mouth, she lowered his zipper. The kiss was hard and desperate. He slid his hands up the last inch to cup her breasts.

"Finally," he breathed, as those soft curves welcomed his touch.

Sammy's head fell back, and the hand that had been poised to dive into the front of his jeans went limp as he brushed his palms over both pebbled peaks. Touching wasn't enough. He had to see her. To taste her.

He pressed her back down on the table and dragged the sweatshirt over her head. The little white tank top obscured nothing from his hungry gaze. She arched her back, putting those beautiful round breasts on display for him.

That trusting acquiescence made him feel things he hadn't known he was capable of feeling.

She was willing to give him this part of her after having known him only a few days. That was a gift. A miracle. She'd seen him on his worst day and *still* wanted him.

He brushed his lips over her cheek, the curve of her jaw. She smelled like sugar cookies and cinnamon. He was a goner.

"More." Her voice trembled, and it made him feel like the luckiest son of a bitch in town. Possibly the state.

"I need you to know I didn't come here with the intent to do this," he whispered as he kissed and licked his way down her neck to her shoulder.

"'K," she said. Her hand returned to his jeans. Only this time, it didn't stop at the waistband.

He lost his breath and his damn mind when she closed her fingers around his swollen shaft.

"I love that you don't wear underwear," she said on a low moan.

Right now, he was pretty happy with that wardrobe choice too. "This is probably a mistake," he admitted on a rasp. A misstep that nothing in the world could stop him from making. "I want to make that mistake with you."

There were too many layers between them.

"Definitely," she agreed. Her fingers tightened on his erection and then began to move, driving him out of his mind and into his body.

On a groan, he lowered himself and sucked a nipple into his mouth through the thin cotton. She bucked her hips against him and tightened her delicious grip on his shaft.

He didn't know how much longer he could stand not being inside her. To distract himself, he shoved up her tank and worshipped her breasts with his mouth.

Sammy's leg spasmed in response, catching the box of jingle bells and sending it flying to the floor.

Bells rang. Cats hissed. Stan the sheep eyed them curiously.

"Shit," she breathed. "Sorry."

He picked her up off the table.

"Ryan, if you come to your senses right now, I will implode," she vowed.

"You've destroyed my senses, Sam. We're going to your bedroom."

"Yay! Condom?"

"Wallet. Bedroom?"

The fireplace was closer and cozy. Maybe even romantic? But Ryan didn't want to have to perform for the first time with a petting zoo for an audience.

"Upstairs and to the left," she said, shivering against him.

She rained kisses over his jaw and neck. And when she sank her teeth into his ear lobe, he almost tripped.

Recovering quickly, he bounded up the staircase. Until she shoved a hand between them and gripped him in her fist. His dick jerked, and his foot nearly missed the next step.

"Don't move a fucking muscle until I get us up these stairs," he commanded.

"Hurry!"

They both survived the last few steps and Ryan kicked open the first door on the left, zeroing in on the bed. He couldn't have described the room or the bed if his life depended on it because he was too busy dragging those Naughty or Nice shorts down her thighs. Underneath, she wore white underwear with snowflakes, and he couldn't stop staring at the tantalizing wet spot on them.

"Help," she whispered, and he realized she was doing her best to shove his jeans to the floor. He held off on touching her for as long as he could. Which was only about 1.5 seconds. Just long enough to get his shirt off and his jeans down.

With his jeans trapped around his ankles and one shoe on, it was good enough, he thought as he dove for her. Covering her warm, soft body with his own. As his mouth took hers in an aggressive assault, he brushed his fingers gently over the hypnotic wet spot on her underwear.

She shivered.

He was afraid to touch her too much. The want welling up inside him threatened to take over everything. He felt alive. Out of control. Scared shitless.

As if sensing that, Sammy brought his hand to her breast and closed his fingers over it. And then he couldn't have stopped if he wanted to.

She was soft and smooth and small. He couldn't understand

how she was here, available to him. How he was the lucky guy who got to taste her and touch her tonight.

He replaced his hand with his mouth and teased her pink nipple until it stiffened against his tongue.

"I need you, Ryan," she whimpered, bucking against him. "Please."

He shoved his hand into her festive underwear and finally found her.

She *needed* him. Her words repeated in his head, echoed in his chest where knots he hadn't known he had untied themselves.

"Say it again," he demanded, spearing two fingers into her tight, wet channel.

Sammy's moan was music to his fucking ears.

"I need you." It was a gasp. A plea. And it was more than enough for him. Slowly, he pulled his fingers out of her, then thrust them back in. Rhythmically. Tauntingly. She was so fucking wet. So fucking ready for him. And had he followed the rules, stuck to the plan, he would have missed out on this.

The thought of that had him diving into another kiss, harder than he'd intended. Her fingers dug into his neck and shoulders.

"Open your legs for me, Sam," he growled, slowly withdrawing his fingers one last time.

She obeyed, dropping her knees open as he fumbled for the condom and rolled it on.

Finally, he settled himself between her legs.

His heart was racing. Her breath was coming in short pants. "If that sheriff shows up right now, I'm not going to be able to stop," Ryan warned her.

Her laugh was soft and breathy. Until the head of his cock pushed insistently, desperately at her entrance. "Please. I need you now." She bucked against him.

It was everything he needed. Right here in this ridiculous

town. In this room. In this incredible, infuriating, inexplicable woman.

His name escaped her throat as he gripped her hips and drove home in one swift, sweet thrust.

It was otherworldly. Being buried inside her as her muscles clenched then slowly relaxed around his cock to accommodate his size only to tighten again. Joined. Melded. Partners in this adventure.

"I know we just started," she whispered in a rush. "But I'm definitely going to die from this."

"Not before you come," he growled. She was so damn tight he was afraid he wouldn't be able to hang on.

"What about you?" she breathed.

His cock flexed inside her in response and she moaned. "I don't think that's gonna be a problem," he promised.

He eased out of her, loving the decadent drag of her walls against him, before pushing back in. "Fuck."

It was too much and still not enough. Her broken cry said the same.

"You drive me insane," he murmured, dipping his head to lap at her nipple.

She gripped his hair and bucked her hips to meet his thrust. "Back at ya."

He couldn't help himself. He pulled out and drove back in harder, faster. Finesse be damned. Meticulous quest to discover exactly what she needed forgotten.

Again. And again he entered her. Her walls opened for him just wide enough to force him up against the edge. Faster. Harder. She was clinging to him, those perfect breasts trembling with every animalistic thrust.

She deserved sweet, romantic. But he couldn't slow it down. Couldn't take his time. He was pumping into her like a piston. Every thrust pushing her a little further across the mattress. His knees and toes dug into the bed for leverage as he drove them both up.

"Dammit, Sammy," he murmured as he felt her start to flutter around him. Her release was going to be the end of him, and he knew it. Bringing his mouth to hers, he continued to hammer into her. His body was desperate for the relief that only her release could bring.

Her nails dug into his skin and dragged across his back. Her breasts were flattened between them, and he wished he had the time to worship them with his mouth, but right now, the only thing that mattered was Sammy coming apart on his cock. He yanked her knees up higher.

"Ryan!" she cried out, and he felt her clamp down on him in the single most erotic experience of his life. Her arms and legs locking around his body while she exploded around him, working his cock in one of biology's perfect miracles.

His own release was right there. Ready to destroy him. One glorious squeeze, one sob from her mouth, and the heat of it seared his balls, blazed up his shaft, and then he was coming—hard, so hard—into the depths of her body.

She throbbed and writhed around him, wringing him out, making him feel like a fucking hero until they were both trembling.

He was spent. Hollowed out. The icy dread of the unknown, all the "now whats" that had circled endlessly in his brain were quiet. Vanished as if they'd never existed. The only thing that existed, that mattered, was the woman in his arms.

∾

"I LIKE YOUR BED," he murmured sleepily against her hair. It could have been ten minutes later or an hour. He had no concept of time as he floated in post-orgasmic bliss.

"Mmph. Thanks," she said, rolling her face out of the pillow. He could hear the smug smile in her voice. "I like having sex with you in my bed."

He would have grinned, but still hadn't regained fine motor control. "I like that thing you did with your mouth and then that other thing you did with your legs. Actually, I liked all the things you did. You were right."

"Right about what?" she asked.

"You're really good at this."

She snickered lazily. "You're no slouch yourself. High five?"

Blindly, he reached out and—after accidentally high-fiving her breast and then her forehead—he found her hand.

"Good in bed. Bad at high-fiving," Sammy mused, snuggling deeper under the covers.

"I'll update my resume," he joked.

She rolled over to face him and folded her hands under that angel face. "What *are* you going to do? Or is that too heavy to talk to after..."

"After all those orgasms?" He reached out and traced a finger down the slope of her nose, over the fullness of her lips swollen from his own mouth. "I don't know. I'd thought about applying at a competitor after my non-compete contract expires. Now I'm not so sure. Maybe I don't have to stay in Seattle? Most of my family is in Pennsylvania and New Jersey. Maybe it would be nice to be closer? To be more involved? Or maybe it's time to do something different. Something on a smaller scale?"

Maybe he could stay in Blue Moon? Or near Blue Moon.

Maybe he could see where things went with the tomboy veterinarian who didn't realize how appealing she was?

Maybe the derailing of his life's plan was just the beginning of a new adventure, not the end of a dream.

"That's a lot of maybes," she said.

"I'm not used to having any," he admitted, moving his leg

restlessly. She had flannel sheets on the bed. He'd never slept on flannel sheets before. He liked the texture. "This one-night stand thing. I'm supposed to leave now, right?"

There was a sweet smile playing on those lips that he couldn't stop staring at. "Well, it does avoid the need to make awkward conversation around the breakfast table the next morning," she mused.

"We already made awkward conversation at the breakfast table yesterday morning," he reminded her.

"Good point."

"'K. I'm just gonna close my eyes for a minute before I go find my pants," he said.

"'K," she yawned.

24

The cat paw poked her in the face twenty seconds before her alarm went off. Sammy hadn't figured out how her cats always seemed to know when the alarm was about to ring or why they couldn't stand giving her the last few seconds of precious sleep.

Cats were assholes. Psychic assholes.

She stretched luxuriously in the pre-dawn dark, dislodging the fur ball from her chest, as she mentally assessed her body. She felt *good*. Sore. Satisfied.

All because Grumpy Ryan Sosa had banged her into oblivion.

Her eyelids flew open, and she slapped a hand to the mattress next to her. It was empty. His half of the bed was already neatly made. Disappointment settled in her chest, dulling the glow of the previous night's satisfaction. The dumb, twittery flicker of hope she'd felt when he'd looked across the pillow at her and confessed his maybes.

"Maybe do something different."

Had she really thought that meant her? *Ugh.*

"Dr. Dumbass reporting for duty," she muttered under her

breath before kicking off the covers and climbing out of bed. For a very intelligent woman, she sure did some stupid things.

Her mood had officially gone surly. Her tiny fluttery butterflies of hope had withered up and died. She had a full day of wreath assembly and booth setup ahead of her. Then there was the stack of grant applications that Mr. Bed Abandoner had offered to help her with. For a second, she thought about just crawling back into bed and pulling the covers over her head until New Year's Day. That would count as self-care. Right?

But duty called.

She'd start fresh in January. Saying no. Blow-drying her hair. *Not* getting pillow talk confused with actual relationship plans. All she had to do was survive the next few days and then she could hit the reset button.

As she trudged down the stairs, her internal pep talk was interrupted by the smell of food. Real food. Not microwaved leftover food. The lights were on downstairs, holding back the dark of the winter morning outside the windows.

Mouth watering, she peered over the railing into the kitchen and blinked.

Ryan stood at the counter very precisely arranging parsley over two plated omelets. He was barefoot. His jeans were left temptingly unbuttoned, and he was wearing what she'd dubbed her I Give Up sweatshirt. An oversized Cornell hoodie that had been washed so many times the front pocket had fallen off. On her it looked sloppy. On him it looked *hot*.

He glanced up and caught her watching him. His smile went straight to her nether regions, making them feel all warm and woozy again.

"You're here," she said.

He gave her a hungry look. "I hope you don't mind that I never found my pants and left last night."

"I don't mind." She sounded as if she'd just run five miles after an ice cream truck.

"It's your fault for having such a comfortable bed," he said, with that swoon-worthy half-smirk on his lips. "And for fucking me cross-eyed."

She tripped over a cat on its way to stare at its food dish and barely managed to not take a header onto the linoleum.

"Nice try, Holly," Ryan said. "I already fed them and your duck."

Holly looked down at her empty dish and back up at Sammy with hostility.

"Wow. Thank you," she said. "Where's Stan?"

"He's outside with McClane and the duck. I hope they're allowed outside because they didn't give me a choice."

She floated over to him on the wings of happy hope butterflies. The part of her brain that was warning her not to get too excited was drowned out by a breakfast she didn't have to cook and fresh coffee she hadn't had to brew. Both served by the still-here, still-smiling, hot accountant in her kitchen.

"They're indoor-outdoor," Sammy explained. "They'll be back for morning treats."

At the word "treats," Holly wove herself in between her legs and pretended not to be evil.

"You said you have three cats," Ryan said, digging forks out of her utensil drawer. "I've only seen two."

"Hans is cat Number Three."

Ryan snapped his fingers. "McClane, Holly, and Hans? Did you name all your cats after *Die Hard*?"

"It's my favorite Christmas movie."

He paused and gave her a long, searching look. "You're telling me that you think *Die Hard* is a Christmas movie?"

"Yeah. Why? Don't you like McClane storming Nakatomi Plaza?"

"I have zero issues with *Die Hard*," Ryan promised, fisting his hand in her shirt and dragging her in for a kiss.

She melted against him, feeling deliciously female.

"But back to your third cat," he said, releasing her and handing her a plate. "Why haven't I seen him yet?"

"Hans is shy. Or maybe he doesn't live here anymore," she said, studying the perfectly plated omelet.

They both eyed the table. The chaotic mess of craft supplies had been made exponentially worse by their bodies rolling over it the night before. There was a distinct butt print outlined in glitter.

At this rate, she'd be sparkling until Flag Day.

"Let's eat on the couch," Sammy suggested.

They gathered plates and mugs and trooped into the living room.

"Are you saying you aren't sure if you have a third cat?" he asked dryly.

Sammy pulled her feet under her on the couch and picked up her mug. "He's this fat, orange cat that's a master of hiding. I only see him every few weeks. I'll wake up in the middle of the night, and this big, dumb, orange face is hovering over me. Or he'll pop out of a kitchen cabinet when I open it looking for cookies. Once, I was in the shower, and I felt someone watching me. I reached for a bottle of shampoo to use as a weapon—"

"Naturally."

"And I found Hans sitting on the edge of the tub between the conditioner and the body wash just staring at me."

"Has anyone else ever seen Hans?" Ryan asked pointedly.

"I know what you're getting at, and the answer will only reinforce your point, so I'm going to go for a distraction instead," she announced. "What's the plan for today?"

Did they still have a plan? She wondered.

Was it weird that she wished they were touching?

Was it weird that they weren't touching?

Was she making it weird by not touching him and overthinking everything?

"The plan is to start with breakfast," he said, pointing a fork at her.

He wouldn't have stayed, wouldn't have cooked if he didn't like her, right?

Unless he felt some sort of gentlemanly obligation to her since she'd put out and rocked his world. But honestly, out of the two of them, Sammy was confident that was more her *modus operandi* than his.

They sat side by side on the overstuffed gray couch and dug into their breakfast. The omelet was—like his performance in bed—impressive.

"Oh mah gawd," she managed around a mouthful of egg, cheese, and tomatoes.

"You've mentioned that sentiment a few times since last night," he said smugly.

"Someone's got their cocky pants on this morning."

While they ate, they ignored Holly's plaintive meows about how she was starving and no one ever fed her. When they were finished, he stacked their plates and utensils on the coffee table next to her clean laundry and rubbed his hands on his knees.

He was nervous. And that made her nervous. She picked up her mug again to give her hands something to do.

"How are you feeling about... everything?" he asked. "Any regrets?"

"None here," she said, trying to watch his face out of the corner of her eye. "How about you?"

"One," he said.

He reached for his coffee, sipped, then cleared his throat. *Uh-oh.* It was coming. The "thanks for last night, but I need to get on with my life" lecture. At least she got two orgasms and a hot breakfast out of the deal. At least he hadn't just vanished. God, she was tired of "at leasts."

"Sam. Last night... it made me see things from a different angle. Thank you for that."

"That's the sex hangover talking," she assured him.

"Maybe. Or maybe it's you."

"Me?" she squeaked. Her stupid hope butterflies landed on her stomach lining, waiting to be crushed by the fly swatter of reality.

"What do you regret?" she asked, hating herself for needing the answer.

"That I wasted a whole night here without you."

Hot. Damn. It was the most perfect sentence ever uttered to her before seven a.m. in her entire life.

Before she could form a sexy, flirtatious sentence, he was taking her mug, setting it on the table with a definitive click and kissing the hell out of her.

The kiss didn't taste like a goodbye. It tasted like a good morning.

Touching was good. Definitely not weird, she decided as his tongue drove her just a little wild. Somehow she found herself on top of him, straddling him on the couch while the cat shot judgmental gazes in their direction.

The denim of his jeans felt rough against the inside of her thighs. But there was a prize beneath it. A long, rigid prize.

"Mmm. Wait," Ryan said, pulling back. "We have things."

"Lots of things," she agreed, rolling her hips in a quest for the friction she was suddenly desperate for.

"Plans. To-do lists. Action items," he murmured, sinking his teeth into her neck.

"We should definitely stop."

"Definitely."

HALF AN HOUR LATER, Sammy found herself on her back, partially under the coffee table. Her sweatshirt was stuck around her neck. She was missing a slipper.

Her legs were tangled up with one of Ryan's limbs, where he sprawled on the floor next to her. His jeans hung over the back of the couch. His shirt was unaccounted for.

"If I'd have known that this would be the upside of some crooked small-town bank trying to screw over my uncle, I wouldn't have complained so much about coming out here," Ryan murmured into the fuzzy area rug.

She blinked. "Wait. What?"

"Rainbow Berkowicz." He yawned. "She's trying to collect on a loan that doesn't exist by threatening Carson with foreclosure if he doesn't make some kind of phony balloon payment."

Forgetting where she was, Sammy sat up swiftly. Well, she tried. She smacked her forehead on the underside of the coffee table.

"Ow! Run that by me again?"

25

"Where are we going?" Ryan demanded, jumping into the passenger seat of Sammy's SUV when she revved the engine. "I told you, I have Rainbow right where I want her."

"You'd like to think that," she said tersely. "But you don't. Buckle up."

She was mad. So mad she could feel her face heating up to 9,000 degrees. The diabolical underhandedness was unfathomable. "What exactly did Carson tell you when he called?" she asked, throwing the vehicle into reverse.

Ryan ran through it again as she sped toward town. "What's this all about?" he asked.

"You're being set up," she snapped. "*We're* being set up."

He looked confused in the early morning sun. Confused and disheveled and sexy as hell. "What are you talking about?"

"Don't worry. I won't let them do this to you." She tightened her grip on the steering wheel and pretended it was Bruce Oakleigh's neck.

"Who?"

"The Beautification Committee."

"You've lost me," Ryan admitted.

"It's only funny when they do this to other people," she muttered grimly.

He was pinching the bridge of his nose now. "Do what, Sam? You've got to stop speaking in code," he insisted.

But she was too angry to explain. The Beautification Committee had toyed with them, manipulated them. There was zero chance Ryan was going to find it "charming" that a band of vigilantes had marked them for love.

She found the enemy in One Love Park where setup for the Solstice Celebration was beginning in earnest. Vendors lugged tables and goods to their designated spots. Pop-up tents in a rainbow of colors dotted the landscape. Food trucks parked and rolled out their canopies. It looked like any other normal town function. Except for the web of lies originating from the small clump of people huddled under a bright yellow tent.

In their little bubble of matchmaking machinations, several Beautification Committee members buzzed about unpacking and arranging a display of their nude fundraising calendar.

"Rainbow Berkowicz, you manipulative puppeteer," Sammy bellowed, as she marched up to the bank manager and her husband, Gordon. Rainbow looked sedate in a black wool coat and ski hat. Gordon shunned the cold with purple corduroy bell-bottoms and a hooded knit poncho.

The couple glanced at each other then back at her. And Sammy saw the unspoken "uh-oh" that passed between them.

"What can I do for you, Sammy?" Rainbow asked.

"What are you two doing here together?" Gordon asked. "You weren't supposed to see each other until tonight." His wife elbowed him in the ribs.

"Did you get Ryan fired just so you could play matchmaker?" Sammy demanded.

"What?" Ryan's question cracked like a whip on the cold morning air.

"Don't be silly!" Bruce Oakleigh bustled up in the bottom half of a Santa costume. The beard and belly were real. "That would be overstepping our bounds just a touch. Don't you think? Although, with all the money we've made on our tasteful nude calendar, we probably could have afforded to orchestrate a firing." He stroked his fluffy silver beard as if he were considering the strategy.

"You're absolutely ridiculous!" Sammy's anger was entering the stratosphere. They'd ruined Ryan's life just to lure him there under false circumstances, dangled him in front of her, and she'd walked into the snare without a backward glance.

"Oh, no, dear. He's quite serious," Willa, proprietor of Blue Moon Boots and known for her matchmaking sneakiness, insisted. "We've made $700,000 so far."

"*Seven hundred thousand dollars*? You know what? Never mind." Sammy shook her head, unwilling to get derailed. "Did you create a fake bank foreclosure just to get Carson's nephew into town?"

"Oh, *that*," Rainbow said. "Yes. We did do that."

"Are you saying she tried to collect on a bogus loan to get *me* here?" Ryan asked. "That's illegal. It makes no sense."

"Nothing they do makes sense," Sammy snarled.

"*Everything* we do makes sense," Bruce countered.

"It's all for your own good," Gordon promised. "But you two shouldn't see each other before tonight. We have it all planned out."

Ellery, in black lipstick, Princess Leia buns, and an ebony cape, hustled over on four-inch platform boots. "Sammy! So good to—"

"Can it, Ellery," Sammy snapped. "Are you or are you not trying to match Ryan and me up?"

"Match us up to do what?" Ryan asked, firmly dragging Sammy out of Ellery's face.

"Get married," Sammy said.

"Excuse me?" Ryan scoffed. "Is that even legal?"

"Now, Samantha," Bruce said jovially. "You can't seriously be asking us to show you how the vegan sausage crumbles are made."

"Oh, I'm deadly serious," she said, trying to advance on the man. But Ryan held her by the waist. "Because if you mess with me, Bruce, the next time your cat Pepper gets stuck in an air duct, I *won't* make a house call." It was a weak threat. *Of course* she would show up to save Pepper.

Bruce gasped theatrically. "You wouldn't *dare!*"

She leaned in and poked him in the shoulder before Ryan picked her up and whirled her around. "Try me," she snarled.

"We *need* a town grump," Bruce insisted. "Everyone here is too cheerful. It throws off the balance. Plus, Mason needs a business partner. And you—"

"If the next words out of your mouth are 'need a man,' Sheriff Cardona is going to be throwing my ass in jail tonight, and you won't be up for any diabolical matchmaking until at least the New Year," she threatened.

"Would someone explain what the hell is going on here?" Ryan asked, tightening his grip on her.

"I was going to say you are 'at the top of our matchmaking list,'" Bruce insisted.

"Aren't you tired of coming home to an empty house, Sammy? Watching all your friends pair off and start spending Sundays naked at home?" Willa pressed.

Now she was picturing all her friends frying bacon naked. *Thank you, Beautification Committee.*

"No. I'm not! I love my life. And I'm *not* marrying a grump that you brought here under false pretenses!"

"Someone needs to explain what the hell is going on right now or I'm letting her rearrange all your faces," Ryan ordered.

"These hippie manipulators are trying to match us up so we fall in love, you move here, and we get married and have babies," Sammy told him.

"Technically the marriage and babies are entirely optional," Ellery cut in. "We don't dictate what constitutes a successful match."

"Carson assures us Ryan is the perfect match," Wilson Abramovich, the town jeweler, said helpfully.

"You *did* have your first kiss with him," Willa reminded her, interlacing her fingers under her chin. "Isn't that romantic?"

"He wasn't my first kiss!" Sammy shrieked.

"Oh, dear. She doesn't even remember her first kiss." Bruce tut-tutted.

Gordon looked perturbed. "Eva and Emma said it was one of your romantic highlights. How could you have forgotten?"

She took a breath and tried to count backward from ten but kept getting distracted by a desire to set all of the calendars on fire. Ryan's arm tightened around her waist.

"I'm not exactly following what's happening here," Ryan claimed. "But I think the two most important things are: the winter solstice already happened on the twenty-first. And you have the wrong nephew. Ryan Shufflebottom was Sammy's first kiss."

Bruce chuckled like he'd told a good punchline. "*You're* Ryan Shufflebottom," he said. "And we can't celebrate the Solstice on the *actual* solstice because the Wiccans would miss out on their celebration."

"He's Ryan Sosa," Sammy announced.

"Ryan Shufflebottom is my cousin."

"Son of a biscuit!" Ellery slapped a hand to her forehead. "We got the wrong Ryan!"

"Oh dear. This is terrible," Willa whispered.

Rainbow held up her hands like she was directing a board meeting. "Let's all calm down. No harm was done. You two didn't accidentally have sex and start having feelings for each other, did you?"

Ryan and Sammy glanced at each other and then looked away again. "Of course not," she said a few decibels louder than necessary.

"Good. We just need you two to stay away from each other until we can get Right Ryan here," Rainbow continued.

"He's not Right Ryan! And Sammy is not marrying my douchecanoe of a cousin!" Wrong Ryan shouted.

"I'm not marrying anyone!" Sammy agreed at full volume. "By the way, where is Carson really?"

"A poker tournament in West Virginia with his cousin Myrt Crabapple," Willa helpfully interjected.

"Hey, quick question. Is Right Ryan an accountant?" Ellery piped up.

"Why does that even matter?" Sammy demanded, pressing her fingers into her eyeballs to make sure they didn't pop out of their sockets.

With a soft smile, Ellery cupped her black lace gloves to her belly. "Well, it looks like we're having a little ghoul or goblin. I'm going to need my Masey home more often."

"Oh, my God, Ellery!" Sammy crooned, temporarily forgetting her anger. "Congratulations! You two must be so excited."

"Mason needs a partner in his firm," Rainbow explained. "It's practically three full-time jobs trying to keep the residents out of IRS prison. Wrong Ryan's skills make him the perfect fit."

And just like that Sammy was back to infuriated.

"That's not actually a thing," Ryan insisted.

"See! Wrong Ryan knows stuff! Maybe after we match up Right Ryan and Sammy, we could pair Wrong Ryan with Moon

Beam Parker. She's due for a new husband," Gordon mused, nervously fingering the fringe on his poncho.

Sammy gasped. "*Not* Moon Beam."

Ryan let go of her to clutch his temples. "What's a Moon Beam Parker?"

"This whole situation can totally be salvaged," Bruce said with confidence.

"No. It can't. You are hereby ordered to leave me, Ryan Sosa, and any other Ryan alone!" Sammy announced.

Ellery's eyes narrowed. "Are you both covered in glitter?" she asked, peering at them.

"Does this mean I don't have to save Carson's farm?" Ryan pressed.

The Beautification Committee members chuckled. "Of course not! Carson has owned the farm outright for more than forty years."

"Damn. I was looking forward to ripping you a new one later today," Ryan said to Rainbow.

"I was looking forward to it too. I've been practicing my villain smoke rings," she told him.

"At least you can quit smoking now that the jig is up," Ellery said. "Rainbow really went method actor for this role."

"Tell you what, Ryan. We can still keep the meeting if it makes you feel better. Maybe grab some lunch while you tell me how you shrewdly deduced there was no loan," Rainbow offered.

"I ran a credit check on Carson. He hasn't had a loan open with your bank or anyone else in the last decade," he said modestly.

"Very clever," Rainbow approved.

Sammy stomped her foot. "No one is having lunch with anyone. I want you to explain how you burnt down a house to get Eden and Davis together, and yet *I* get some half-assed attempt with mistaken identity!"

Bruce Oakleigh shushed her and looked frantically over his shoulder. The fire—like most secrets in Blue Moon—was a poorly kept one. "I assure you, Samantha, we full-assed this campaign. And I would very much appreciate it if you kept any mentions of any f-i-r-e-s quiet."

"Sheriff Cardona can spell, Bruce," Sammy said dryly. "I am very disappointed in you all."

"Sammy—" Ellery tried.

"*Very. Disappointed*," Sammy announced, cutting her off.

"Okay, Sparkle. Let's regroup," Ryan said, dragging her a few steps away, leaving the Beautification Committee clucking like worried chickens. "Take a breath and explain to me what just happened."

She sucked in oxygen as she watched vendor tents going up around them.

There was an empty spot between the vegan wiener truck and the alpaca dung incense stand where her booth was supposed to be.

"Sam." Ryan gripped her shoulders. "Talk to me."

"I don't mean to butt in, but you should keep your hands to yourself, Wrong Ryan. Your cousin might not like it," Bruce called.

"My hands are the last body parts you need to be worried about where Sam is concerned, Santa," Ryan snarled.

"Ryan!" she hissed.

"Sammy, since you're here, we could use a hand putting up the—"

"No!" Ryan cut off Willa's request. "Sam is not doing anyone else any favors. She's not lending a hand, helping out, or stepping in. From now on, you people need to give her space to do her things. Better yet, why don't you offer *her* a hand?"

"Do you see what I mean?" Bruce clapped his hands in glee. "He's the perfect town grump."

"We need to get you in front of Moon Beam," Rainbow agreed. "How do you feel about excessive gum chewing and inappropriate flirtation?"

"These people aren't right in the head," Ryan said, gesturing toward the clump of master manipulators. "Falsifying loan documents and trying to collect on them? Orchestrating some scheme just to get a stranger to fly across the country and get married?"

"Trust me," Sammy said, pulling him farther away. "It's not the worst thing they've done. Though I kind of expected more out of them. This was a half-assed scheme compared to some of their more recent matches. Usually their efforts are more elaborate."

"It really was whole-assed," Ellery called to her. "I'll admit we had a few shortcomings in our research department. But our whole asses were in it."

"This is exactly why you shouldn't get to know your neighbors," Ryan lectured her.

"They mean well," she said lamely.

"They just tried to *arrange a marriage*, Sam. That's not normal."

"Hey, I said they mean well. Not that they're normal," she countered. "I am so sorry about this. I don't blame you for booking the earliest flight out of this patchouli-scented loony bin."

He would, she knew. The BC had just blown their chance of landing a town grump with their botched string pulling. All those maybes from last night couldn't stand up under the harsh light of morning. It made her feel cold inside. Cold and sad.

"Sam—" Ryan's phone rang and he fished it out of his

pocket. She saw his eyes widen in surprise when he looked at the screen. "It's one of the partners from the firm."

"Answer it," she said, her throat tight.

He looked like he wanted to say something to her, but words weren't necessary when she saw the conflict written plainly on his face. "Go on," she insisted, giving him a sad smile.

She watched helplessly as he wandered a few steps away, stopping in the middle of the half-assembled Mistletoe Corner to answer the call. Her heart gave an odd, painful lurch.

She hadn't even known she wanted a relationship until Ryan and his dirty sheep had wandered into her life.

"Excuse me, Samantha," Bruce said, trotting over. "Rainbow wanted me to ask you to ask Ryan if he was still going to help us out with our little state audit problem."

"That was real?" she asked.

His eyes were wide and guileless. "I would never joke about accidentally bankrupting our town, not even for the right match," he insisted.

Ryan was watching her intently even as he listened to the person on the other end of the call. A partner who hadn't fought for him or believed in him when it counted. One who didn't recognize his value until Ryan was already gone. That was the problem. She *had*. So had her inept, good-hearted, manipulative neighbors. And he was going to walk away from them.

She could read it on his face.

"Sorry, Bruce," she said sadly. "Ryan's flying home today."

"This is a travesty," the man wailed.

Sammy couldn't agree more.

"Amethyst and I are not cut out for prison. Orange washes out her complexion," Bruce muttered as he walked away.

Ryan's call was over. She held her breath as he returned to her. One last hope butterfly struggling to stay in the air.

"They want you back?"

He nodded. "My clients are unhappy with Bart Lumberto stepping in. The partners think they were too hasty and want me to fly back tonight for a meeting in the morning. A fresh start."

The last little butterfly in Sammy's stomach hurled itself into the bug zapper.

"Tonight? Wow," she croaked. Her eyes were filling with tears. Tears she had no right crying after only a few days. "Tomorrow is Christmas Eve."

"Corporate accountants aren't big on the holidays," he said, shoving his hands in his pockets.

She shook her head and blinked hard. "Congratulations, Ryan. You got what you wanted. I'm happy for you," she said with feigned brightness.

"Then why do you look like your eyeballs are going to pop out of your head?" he asked. He nudged her chin higher.

"What are you talking about?" she scoffed, looking everywhere but his face. Looking at him would force her to face the fact that she was losing what she'd only just found.

She blinked, and her right eye promptly overflowed. *Crap.*

"Look at me, Sparkle."

"No, thanks." She stared down at their feet.

Again, he took her chin in hand and lifted it. "You're killing me, Sam," he said softly.

"I'm not sad," she lied. "I'm..." *Dejected. Miserable. Ruined for all future non-glittery sex.* "Happy for you."

"This doesn't have to be over. Isn't that what video calls and plane tickets are for?" he said gripping her arms.

She gave him a small, watery smile. "You work sixty hours a week. I have an erratic schedule. And I can't stay up late enough for West Coast sexting."

"I'll reschedule the meeting," he insisted. "Those grant applications aren't going to fill themselves out."

She shook her head. "This is what you wanted. Losing it

showed you how much you loved it. There's no point delaying it. You need to go home."

"What about your grants? The wreaths?"

"It's time for me to face facts. I spread myself too thin and now I'm learning my lesson."

"I don't want to leave you like this," he said earnestly.

"Me? You should be more worried about Bruce. I told him you weren't going to be able to help with that whole auditor thing."

The man in question was behind them loudly lamenting his fate to the vegan wiener lady.

"Sam," Ryan began. "I'm not ready to say goodbye to you."

"Doc!"

They both looked up and spotted Sheriff Donovan Cardona jogging toward them across the park.

The Beautification Members scattered like cockroaches.

"Just got a call from Animal Control over in Lewisberry," Donovan announced. "Hoarding situation on a farm. They need help triaging the animals."

"I'll be right behind you," Sammy told him. "Tell Rainbow I'm canceling my booth for tonight. She's hiding from you behind that tree."

Donovan gave her the thumbs up and hurried off.

She took a breath before she turned back to Ryan. "These situations take a while to sort out. Can you find a ride back?"

He nodded, then reached for her hand and held on. "I meant what I said. I'm not ready to say goodbye."

"Me neither," she admitted softly. "Maybe it's for the best. Less time to make it awkward."

Ryan sighed and stroked his knuckle over her cheek. "You're one of a kind, Sparkle."

"I hope you get everything you want. Give 'em hell." She rose on tiptoe and pressed a soft kiss to his stubbly, sparkly cheek. "I'll think of you every time I see glitter. Goodbye, Wrong Ryan."

He shook his head as she stepped back. "I'll see you around, Sparkle."

With a sad little wave that almost broke her heart, she turned and started to jog after Donovan.

To: *Beautification Committee Members*
    Subject: *Operation Wobbling Osprey*
    Dearest Beautification Committee Members,

We have hit a tiny, insignificant snag in Operation Wobbling Osprey. Not to worry! We will have everything sorted out in time for tonight! Don't forget to share your favorite nude photos of fellow committee members on your social media to increase sales of our fundraising calendar!

Bruce Oakleigh

P.S. If any of you are willing to spend the next eighteen hours working with some very fun and exciting paperwork, you will be excused from your booth shift at the Solstice.

26

———

$\mathcal{R}$yan watched the Volkswagen Bus Lyft pull away from Carson's farmhouse.

He waved at Fitz, the skinny driver with the receding hair-line compensated for with a foot-long rat-tail down the back. Fitz tooted the horn a little too hard. It got stuck and blared the entire way down the lane.

Stan trotted over to investigate a spot under one of the big pine trees in the yard. Only in Blue Moon would a Lyft driver not bat an eye when the passenger requested a pick-up for a sheep.

Ryan kicked at the bottom step and looked up at the cozy, white farmhouse. The snow was almost completely melted, but the heavy clouds above hinted that there was more to come. He most likely wouldn't be here to see it.

He'd be on his way back to normal.

So why wasn't he jumping up the stairs two at a time and throwing his shit in a bag? Hurrying back to the life he'd missed?

Back to anonymous neighbors. Back to co-workers pitted

against each other, kicking and scratching their way to the top for sport.

All for what?

He glanced around. There must be something stupid in the air on this side of the country, he decided. The competitiveness had never bothered him before. Neither had the toxic leadership or long hours behind a desk that ate away at his life outside the office.

It was still what he wanted. Still what he'd planned for. It was still better than some arranged marriage by a deranged nudist colony. Even though the bride was Dr. Sammy Ames, a woman he hadn't known he'd been looking for.

Ryan's Newest Plan
> *1. Book the ticket.*
> *2. Pack his bags.*
> *3. Steal a casserole out of Uncle Carson's fridge for the road.*
> *4. Leave Blue Moon... and Sam in the rearview mirror.*

Sam. Pictures of her flipped through his mind like a collection of Polaroids. Her amusement with his hangover. Those big lavender eyes full of anxiety when he held up that fat stack of paperwork. Her face softening with pride over her horse's growing confidence. Her body spread out under him, naked and needy.

"I need you, Ryan."

Those words had filled a hole inside him he hadn't known existed.

Instead of going inside, he veered off toward the barn. He would at least bring the chickens in to roost so Sammy wouldn't need to do it that night. She'd be tired after a long, hard day. Disappointed in herself for not finding a way to make it all work. Dejected at failing. And he wouldn't be there for her.

He'd seen the pang in those blue eyes just before she covered it up. The realization that there would be no grants this year, no wreaths, no booth, no fundraiser. Everything she'd hoped for had been swept off the table in one fell swoop.

Meanwhile, he'd gotten everything he wanted. A reprieve from the tailspin of the unknown. A second chance at his old life.

His clients hadn't been "impressed" with Bart Lumberto in Ryan's week-long absence. That's how Randall Finnegan, senior partner, had put it in the phone call. The firm had been "too hasty" in their decision to let him go and would welcome him back. It wasn't exactly the groveling apology he'd fantasized about immediately after his unceremonious firing. However, it would put him back where he belonged.

Sammy had lost, and Ryan had been victorious. Yet they'd both go home tonight alone.

And that felt wrong.

Instead of heading to the door of the barn, Stan disappeared around the side.

"Don't even think about running away," Ryan called.

He followed the sheep's path past the open bay of rusty equipment and around the far side. Stan hadn't gone far. Tail flicking, he stood in front of the first of several short, neat piles of cut Christmas trees wrapped with green tarps.

They'd be going to waste, Ryan realized.

Just like the Beautification Committee's bizarre, convoluted plot.

Just like the wreaths and grant applications.

Just like a team of inexperienced volunteers trying to recreate six months of state reporting.

Just like a funny, sparkly, sexy veterinarian with a pathological helpful streak getting matched to his unworthy, loser cousin.

Ryan *hated* waste. And he hated the idea of his cousin getting within one hundred yards of Sammy. No one in their right mind would try to match her up with a shiftless, immature, over-grown, entitled child.

Of course, no one in their right mind would concoct a fraudulent mortgage scheme just to hook up two complete strangers either. That was the problem. He'd be leaving Sammy in the unfit hands of the deranged Beautification Committee.

"They can't be serious," he complained to the sheep. "My cousin and Sam? It's laughable. She deserves someone who's going to reel her back in, to keep her focused on her own plans. Not someone who's going to take advantage of her."

Stan didn't seem nearly upset enough at the prospect of Sam and Shithead Ryan ending up together.

"You'd hate him if you met him," he insisted. The idea of it made Ryan mad enough that he picked up a stone and hurled it into the adjoining pasture.

"This is crazy. This makes no sense," he muttered to himself, pacing in front of the trees. "I can't just move here for a woman I met less than seventy-two hours ago. I don't owe a town full of strangers anything. People will survive without wreaths, and trees, and state funding... Well, maybe not that last one. But Sam's smart. She can take care of herself. And everyone else will figure things out."

The sheep ignored his argument and turned his attention to grazing.

"I don't owe anyone anything," Ryan said emphatically.

And yet he couldn't quite stop his plan from rearranging itself. Couldn't stop plotting out the steps as his mind turned the problem over, examining it from all angles.

"Shit." He pinched the bridge of his nose.

His plan felt *wrong*. Worse, the only thing that felt right was the one that made absolutely no sense. It was Blue Moon's fault.

This trippy town had finally got its psychedelic hooks in him and macraméd him into a cocoon of crazy.

"Come on, Stan," he said. "We have some phone calls to make."

The sheep pranced ahead of him on the way back to the house while Ryan pulled out his phone and dialed.

"Hey, Mom. I know it's not Tuesday, but..."

27

It was after seven by the time an exhausted Sammy found a parking spot two blocks from One Love Park. Her muscles sang, her head ached, and her heart... well, it felt a bit dented. She'd been tempted to go straight home and dive headfirst into a shower. But missing out on the Winter Solstice and Multicultural Holiday Celebration wasn't an option. She'd never missed a year. And despite her weary body and belly full of murdered hope butterflies, the lights and laughter coming from the park were too much to resist.

Besides, she wasn't ready to face the ghost of naked Ryan in her bedroom... and living room... also the dining room.

She'd grab a bite to eat, a hot chocolate for old time's sake, avoid Mistletoe Corner, and head home when she was too tired to remember how much she liked Ryan Sosa.

Solid plan.

It had been a long, tough day. The farm had been a series of dilapidated outbuildings, each one in worse disrepair than the one before. The owner was a frail seventy-year-old suffering from a mental illness.

Love hadn't been the issue. But resources and cleanliness had.

Thanks to the efforts of dozens of people—some professionals, some volunteers—forty-two animals were in safe homes that night.

A local farmer with two daughters in 4H had taken the four painfully thin Jersey cows. An organic lavender farm stepped up to take the goats and chickens. Two dog groomers showed up with their mobile grooming van and volunteered for several hours. Once checked and groomed, the dogs and cats—so many of them—had been divvied up between three foster rescue networks.

Best of all, thanks to the Blue Moon gossip group and a sympathetic TV news reporter, adoption applications were already pouring in.

The helpers, the people who showed up and stepped up, were what gave Sammy hope for the world. Especially on her darkest days. But today, she couldn't help but think how much closer she'd be to making a bigger impact if she'd prioritized those grant applications.

It was a painful lesson learned.

If Ryan Shufflebottom had helped guide her toward veterinary medicine, Ryan Sosa had dragged her to a mirror and made her take a hard look at her priorities. She would do better and have Wrong Ryan to thank for it.

"Happy Solstice, Dr. Ames," Mrs. Quan trilled from the other side of the street. She had a wreath looped over her arm like a gigantic purse. It jingled with every step. Apparently, the festival committee had found a more reliable wreath maker.

"Hi, Mrs. Quan," she called back with a weary wave. She turned the corner and let Blue Moon in the middle of a good time draw her back to the present. The drumming circle was working their way through holiday classics. The scents of roasted peanuts and wood smoke mingled together while thousands of Christmas lights glowed above and around the festivities.

"Sammy!" Layla, in her deputy's uniform, waved her down.

Sammy crossed the street. "Hey," she said, hunching her shoulders against the cold. They hadn't talked since the lecture at Peace of Pizza and she didn't have it in her to jump into an argument.

"So listen," Layla began, falling into step with her. "I feel like I owe you an apology."

Someone walked by eating a slab of lasagna out of a biodegradable container. Sammy's stomach grumbled. She'd missed lunch *and* dinner and had been forced to break into her protein bar stash between animal exams.

"Apology for what?" Sammy asked.

"For the tough love routine yesterday," Layla said, shoving her hands into the pockets of her Blue Moon Sheriff's Department coat.

Sammy waved a dismissive hand. "Don't worry about it. It was overdue."

"I also wanted to say that Ryan seems like a pretty decent guy," her friend said, keeping an eye on a toddler trying to gnaw his way through the child safety tether attaching him to his father's parka.

Sammy wondered how long it would take before she could hear his name and not feel painfully disappointed. Or think of him without her vagina rising for a standing ovation. It had only been about twelve hours since he'd last wowed her. She'd give it some time.

"Yeah. He was pretty great," she said lamely.

"Was?" Layla asked. There was something inappropriately smug about her smile.

"His old job called him this morning and wanted him back. He's probably deplaning right about now," she guessed.

Layla stopped in her tracks and peered into her face. "Well, holy shit. You slept with him didn't you? You slept with the guy and you didn't tell us. Not cool, Ames."

"There wasn't much time between the having of the sex, me getting an emergency call, and him leaving town," Sammy said dryly.

"That sucks. I'm sorry. Do you want me to run him through the system to see if he has old arrest records? That always makes you feel better," Layla offered.

She shook her head. Nothing short of a miracle would make her feel better.

Layla pointed to the Pierce Acres petting zoo. "Remember the great sheep escape?"

"Oh, I remember," Sammy said. And for a moment, she could picture John Pierce grinning at her from across the path, could taste the Butterfinger hot chocolate on her tongue, could feel the excitement of a new crush.

"What are the odds of two sheep and two Ryans on two solstices?" Layla mused.

"The odds are zero. I'm the first official Beautification Committee failed match," Sammy explained. "They got the wrong Ryan."

"The wrong Ryan?"

She filled in her friend on the particulars while they got in the fried tofu line for old time's sake.

"But did they *actually* get the wrong Ryan?" Layla asked.

"He wasn't the one who kissed me fifteen years ago."

"Yeah, but you liked *this* Ryan enough to sleep with him. And now that he's gone, you're mooning like a lovesick teenager."

"Who's mooning? I'm not mooning," Sammy snapped, taking offense. "I'm tired. I didn't accomplish any of the things I set out to do. And the guy I stupidly let myself fall for left town today."

"I'm sorry, Sammy. I don't think any of us realized how hard you were working to help everyone else and how far behind you were with your own stuff."

"Yeah, well, I guess I didn't either." She took a breath and blew it out slowly, trying to dull the ache. "I really wanted him to stay," she admitted.

Layla slung an arm around her shoulders. "If it were up to me, you'd get everything you want."

Sammy gave her a small smile. "Thanks, friend."

They got their tofu and continued their tour of the park. Sammy's booth had been taken by a crochet lingerie artisan that was doing a brisk business with the over-eighty crowd. A couple wandered by with two stylish wreaths looped over their arms. They looked better than any wreath Sammy had cobbled together. The thought served to depress her further.

"What's all the fuss down there?" she asked, pointing to the end of the park where a crowd was gathered.

"Just the tree farm."

"Did Carson come back?"

Layla shook her head. "Nope."

"Wait a second." Sammy stopped on the concrete. "Layla Gunnarson, why do you have glitter on your face?"

Layla grinned and pulled her toward the crowd. "Hang on to your heart, Sammy."

Between Mooners with fists of cash, Sammy spotted the hand-lettered signs for Fresh Cut Trees and Handmade Wreaths.

All proceeds benefit Down on the Farm.

"How did you do all this?" Sammy asked. Her throat felt tight.

"I helped. But I can't take credit for it."

Sammy watched in shock as Carter Pierce and Nikolai

Vulkov fed Christmas trees through a baler. Emma sat nearby wrapped in a blanket with her feet up and a plate of French fries in her lap. Evan and his stepdad Beckett schmoozed the hell out of the dozens of customers while Phoebe and Franklin made change. Next to them, Eden and her boyfriend Davis were pouring samples of mulled wine and hot cider.

The donations jars on the tables were overflowing.

"Hey, Mom," Jax and Joey elbowed their way to the front of the line. They were both wearing Santa hats. "Are you up for taking Caleb overnight on New Year's Eve?" Jax asked.

Phoebe and Franklin exchanged a devious look. "I don't know," Phoebe mused. "It's *awfully* short notice."

Joey placed her palms on the table. "What's it gonna take?"

Phoebe and Franklin shrugged in unison. "Gosh. I don't know. What's the name of that spa you like in Pennsylvania?" Franklin asked his wife.

"Oh! The Hershey Spa," Phoebe said. "I adore their chocolate massages."

"Would a gift card to the Hershey Spa make you available for babysitting New Year's Eve?" Jax asked.

Eden spotted Sammy and Layla and skirted the table to throw her arms around them.

"I can't believe you guys did this for me," Sammy whispered, hugging her friend back.

Elvira Eustace breezed past with four wreaths, two on each arm. "Happy to support you, Sammy, my dear," she said.

Carter wandered over when the hug broke up. He looked like a magazine-worthy lumberjack in a heavy barn coat with a thick scarf that matched his wife's eyes. "You do a hell of a lot for our farm and this town," he said. "It's about time you let us do something for you."

"I don't know what to say," Sammy said, feeling her eyes well up for the second time today.

"How about 'cheers'?" Davis suggested, handing them each a glass of wine. He slid an arm around Eden's waist and pressed a kiss to her forehead.

"Davis, how are you here? Shouldn't you be manning the winery stand?" Sammy asked.

"The dads are handling the stand while the moms hand out samples to the parents in line for Santa," he explained.

"*All* of the parents?" she asked. The feud between the Moody and the Gates families had come to a very recent end. A little too recent to expect Davis's two fathers, his mom, and Eden's parents to be around each other for any extended period of time.

"No bloodshed yet. But Sheriff Cardona is keeping a close eye on them. We believe in what you're doing, what you plan to do," Eden said. "All of us. Especially Ryan."

"Ryan?" Sammy asked.

"He called us," Layla said. "And half of Blue Moon."

"He berated us for being too self-absorbed to notice that you were floundering," Eden added. "Then he let us into your place."

"Ryan did this?" Sammy asked, certain she'd heard them wrong.

"You've got yourself a good man, Sammy," Phoebe said, joining their little circle with a glass of her own.

"He's a great guy," Sammy agreed. "But he's not *my* great guy. He went back to Seattle today."

There. She said it without bursting into tears or curling up into the fetal position.

In her self-pity, she noticed everyone exchanging knowing glances.

"What?" she demanded.

"I think it's time you wandered over to Mistletoe Corner," Phoebe suggested, pointing her in the right direction.

"If I find the Beautification Committee and Ryan Shufflebottom from Des Moines there, I will start throwing tofu," Sammy warned.

"You never know what you'll find unless you start looking," Phoebe said innocently.

"Good luck," Layla whispered, her no-nonsense gaze looking just a little misty.

Sammy followed the path in the direction of Mistletoe Corner and tried to talk herself out of hoping. Those little bastard butterflies were starting to show signs of life again, despite her best efforts.

"He's not here," she reminded herself. "He went home. He wouldn't give up his shot at normal to spend another day in a town that tried to force him into an arranged marriage."

The cozy clearing was the same as it always was, the tall spruce decked out in multi-colored lights from tip to trunk. More strands of lights, soft and white, crisscrossed over her head. Tiny clumps of mistletoe hung every six feet.

But there was one thing that was different this year. One perfect, grumpy thing.

28

Ryan Sosa stood scowling at the flowers in his hand as he muttered to himself.

"Why aren't you thousands of miles away from here?" Sammy demanded.

He looked up at her, surprised out of the argument he was practicing. "Christ. It's about damn time, Sam."

It was such a Grumpy Ryan thing to say that she couldn't help but smile.

"Gee, sorry. I was busy doing my job and saving animals."

He rolled his eyes. "You got to the park almost twenty minutes ago. I've been freezing my ass off waiting for you since Layla texted that you were here."

"Why *are* you here freezing your ass off?"

"You know why, Sam." He crooked his finger, in that deliciously bossy way of his, and she couldn't fault her feet for automatically carrying her toward him.

She stopped when she was a foot away, not willing to throw herself at him in case this was some unfortunate misunderstanding and he was here holding flowers because something terrible had happened.

"Is Carson okay?" she asked.

Ryan frowned. "He's fine. He's on his way home. Why?"

"What about Stan? The chickens?"

"You think I'm standing here under mistletoe with stupid flowers in thirty-degree weather to break bad news to you?"

"It's a possibility."

"Goddamn it, Sam. For a doctor, you can be incredibly obtuse sometimes. I'm here because of you."

She tried to rewind the words and listen to them again, but nothing made sense. "I'm sorry. I think I'm not processing language correctly."

He growled, and the sound of it both delighted and terrified her.

"You're just doing this because of the Beautification Committee," she insisted. "I don't know how they do it. Maybe it's mind control or something. But you aren't here of your own free will. Did they make you drink anything or force you to watch a slide show or something?"

He was in her space now, the toes of their boots touching. "I'm here for you. I'm staying for us," he said, his voice low and rough.

"You're not thinking straight," she insisted. She couldn't think with him this close to her. But when she tried to take a step back, he reached and grabbed her by the front of her vest.

"Snap out of it, Sparkle," he warned, dragging her against him. "I'm here because I want to be. Not because a couple of nutcases pulled some half-assed stunt. I'm here for you. I'm here because the thought of waking up and not seeing you tomorrow scared the hell out of me."

"Oh," she said weakly. This was happening. Really happening. She was getting her happily ever... scratch that. She was getting her grumpily ever after.

266

Someone cleared their throat theatrically. "Is this where the line starts?"

Sammy and Ryan dragged their heated gazes away from each other to find Fitz standing indecently close to them.

"The line?" Sammy managed.

"The kissing booth line?" He took a hit of breath spray and licked his thin lips.

Sammy shuddered.

"Fitz, if you don't get the hell away from my girl, I'll send you to IRS jail," Ryan threatened.

"Jeez. Okay," Fitz said, holding up his mittened hands. "Mind if I hang out?"

"Aren't you late?" Sammy asked.

He frowned. "Late for what?"

"The Pants Off Dance Off at the gazebo," she improvised.

Fitz's face lit up. "Sweet! Finally some real entertainment. Later, dudes!" He hurried off toward what would soon be a very confused audience.

"Now, where were we?" Ryan demanded.

His fiercely frowning mouth was so close. She could feel his breath, warm and sweet on her face. "Is this happening?" she whispered as her heart thudded in her chest.

"You're damn right it is," he said. "Now get used to it."

She melted against him, ready to seal the Official Most Romantic Moment of her life with a kiss under the mistletoe. "In that case, I think we were right about here," she said, rising on tiptoe.

"Wait!" someone yelled, breaking the spell.

Chest heaving, Sammy tried to jump back, but Ryan merely tightened his grip on her vest.

"Stop! He's the wrong Ryan!" Ellery stormed into the clearing, dragging a man behind her.

"You've got to be fucking kidding me," Wrong Ryan groused.

"Is that you, Ry?" the newcomer asked with a lazy grin. He was wearing white pants, a pink Oxford, and a long wool coat. He had a green sweater wrapped around his neck like a scarf. "Heard you got shit-canned. Sucks to be you."

There was something unsettlingly familiar about him, Sammy thought.

"What the hell are you doing here, Shufflebottom?" snapped Wrong Ryan.

Oh, shit. Ryan Shufflebottom, the Original Mistletoe Kisser, was back.

"Dude, Esme here told me there was an emergency and paid for my plane ticket," First Kiss Ryan said.

"Ellery," Wrong Ryan corrected. "And there's no emergency. You can go."

"Dunno. I kinda like this place," he said, shoving his hands in the pockets of those blinding white pants. "It's sexy."

"What the hell is happening?" Sammy demanded.

"This only works if you kiss Original Ryan in the same spot as your first kiss. It's all about symmetry," Ellery insisted knowledgeably.

"Original Ryan?" Wrong Ryan scoffed.

"Holy shit! It's Fried Tofu Chick," Original Ryan said, chewing his gum harder. "I totally remember you. You got even hotter. Man, we could have had some real fun that night if my parents hadn't caught me stealing cash from the Salvation Army kettle in the park."

"Ellery, if you don't want a murder on your conscience, get this douchewaffle out of here now," Wrong Ryan warned.

"So, you want me to just kiss her, or can I try for a little third base action?" Douchewaffle Ryan asked, firing off pistol fingers and a lecherous wink in Sammy's direction.

"Ew," she said.

"What are we working with here? B cup? C cup?" Gross Ryan

asked, walking toward her with outstretched palms at boob height.

"Not happening," Accountant Ryan said briskly. "Hold these." He shoved the flowers into Sammy's hands.

"Ryan," she warned.

"What?" both Ryans said at the same time.

"Dude, pretty sure she was talking to me," Boob Grabber Ryan said, wriggling his eyebrows. He no longer had the boy band swoop of hair. Instead he'd graduated to a slicked back, heavy-on-the-gel style.

"Fuck symmetry," Grumpy Ryan growled. His fist flashed out and connected with Original Ryan's jaw. The man crumpled to the ground like a deflating Santa lawn display.

"Ryan!" Sammy yelped.

"What?" Wrong Ryan said as he stalked toward her.

"Ow! I can't believe you hit me. I'm suing your ass! Tofu Girl, you and Ellen are my witnesses," whined Inappropriate Conduct Ryan.

"Let's do this right," Wrong Ryan insisted. Once again, his hands fisted in her vest. The flowers fell uselessly from her fingers to the ground as their bodies connected. He didn't give her a chance to breathe before crushing his mouth to hers.

There under the mistletoe, their tongues twined, teeth grazed, lips crushed.

There was nothing sweet or safe about the kiss. But there was fire and heart and hope. Even romance. And a host of other feelings drowned out by the pulsing need of more. More. So much more.

"Now, *that's* a kiss," Ellery mused from what sounded like a long way off.

"Can someone get me some ice? And some vodka?" Punched-in-the-Face Ryan asked.

"Come on, Subpar Ryan," Ellery said. "I'll buy you some wassail."

Wrong Ryan broke away from the kiss. "Wait," he ordered. He unraveled the green scarf from Sammy's neck and threw it at his cousin. "You can have this back."

"Hey! I shoplifted this from Nordstrom's when I was like fifteen. I wondered what happened to it."

"You're not a great person, are you?" Ellery asked as she led Criminal Ryan away.

"Not really," he agreed.

"Oh my God," Sammy breathed. She'd been wearing a stolen scarf for fifteen years.

"I paid for this one after I saw it and it reminded me of your eyes," Ryan said, reaching into his coat and yanking out a deep blue scarf. She buried her face in the yarn and breathed in his scent.

He cleared his throat. "Now it's time to get a few things straight. Number One, I won't tolerate you making out with anyone who isn't me from here on out."

Her butterflies had exploded into a glorious, golden glow that filled her chest.

"Is that so?"

"That's right, and you'd better get used to it. Because Number Two, I'm sticking around. One night with you wasn't enough for me. I want more of you. *All* of you."

"Even though it doesn't make sense? Even though this isn't part of your life plan?" she pressed.

"Somehow you make more sense than any other decision I've ever made," he insisted, sliding his hand up her jaw to her neck and into her hair.

Sammy's blood felt thick in her veins. The night air was chilly, but in the moment, she felt like she'd never be cold again. She slid her hands up his chest and was surprised by the heat pumping through his sexy thermal shirt under the flannel coat.

He didn't look like a snooty accounting robot.

He looked like a man who wanted something. And that something was *her*.

His hand fisted in her hair, tugging hard enough that she opened her mouth on the softest moan. Something like triumph lit up his gray eyes, and she felt rather than heard the rumble in his chest as he took her lips again.

He'd barely touched her, and she was reacting like an orgasm was on its way.

His other hand slipped under her jacket to her waist, where it curled into the curve of her hip and drew her against him in one swift pull.

Oh. God.

Her chest pressed against his torso, hips to his denim-clad thighs, and her stomach up against the erection demanding full attention.

She wanted. Was wanted. Craved. Was craved.

She wanted to wrap her legs around his waist. Wanted to run away. Wanted to stay right here in this exact moment of anticipation for the rest of eternity.

He leaned in, nuzzling his nose against her cheek. "I like when you look at me like that," he whispered darkly in her ear.

"Like what?" she asked breathlessly.

"Like this isn't just a kiss. Like this is forever."

She made some kind of unintelligible moan.

"What was that, Sam?" he asked smugly.

She could feel the hardness of his erection where it pressed into her, and she wanted more. Friction. Skin. Sweat. She wanted to taste him and be tasted. He lowered his forehead to hers.

"How is this going to work?" she whispered.

"I'm going to take you home and strip off every piece of your clothing in front of the fireplace."

She sucked in a breath. "I mean, you staying. What does it mean?"

"It means Number Three, we're together," he said firmly. "This isn't a marriage proposal, but it's a notice of monogamy."

"If you were proposing right now, I'd be concerned about head trauma or hypothermia."

"I *am* moving in with you," he informed her.

"Are you feeling feverish? Did Bruce Oakleigh come near you with a comically large mallet?"

"I'm feeling alive. And I'm not moving the whole way across the country unless it means I can see your face every morning, Sparkle."

Swoon.

"Besides, we need to figure out how annoying the other is on a day-to-day basis. We'll start with a one-year probationary period," he continued.

"How romantic," she teased.

"I punched a guy in the face for you after selling fucking Christmas trees in a small town. I'm the master of romance," Ryan insisted.

"So one year. What happens during that year?" she asked.

"I make love to you on every flat surface in the house until I know your body better than you do. We renovate that God-awful kitchen. I buy into Mason's practice. We launch the sanctuary. I wait a respectable amount of time before I tell you that I am so in love with you that it hurts to look at you because I'm afraid you'll disappear and this whole thing will be a dream."

"Ryan," she whispered. Her heart was soaring.

"Then you'll tell me you've loved me since I tried to abandon a sheep."

"And then what?"

"Then after twenty-four months we get engaged. Get married. Live happily ever after."

A single fat snowflake fell from the sky and landed on her cheek.

She could feel herself nodding as if it was all perfectly logical. "I like this plan. How do we seal this deal?"

He looked above them at the mistletoe. A few more fat flakes drifted toward the ground. "I've got a few ideas."

"How many of them are family festival friendly?" she teased.

He nuzzled into her neck, then bit her earlobe. "Zero."

"Take me home, Wrong Ryan."

29

$\mathcal{M}$agic really did happen. And this time it was happening to her, Sammy thought as Ryan kissed her across the threshold of her front door. *Their* front door. That would take a little getting used to. She couldn't wait.

"Mmm, wait," she said, breaking away from the kiss. "Why is it so clean in here—Oh my God! There's a Christmas tree!"

Her little farmhouse was immaculate. The crafting supplies, laundry, and dishes were gone. There was a garland draped over the mantel above the warm glow of a fire. A Christmas tree topped with mistletoe stood in the corner, strands of colored lights casting a soft glow.

There were candles in her windows. Instrumental holiday music played softly in the background. *Die Hard* was cued up on the TV screen.

It smelled like sugar cookies and happiness.

"How did you do this?" she asked, bringing her fingers to her mouth.

He stroked a hand over her hair. "I asked for help."

"I can't believe you did this for me." She blinked back tears that blurred the lights into starbursts.

"I didn't do it alone. You have a whole town of people who love you, Sam."

McClane padded by, a plaid bowtie on his collar. Stan the sheep let out a snore from a dog bed next to the fireplace. "What's that under the tree?" she asked, spying a small, flat box wrapped with a red ribbon.

"Go find out," Ryan suggested. "But lose some layers first."

With a grin, she shrugged out of her vest and handed it to him. When he wasn't looking, she pressed her face to the scarf and took a breath.

While he hung up their coats, she toed off her boots and pounced on the package.

Ryan sauntered over to her and joined her on the rug. As she worked the ribbon free, he pulled off both her socks.

When she started to lift the lid, he stripped her sweater off over her head.

"This isn't how unwrapping presents usually goes," she said as he sank his teeth into her shoulder next to her bra strap.

"Mmm, are you sure? Because I think the rest of the world is doing it wrong," he said as he worked open the button on her jeans.

Her breath caught in her throat as his fingers dipped into the waistband. "I can pay attention to this later," she decided, sliding the box away and reaching for him.

"Open your present, Sam, and let me open mine." His gray eyes glittered in the soft light of the fire, the tree. Dangerously romantic, she thought. Then he maneuvered her onto her hands and knees, and she was left with just dangerous.

Her heart hammered away in her chest as he knelt behind her and slowly slid her jeans down her trembling thighs.

His laugh was soft, ragged, as he traced one finger lightly over her underwear. "Mistletoe here too, Sparkle?"

She shivered. "I don't make the rules," she teased, her voice quivering.

"And I love to follow them," he said softly. She could feel his breath on her back. Held her own as he deftly unhooked her bra, then ran a palm down her spine. His fingers snagged the band of her underwear and dragged them slowly down to her knees.

Her breath caught in her throat, and she squeezed her eyes closed. She was bared to him, vulnerable to him.

"Open," he growled.

She wasn't sure if he meant the box or her legs. So she did both and was rewarded with two of his deft fingers sliding into her entrance.

Her breath released on a strangled cry, and she felt his teeth graze the curve of her hip. "Look at your gift, Sam," he ordered.

She forced herself to open her eyes and stare down at the papers neatly stacked in the box. She shook her head, trying to clear it.

"Are these—"

But the thrust of his fingers was replaced by the stroke of his talented tongue. She nearly collapsed to the floor. Her elbows shook with the effort to keep her upright.

"Ryan," she breathed.

"What are they, Sam?" he whispered, kissing her again where she needed it most.

"Oh my God. Oh my God. Oh my God," she chanted. He was expertly driving her toward an orgasm while expecting her to carry on a conversation. Her entire core was trembling now. She felt him slide back from between her legs and heard the hasty removal of clothing, the tear of a wrapper.

"These are my grant applications," she whispered.

"That's right," he said, stroking over her back, her hip, the curve of her backside.

"They're filled out." She managed to get the words out as he notched the head of his erection at her entrance. She was going to cry and had no idea if it was from being so wound up sexually or so bowled over emotionally.

"And submitted." Ryan said the word tenderly.

"All of them?" she asked on a broken groan as she felt the blunt crown nudge at her sex.

"All of them, my sweet Sam," he whispered, clamping his hands on her hips and thrusting home.

30

---

*S*he woke with a crick in her neck and a heavy arm locked between her breasts, anchoring her to a hard body. Dawn was breaking outside the windows, and it was still snowing.

It was Christmas Eve, and she was waking up naked under a Christmas tree next to her former one-night stand.

"Magic," she whispered.

Ryan grumbled something into her hair, and she smiled to herself.

"Stop poking me in the face," he said sleepily.

"I'm not poking you in the face."

They both looked up. Perched on the couch cushion above them was a fat orange cat glaring down at them.

"Hi, Hans," Sammy yawned.

"Oh, thank God," Ryan murmured. "There really is a third cat."

She snickered as the orange ninja vanished above them. "You were willing to commit to me for a year when you thought I had an imaginary cat friend?"

"That's how into you I am, Sparkle. Don't forget it."

Sammy rubbed her eyes and stretched luxuriously. Ryan's arms belted around her again, pulling her back against his heat, his hardness. "Where do you think you're going?"

Her smile was so wide it hurt her face. "Absolutely nowhere," she promised.

"Good. We can start establishing a morning routine," he said, nestling his erection against her behind.

"I can't believe this is happening," she sighed happily.

"Neither one of us is allowed to come to our senses," he insisted.

She laughed. "Do we have to tell the Beautification Committee?"

"First, you have to explain to me exactly what the Beautification Committee is because they seem less about maintaining common spaces and more about meddling in love lives," he told her.

"You just answered your own question."

"I don't see how they could take credit for us. They wanted to match you with my idiot cousin. Technically, you're being very rebellious right now." He rolled her on to her back.

"Mmm. I like being a rebel," she said, taking his lower lip between her teeth.

He groaned his approval.

The knock at the door startled them apart.

"Ow!" Ryan held a hand to his lip.

She winced. "Sorry."

"Whoever is at your door is the one who's going to be sorry," he growled.

She jumped up and wrapped a fuzzy blanket around herself.

Ryan rose and snatched a Merry Kiss This pillow from the floor and held it in front of his hard cock.

She gaped at him. "You are *not* going anywhere near my door like that," she hissed as he stalked toward the front door.

"*Our* door, Sam. And whoever it is deserves what they get for showing up unannounced at seven-thirty in the morning on Christmas Eve."

She made a run for the door but tripped over Holly. The cat shook her jingle bell collar in derision.

Ryan yanked open the door.

Ellery stood on the front porch in a gray plaid cape trimmed with faux black fur. She cocked her head and took in the view. Her purple lips curved. "High five, Sammy!" She held up a skull gloved hand.

Sammy felt a little like high fiving the entire town and obliged... promptly losing her grip on the blanket.

Ryan grabbed it and tucked it back in place.

"We're about to have sex. This better be good," he announced.

Ellery clapped her hands in glee. "See? We totally needed a town grump! Everyone is going to love you. I am so excited this worked out."

Sammy put herself in front of Ryan, who looked like he was ready to slam the door in Ellery's face.

"This *didn't* work out," Sammy reminded her. "You got the wrong Ryan."

"Oh, *sure* we did," Ellery said with a wink. "Silly us! Anyway, I wanted to give you both your Christmas present in person." She held out a flat package wrapped in black paper with a silver-and-black bow.

With more than a little reticence, Sammy accepted it.

"Ellery, go away," Ryan insisted.

"Not until you open your gift," she said firmly. "It's the least we could do since you pulled your accountant magic and filed that audit extension for the town."

"You did?" Sammy asked.

"It was one dumb form," he said dryly. "Blue Moon has three months to compile the reporting to the state with no penalties if everything is in order."

"I can't believe you did that for us," Sammy said.

"Yeah. Yeah. I'm a hero," he said. "Now open this damn thing so we can get back to being alone and almost having sex." Ryan slipped his fingers in the seam of the wrapping paper and shredded it open.

When the gift came into view, Sammy nearly dropped it. "Oh God."

"It's your very own Beautification Committee Nude Calendar," Ellery said proudly. "We've raised almost $800,000 so far. Just imagine the matchmaking resources we can afford now."

Sammy *was* imagining, and it made her feel a little ill.

"Great. Bye, Ellery," Ryan said, trying to shoo her out of the doorway.

"Oh, baby brain!" she said, tapping her forehead. "I almost forgot to thank you for taking care of Edgar for me."

"Edgar?" Ryan was incredulous.

She whistled, and Stan the sheep trotted up to the door. It baa-ed and flicked his tail in greeting.

"You didn't!" Sammy brought her hands to her face, forgetting she was holding the calendar. The view of Gordon Berkowicz's flat white ass on the cover had her losing the blanket again.

"Aww! Look at those love bites," Ellery said, staring at Sammy's chest. "Nice job, Ry. High five."

Scrambling, Ryan grabbed Sammy around the waist and tucked her behind his back. "You listen here, Queen of the Damned—"

Ellery curtsied. "Aww, thank you! How sweet!"

"Not a compliment."

Ellery shrugged. "Agree to disagree."

"Wait a minute. Did Dr. Turner even have food poisoning?" Sammy asked.

"Nope. He's vegetarian, by the way. No hot dog eating contests for him," Ellery said with a smug smile.

"I can't believe this. I almost ran over that poor sheep just so you could pull strings?" Ryan was getting himself worked up. "What kind of a fucked up—"

"Don't be silly," Ellery said, waving his concerns away. "Edgar was never in any real danger. We had Ernest Washington rig the front sensor on your little tiny car while you were inside. You didn't get within six feet of my sweet little sheep."

"But the thump? The limping!"

Sammy put her hand on Ryan's back to calm him.

"Wilson Abramovich is an excellent shot with a water balloon, and sheep are very intelligent. You can train them to do tricks just like horses. Watch. Hey Edgar, limp!"

The sheep toddled down the walk toward Ellery's jacked up hearsemobile, limping like he'd broken his leg.

"Good boy! Now play dead!"

Edgar flopped over on his side and rolled until all four hooves were in the air.

"He's so smart, isn't he?" Ellery beamed.

"Oh, for fuck's sake." Surprise had Ryan bobbling the pillow and dropping it.

Ellery's eyes widened as she took in the view. "Mazel tov, Sammy! I'll let you two get back to it. Merry Christmas, guys. I've got to get Edgar home, and I need to swing by Moon Beam's place. Rumor has it Subpar Ryan spent the night, and the Beautification Committee wants to confirm its first two-fer."

"Mazel tov," Sammy croaked. "Happy Solstice."

Ryan grabbed the pillow and covered his nether region.

"Oh! One more thing," Ellery said. "Eden asked me to let you know that she just had a few last-minute reservations at the inn. It sounds like Ryan's family is in town. His mom said something about Ryan calling her and telling her he'd gotten fired and quit and fell in love with a girl. They'll be by this afternoon to meet Sammy and assess you for a mid-life crisis."

"You told your mom you were in love with me before you told me?" Sammy asked him.

"Technically, I still haven't told you I'm in love with you because I'm waiting for the right moment. Preferably after we've known each other longer than a week," he said dryly.

"It does seem awfully irresponsible of you to fall in love with me that fast," she agreed.

"Are you trying to say you're not in love with me?"

"Of *course* I'm in love with you," she scoffed. "But *I'm* the romantic. It's expected from me."

"Well, it sounds like you two have a lot to work out here. So I'll be on my way," Ellery said, turning to leave. "Oh, gosh. I almost forgot. Sammy, your parents just arrived in town, too. Your mom skipped brunch with the Secretary of Agriculture, and your dad brought a copy of *Die Hard*. They're looking forward to seeing you tonight."

"Is it too early to start drinking?" Sammy murmured.

"How soon does the liquor store open?" Ryan asked.

They stood there watching Ellery as she unfolded a ramp from the back seat and guided the sheep up into the vehicle.

She tooted the horn, an oddly cheerful funeral dirge, and drove off.

"Was that a hearse?" Ryan asked.

"Yep."

"With reindeer antlers and a red nose on the grill?"

"Uh-huh."

"And she planned this entire thing?"

"It would appear so." Sammy sighed. "You changed your mind, didn't you? You're rescheduling your flight in your head right now."

He threw the pillow over his shoulder and reached for her. His hands were hot, his grip firm. "It's gonna take more than a handful of Machiavellian hippie manipulators to scare me off."

"Good," she breathed. "Because there's more than a handful around here."

"Sam?"

"Yeah?" she asked breathlessly.

Ryan pointed up. Hanging in the doorway was a sprig of mistletoe. "Let's make it official."

"How many of these did you hang up?" she asked.

"One in every room."

She beamed up at him as she looped her arms around his neck. "I'm looking forward to that reasonable six-month timeline to tell you that I love you, Wrong Ryan."

He slid his hands down to cup her butt. "Six months was more of a place to start negotiations. I don't see anything wrong with moving up the timeline."

With a soul-deep smile, Sammy rose on tiptoe and kissed her Mistletoe Kisser as the snow fell outside.

∼

To: Beautification Committee Members
 Subject: Operation Wobbling Osprey

Dearest Friends,

We have once again brought love to our little corner of the world. Not only did our primary match stick, we also achieved our first ever two-fer thanks to Moon Beam Parker and Sub Par Ryan. Our karmic *rewards are many. Including the $789,425 we've raised in online calendar sales.*

Enjoy your holidays. The matchmaking begins fresh in the new year!

Happy Holidays and Ever Afters,

Ellery Cozumopolaus-Smith

EPILOGUE

One year later

"*B*abe?" Sammy called as she let herself into the house. "I'm home. It was a false alarm. The goats were fine. You'd think Jax would know by now when Thor is faking a limp for attention."

She managed to shuck off her boots and put them on the tray just inside the door before a blur of fur and paws raced down the stairs to greet her.

"Yes. Hello. It's been a whole hour since I've seen you," she crooned, ruffling Sergeant Powell's fluffy face. Sixty-five pounds of mutt scrabbled at her legs, deliriously thrilled to see her. "Where's your daddy?"

Holly the cat meandered by, shooting her a disinterested look.

Sammy looked up expecting to see her grumpy boyfriend standing in the doorway to his office, the former sun porch. But he wasn't there. The house was also tidier than when she'd left.

Fresh wood crackled and split in the fireplace. Neat stacks of glasses and dishes lined the buffet in the dining room. And the pot of corn chowder that she was going to start when she came home simmered on the new range.

A year later and she was still tickled by the fact that Ryan's favorite way to spoil her was to chip away at her chore list. His patented "useful romance" had made Eva Cardona's latest grumpy hero a huge hit with readers.

"Ryan?" she called.

McClane poked his head out from under the Christmas tree, then returned to batting at a cat ornament.

Instrumental Christmas music played on the wireless speakers Ryan had insisted on during the spring renovation.

She really only had to open some wine, pull out the appetizers she'd made, and don her pajamas to be ready for their Christmas Eve Happy Hour. Their second together. Last year, things had been a little awkward, what with Ryan's family worried that he'd jumped head-first into a life crisis and Sammy's mother complaining about all the work a farm sanctuary was going to take for no gain whatsoever.

This year would be easier. Tonight was just friends, and babies, and dogs. Tomorrow, they would enjoy brunch with her parents and head to Philadelphia for Ryan's family's festivities.

The front door flew open behind her, allowing a gust of winter air inside.

Ryan, looking ruggedly delicious in jeans and a heavy farm coat, stomped snow off his boots. "It's about damn time," he complained.

"What? Miss me already?" she teased.

He looked down at her, gray eyes fierce and hot.

She couldn't help herself. She gravitated to him, toward that grumpy mouth of his and rose on tiptoe. He didn't seem to mind it when she slid her arms around his waist.

The kiss was hot and hard and over much too fast.

"Let's go, Sparkle," he said, pulling away and giving her arms a squeeze.

"Go?" she repeated.

Sarge the dog gave a happy bark and danced out the door on the porch.

"You and me and Sarge," Ryan said, pulling her scarf off the rack and winding it around her neck. "We've got just enough time for an afternoon ride before we're forced to spread holiday cheer."

He made drinking alcohol and eating snacks in their pajamas sound like a hardship.

"What kind of ride?" she asked, hiding her grin.

"The kind where you put your boots back on and we go outside."

"Oh. *That* kind of ride."

One of the best surprises of the past year was just how involved with the sanctuary Ryan got. He didn't just keep the books. He fed the animals. Shoveled manure. Collected eggs. And, yes, even rode the horses. They had two now.

Plus four cows, three pigs, two sheep, a flock of ducks that welcomed Willis like family, a pair of cantankerous donkeys, and a three-legged goat named Mabel. Not bad for only having been incorporated for six months.

"Are you sure you don't want to use the time preparing?" Sammy asked.

He glanced down at his watch, then picked up her boots and handed them to her. "Preparations are done. We're burning daylight, Sam."

"Okay. I guess we're going for a ride," she laughed.

She dragged on her boots and let her handsome boyfriend haul her back out the door. The dog trotted on their heels, pausing every few feet to shove his face in the snow.

He had Magnolia and Teddy saddled and tethered just inside the fence.

"Wow, you really mean business, don't you?" she asked.

"Damn right I do. I've never been more serious in my life," he said, patting his jacket pockets. He seemed tense.

"Is everything, okay?" she asked, unlatching the gate.

"Everything is fine," he said, not sounding fine at all as he untethered both horses. Maggie nudged Teddy, the big chestnut bay, with her nose and snorted softly.

Sammy gave her mount a pat on the neck and swung up into the saddle.

"Let's go this way," Ryan said, pointing to the north.

The snow was falling in fat, lazy flakes, landing with a hush on the already white carpet. They rode across the field in silence, Sammy feeling more and more nervous with each creak of the saddle.

"You're not bringing me out here to murder me, are you?" she asked suddenly.

He glanced at her and waited a suspiciously long time before responding. "Why would I do that?"

"That wasn't a no!"

He sighed. "No, Sam. I'm not taking you out here to murder you."

Was he breaking up with her? Hadn't he broken up with his old girlfriend just before Christmas? *If he'd orchestrated a romantic snowy ride on Christmas Eve to break up with her, Ryan Sosa was the one getting murdered out here.*

He patted a hand over his pocket again. She wondered if he had a murder weapon tucked inside his coat.

"You can't murder me and you can't break up with me on horseback on Christmas Eve," she said.

"Relax, Sam."

"You relax. You're the one who looks like he's sweating through his long johns."

"I'm completely relaxed!" His mount shook its huge head as if to disagree.

"Oh, yeah. You sound like it," she scoffed.

"You're going to feel like a jerk in about ten seconds," Ryan warned her as they began to crest the hill. They were heading toward a neighboring plot of land that Sammy had her eye on for future expansion.

"I find that hard to be—"

Well, hell.

"Oh, *now* you're quiet," Ryan teased.

She was too busy feeling like a jerk as she took in the scene before them to answer. There was a gate in the fence where there hadn't been one three days ago. Above the gate, carved in wood was a sign that said Down on the Farm. It was wrapped in fairy lights and evergreen boughs. Candles flickered in glass jars in the snow.

Sarge jogged out in front of them and turned around, his tail wagging.

"What is this?" she asked.

Ryan dismounted next to her, then reached up and plucked her off her horse.

He took her trembling hand in his and led her toward the gate.

"A year ago, I was fired. Depressed. Pissed off about having to fly across the country to this hippie holiday hellhole," he said.

"I remember," she said, not quite trusting her voice.

"A year ago I thought what I wanted was a partner. But I found something else. Something better than I ever could have planned."

He stopped in front of the new gate and turned to face her.

He was so tall and warm and wonderful. Beneath that broody exterior, Ryan Sosa had a soft heart.

"I found you, Sam." He cupped her chin in his hand. "I found you, fell for you when I wasn't even looking. When all my plans had gone to hell."

"I was looking for a partner," he said again. "But I found the love of my life."

"Oh, crap," Sammy whimpered, tears beginning to slip from the corner of her eyes. Her mascara wasn't going to hold up to this.

He brushed the tears away one at a time.

"You took me for a ride and you changed my life," he continued. "You changed my plans and my path and I've been grateful every day since."

"Maybe I'm not the most romantic guy out there, but I want to spend the rest of my life with you. I want to build a plan together, grow together. So I got you this."

Sammy was too bamboozled to be surprised when he didn't get down on one knee. Instead, he pointed to the other side of the gate.

"Huh?" she sniffled ineloquently.

"That acreage you've been eyeing for the past eight months."

More tears fell, scalding hot on her icy cheeks. "You did *what*?" This was better, more meaningful than any shiny bauble in a stupid jeweler's box.

"Catch up, Sparkle," he admonished. But his smile was soft. "I bought the land. More land means a bigger sanctuary, right?"

"That's right," she whispered, stepping up to the gate and picturing it. More land. More animals. He just kept making her dreams come true.

"I believe in you," Ryan said behind her. "In what you're doing. And I want to be part of it."

She mopped at her eyes and turned around. The "thank

you" died on her lips when she saw him kneeling in the snow, a stupid jeweler's box in his hand.

"Oh my God," she whispered.

Sarge darted between them, flinging fresh powder in all directions. Maggie softly whickered her approval.

"Samantha Ames, will you marry me?"

"But... but it hasn't been two years yet. You have a timeline."

He rolled his eyes. "I don't need another year to be certain. I've *been* certain since last Solstice. I love you, Sam. I've loved you since you called me dirty hot and yelled at me over a sheep."

She brought her gloved hands to her mouth. "You're sure?" she pressed. "Absolutely sure? Because I want this. I want this so bad. But if you have any doubts or feel pressured or—"

"Sparkle, I'm freezing my ass off down here. I need you to say yes so I can stand up, put this ring on your finger and kiss the hell out of you."

"Yes." She whispered it. Then said it again. And a third time for good measure as he swept her up in his arms and spun her around.

When he released her, it was only long enough to slip off her glove and slide the diamond band onto her finger. "I didn't want to get you some honking solitaire you wouldn't be able to wear to work," he said, holding up her hand to admire the glint of snow and diamonds.

She still felt dizzy, but in a warm, happy, drunk kind of way. "I love it." She raised her eyes to his face. "I love you. So much that it leaves me breathless."

He pointed above their heads, a wicked grin on his kissable mouth. She looked up and saw the mistletoe hanging from the sign.

"Damn. For a guy who doesn't do romance, you did good."

"Just don't tell Eva. I don't want to have to consult with her on another hero," he said, dragging her into his arms. He buried his face in her hair.

"I'm going to keep you to myself," she promised.

"Merry Christmas, Sam."

"Happy Solstice, Ryan."

He kissed her as the snow fell. As the dog barked. As her heart beat steadily against his.

"By the way. I looked at our finances and I ran a few preliminary budget numbers for the wedding and honeymoon..."

AUTHOR'S NOTE TO THE READER

Dear Reader,

I hope you found The Mistletoe Kisser to be the warm, fuzzy hug escape that I intended it to be. I tried to turn a short story into a quirky novella and ended up escaping into Blue Moon to leave 2020 behind for a few hours a day. Hence the quirky novella turning into a full-length novel.

It's my love letter to you. You're doing great. Even on the days when you don't think you are. Keep hanging in there because there is always light at the end of the hippie, dippy, most-likely-manipulated-by-the-Beautification-Committee tunnel.

If you loved this book, feel free to leave a review and tell all your reader friends! If this is your first Blue Moon book, No More Secrets where the fun starts! Thank you from the bottom of my heart for reading my books!

Xoxo
    Lucy

ABOUT THE AUTHOR

Lucy Score is a *Wall Street Journal* and #1 Amazon bestselling author. She grew up in a literary family who insisted that the dinner table was for reading and earned a degree in journalism. She writes full-time from the Pennsylvania home she and Mr. Lucy share with their obnoxious cat, Cleo. When not spending hours crafting heartbreaker heroes and kick-ass heroines, Lucy can be found on the couch, in the kitchen, or at the gym. She hopes to someday write from a sailboat, or oceanfront condo, or tropical island with reliable Wi-Fi.

Sign up for her newsletter and stay up on all the latest Lucy book news.
And follow her on:
Website: Lucyscore.com
Facebook at: lucyscorewrites
Instagram at: scorelucy
Readers Group at: Lucy Score's Binge Readers Anonymous

ACKNOWLEDGMENTS

- Joyce and Tammy and Mr. Lucy for all the hand-holding you do for me
- Audio Dan who is now also Newsletter Dan
- Binge Readers Anonymous for their undying, over-the-top support of Blue Moon
- Everyone who didn't judge me for putting up the Christmas decorations the second week of November
- Kari March Designs for the fabulous cover
- Jess and Heather for their eagle eyes
- My Street and ARC teams for being tireless cheerleaders
- Cleo the cat for being a pain in my ass
- Readers for having superb taste in books
- Sushi delivery
- My new sweater that feels like the innards of a teddy bear

LUCY'S TITLES

Standalone Titles

Undercover Love

Pretend You're Mine

Finally Mine

Protecting What's Mine

Mr. Fixer Upper

The Christmas Fix

Heart of Hope

The Worst Best Man

Rock Bottom Girl

The Price of Scandal

By a Thread

Forever Never

Riley Thorn

Riley Thorn and the Dead Guy Next Door

Riley Thorn and the Corpse in the Closet

The Blue Moon Small Town Romance Series

No More Secrets

Fall into Temptation

The Last Second Chance

Not Part of the Plan

Holding on to Chaos

The Fine Art of Faking It

Made in the USA
Monee, IL
18 November 2024